Erle Stanley Gardner and The Murder Room

>>> This title is part of The Murder Room, our series dedicated to making available out-of-print or hard-to-find titles by classic crime writers.

Crime fiction has always held up a mirror to society. The Victorians were fascinated by sensational murder and the emerging science of detection; now we are obsessed with the forensic detail of violent death. And no other genre has so captivated and enthralled readers.

Vast troves of classic crime writing have for a long time been unavailable to all but the most dedicated frequenters of second-hand bookshops. The advent of digital publishing means that we are now able to bring you the backlists of a huge range of titles by classic and contemporary crime writers, some of which have been out of print for decades.

From the genteel amateur private eyes of the Golden Age and the femmes fatales of pulp fiction, to the morally ambiguous hard-boiled detectives of mid twentieth-century America and their descendants who walk our twenty-first century streets, The Murder Room has it all. >>>

The Murder Room
Where Criminal Minds Meet

themurderroom.com

Erle Stanley Gardner (1889–1970)

Born in Malden, Massachusetts, Erle Stanley Gardner left school in 1909 and attended Valparaiso University School of Law in Indiana for just one month before he was suspended for focusing more on his hobby of boxing than his academic studies. Soon after, he settled in California, where he taught himself the law and passed the state bar exam in 1911. The practise of law never held much interest for him, however, apart from as it pertained to trial strategy, and in his spare time he began to write for the pulp magazines that gave Dashiell Hammett and Raymond Chandler their start. Not long after the publication of his first novel, *The Case of the Velvet Claws*, featuring Perry Mason, he gave up his legal practice to write full time. He had one daughter, Grace, with his first wife, Natalie, from whom he later separated. In 1968 Gardner married his long-term secretary, Agnes Jean Bethell, whom he professed to be the real 'Della Street', Perry Mason's sole (although unacknowledged) love interest. He was one of the most successful authors of all time and at the time of his death, in Temecula, California in 1970, is said to have had 135 million copies of his books in print in America alone.

By Erle Stanley Gardner
(titles below include only those published in the Murder Room)

Perry Mason series

The Case of the Sulky Girl (1933)
The Case of the Baited Hook (1940)
The Case of the Borrowed Brunette (1946)
The Case of the Lonely Heiress (1948)
The Case of the Negligent Nymph (1950)
The Case of the Moth-Eaten Mink (1952)
The Case of the Glamorous Ghost (1955)
The Case of the Terrified Typist (1956)
The Case of the Gilded Lily (1956)
The Case of the Lucky Loser (1957)
The Case of the Long-Legged Models (1958)
The Case of the Deadly Toy (1959)
The Case of the Singing Skirt (1959)
The Case of the Duplicate Daughter (1960)

The Case of the Blonde Bonanza (1962)

Cool and Lam series

The Bigger They Come (1939)
Turn on the Heat (1940)
Gold Comes in Bricks (1940)
Spill the Jackpot (1941)
Double or Quits (1941)
Owls Don't Blink (1942)
Bats Fly at Dusk (1942)
Cats Prowl at Night (1943)
Crows Can't Count (1946)
Fools Die on Friday (1947)
Bedrooms Have Windows (1949)
Some Women Won't Wait (1953)
Beware the Curves (1956)
You Can Die Laughing (1957)
Some Slips Don't Show (1957)
The Count of Nine (1958)
Pass the Gravy (1959)
Kept Women Can't Quit (1960)
Bachelors Get Lonely (1961)
Shills Can't Cash Chips (1961)
Try Anything Once (1962)
Fish or Cut Bait (1963)
Up For Grabs (1964)

Cut Thin to Win (1965)
Widows Wear Weeds (1966)
Traps Need Fresh Bait (1967)
All Grass Isn't Green (1970)

Doug Selby D.A. series

The D.A. Calls it Murder (1937)
The D.A. Holds a Candle (1938)
The D.A. Draws a Circle (1939)
The D.A. Goes to Trial (1940)
The D.A. Cooks a Goose (1942)
The D.A. Calls a Turn (1944)
The D.A. Takes a Chance
  (1946)
The D.A. Breaks an Egg
  (1949)

Terry Clane series

Murder Up My Sleeve (1937)
The Case of the Backward
  Mule (1946)

Gramp Wiggins series

The Case of the Turning Tide
  (1941)
The Case of the Smoking
  Chimney (1943)

Two Clues (two novellas) (1947)

The D.A. Draws a Circle

Erle Stanley Gardner

An Orion book

Copyright © The Erle Stanley Gardner Trust 1939

This edition published by
The Orion Publishing Group Ltd
Orion House
5 Upper St Martin's Lane
London WC2H 9EA

An Hachette UK company
A CIP catalogue record for this book is available from the British Library

ISBN 978 1 4719 0936 8

www.orionbooks.co.uk

CAST OF CHARACTERS

IN THE ORDER OF THEIR APPEARANCE

CHAPTER I

THE WOMAN ACROSS THE DESK FROM DOUG SELBY WAS IN her early thirties. Her dark eyes, flashing with emotion, long-lashed and subtly emphasized by skillful make-up, were fixed on the district attorney. Her mobile lips, a vivid red in contrast with her smooth olive skin, moved expressively as she talked. "He isn't the sort of person we want in Madison County," she said. "He's a big-time, crooked shyster. He can bring nothing to this community that is either desirable or healthy. He . . ."

"But, Mrs. Artrim," Selby interrupted, "I can't stop him from buying property here."

"Why not?" she asked.

"Because," Selby said, "the person who owns the property is willing to sell. Mr. Carr is willing to pay the price."

"But he's an undesirable citizen."

"Perhaps from your standpoint," Selby said, "but not from mine. He's never been convicted of crime."

"He's a criminal lawyer."

Selby said, "By that you mean he specializes in defending persons accused of crime?"

"Yes, of course."

Selby said, "The law provides that a person accused of crime is entitled to employ counsel. Alphonse Baker Carr is the lawyer they frequently select."

"Oh, but you know what I mean," she said, putting feminine appeal into her eyes and into the quick smile of her lips. "He isn't the sort one would want for a next-door neighbor. You wouldn't want him yourself, would you now, Mr. Selby?"

"Probably not," Selby said, "but you understand my po-

1

sition. I'm the district attorney of this county. If Carr violates any law, I'll prosecute him. If he doesn't, there's nothing I can do."

She surrendered so easily and quickly that Selby realized she was arguing a lost cause. "Well," she said, "I guess there's nothing I can do. I've been to the president of the Chamber of Commerce, the chief of police, and the mayor. They said you might know of something."

Selby said, with a smile, "Technically, Mrs. Artrim, that's known as passing the buck. There's nothing anyone can do."

"But isn't there a zoning ordinance covering Orange Heights?"

"Yes," Selby said. "It's made residential property by the zoning ordinance. There are also building restrictions barring houses costing less than fifteen thousand dollars. The house Carr is buying is one that cost thirty thousand to build. I understand he's paying thirty-five thousand for the house and lot—and it's an all-cash transaction."

"Well, it seems to me you could do *something*. I notice that whenever gangsters try to locate in other exclusive residential districts, the authorities manage to give them the impression that they are *persona non grata,* and the deal falls through."

Selby said, "Why don't you buy the property yourself, Mrs. Artrim? It might be worth while for you to pay two or three thousand more than he is offering."

"I didn't learn of the deal in time," she said. "I tried to do that. The papers have already been signed."

Selby said, "Well, I'm sorry. There's nothing I can do."

"Suppose he uses the house as an office? He undoubtedly will. Wouldn't that violate the zoning restrictions?"

Selby said, "That's a matter you'd have to take up with an attorney who could give you advice on civil law. I'm the district attorney and not permitted to engage in private practice."

She pushed back her chair. Selby rose. She gave him a quick, impulsive hand, and said, "At least, Mr. Selby, you haven't tried to avoid the responsibility by passing me on to the sheriff. That's something. I suppose I'll have to reconcile myself to wild orgies within a stone's throw of my house. I suppose notorious crooks will be frequent visitors. I'll probably have to employ a guard to watch my premises—and it knocks my own chances of sale into a cocked hat."

"Were you trying to sell?" Selby asked.

"Yes," she said. "I was thinking of it. I bought that big house because I thought father and mother would come to live with me, and—and they won't touch a cent of my money." She turned abruptly away as her voice broke. For a long instant she seemed to be fighting for control; then she gave him a quick radiant smile. "But I won't bother you with my private affairs. Do I go out through this door?"

"Yes," Selby said, and watched her lithe, well-groomed figure across the office and through the door.

Selby pulled open a drawer, took out his favorite briar, thoughtfully stuffed tobacco into the bowl, and was just reaching for the telephone when Amorette Standish, his secretary, slipped quietly into the room from the outer office. She carefully closed the door behind her. "What is it, Amorette?' Selby asked.

"I wanted to make certain she'd gone. I thought I heard her walking down the corridor."

"Yes. She's gone. Why?"

"Mr. Carr is in the outer office. He wants to see you."

"A. B. Carr?" Selby asked.

"In person."

"Did he say what he wanted to see me about?"

"No. He said his business was private."

Selby scraped a match on the underside of his desk. "Send him in," he said.

Alphonse Baker Carr, known affectionately among the

3

class of clients who found use for a mouthpiece as old A.B.C., was a tall, rather slender man in the middle fifties. His face, deeply etched with lines of character, broke into a smile as he crossed the office with outstretched hands. "Mr. Selby," he said, "I'm glad to meet you. While I'm usually on the other side of the case from district attorneys, I number among my close friends many of my courtroom opponents." Selby shook hands and indicated a chair.

The lawyer dropped into the chair in which Mrs. Artrim had but recently been seated. Under the pretext of taking time to snip off the end of a cigar and light it, his shrewd gray eyes sized up the young prosecutor. He puffed the cigar into a glowing end, and said, "I'm going to reside in your county. I thought I'd drop in and pay my respects."

"Thank you," Selby said.

"I've bought Pittman's place out in Orange Heights."

"I've heard you had."

Carr laughed and said, "So have several other people." Selby said nothing. Carr held the cigar between the two fingers of his right hand, fingers that were long, tapering, and given to motion. The man looked more like a successful actor than a practicing attorney, and his voice, smooth-flowing, effortless, and magnetic, seemed capable of expressing every subtle nuance of emotion. "I understand," he said, "there's some objection to my becoming a resident of Madison County."

Selby puffed silently at his pipe. The lawyer, radiating calm assurance, shifted slightly in the chair, and crossed his long legs, his manner that of one who is accustomed to making himself at home under all conditions. His eyes, having completed their appraisal of the prosecutor, shifted to the end of his cigar. He said, "Some of the owners of adjacent property are, I believe, trying to stir up trouble."

"Are you," Selby asked, "consulting me professionally?"

4

The lawyer flashed him a swift glance, and his long mouth twitched into a smile. "Hell no," he said.

Selby smiled. "I'm just talking," Carr explained.

"Did you have some particular reason for talking—in this office?"

Carr laughed. "District attorneys are elected by their local constituents. Sometimes an outsider finds the sledding rather rough. In some respects, at least, this is a free country. As a citizen, I'm entitled to purchase property wherever I damn please."

Selby said, "That, I believe, is a matter of routine law—although it's hardly routine for prospective purchasers to call upon me just to advise me of their rights."

Carr threw back his head and laughed. The laugh showed genuine amusement. "Okay," he said, "you win." There was a moment of silence. Carr smiled musingly at the thin wisp of smoke which spiraled upward from his cigar. He conveyed the cigar to his mouth, puffed thoughtfully for a moment, then said abruptly, "What's the use of you and me mincing words, Selby? I know damn well there's been pressure put on you to keep me out. I dropped in to size you up and tell you I wouldn't be put out. I intended to tell you that I've found it pays me to do what I want to do, rather than to do what other people want me to."

"I see," Selby said.

"No, you don't see," Carr said, with a quick, disarming smile which seemed so characteristic of him. "I came to tell you that. I'm not going to tell you that, because I don't have to. I expected to find some zealous young crusader who would tell me there had been complaints, warn me that this was a law-abiding community, that while the officers couldn't keep me from buying property, they wouldn't tolerate any of the things that would get by in the big city. I thought you'd try to bluff me. I thought I'd show you that I didn't bluff easily. I find that you're not one who tries to bluff, so there's no need for me to say anything, except that I'm glad I met you, that I don't intend to practice law in Madison County, so we won't be on the opposite sides of the courtroom fence. And incidentally, if you ever decide to move into the big city and would like to take a fling at the defense instead of the prosecution, it might pay you to look me up. I need brains in my business and pay for them."

"Thanks," Selby said. "I'm quite well satisfied with my present niche."

Carr rose and shook hands again.

"Going to commute back and forth to the city?" Selby asked.

"No. I'm going to live here. I don't keep regular office hours. When I'm trying a big case, I'll stay in the city. In between times, I'll use this as a hideout. I don't want to be too accessible. I have junior partners who can take care of the routine stuff. I'm trying to take life a little easier." In the doorway he turned back to say, "You play them pretty close to your chest. If I hadn't seen Mrs. Artrim walking down the corridor ahead of me, I'd never have known she'd been in. Good morning, Mr. Selby."

"Good morning?" Selby said.

His telephone was making noise before the sound of Carr's steps had died away in the corridor. Selby picked up the telephone and heard Sheriff Brandon's voice on the other end of the line. "Busy, Doug?"

"No."

"Okay. I'll be right in." He hung up, and Selby walked over to unlatch the exit door.

Rex Brandon was twenty-five years older than Selby. His face was tanned by the years he had spent in the saddle as a cattleman. His waist was several inches smaller than his chest. His motions spoke of perfect muscular co-ordination, and he was optimistic enough still to cling to the belief of the top-string cowpuncher that he could ride any animal

God ever made, from a goat to a Brahma bull. "Hi, Doug."

"Hi, Rex. What's new?"

Sheriff Brandon dropped into a chair, fished out a cloth tobacco sack from his pocket, extracted a book of cigarette papers, and spilled tobacco into the paper. He rolled the cigarette deftly with one hand, moistened the paper into place, and snapped a match into flame. "Been having visitors?" he asked.

Selby nodded. "You too?"

"Uh huh."

"Before or after?" Selby asked.

"Before," the sheriff said. "She told me she was coming in to see you. I told her I didn't think it would do any good."

"It didn't," Selby said. Brandon grinned. "Immediately after she left," Selby said, "I was favored by a visit from A. B. Carr."

"What's he look like?" Brandon asked.

"Around fifty-five, tall, magnetic, and personable," Selby said. "You can see where he'd be deadly in front of a jury. He's a consummate actor."

"What did he want?" Brandon asked.

Selby grinned. "He wanted to tell me that he didn't intend to practice law in Madison County, that he had found it paid him best to do the things he wanted rather than the things other people wanted, that I wasn't the type he'd expected to find, that he had a great deal of respect for my ability, and that if I wanted to give up the office of prosecutor in Madison County and go to the city, he'd make me an offer."

Brandon's eyes showed surprise. "The hell he did," he said.

Selby said, "Exactly. He put it in such a clever way that he really didn't say it."

Brandon smoked for a moment in thoughtful silence, then said, "It's not so good having him come in here."

7

"I know it," Selby said, "but what are you going to do? My hands are tied. After all, Rex, he's a big-time lawyer. His clients may be crooks, but it's pretty hard to get juries to look at it that way. There's a rumor that he's being retained by some of the big gambling interests. There's a general feeling that he's pay-off man for some of the bookies. I really don't think he intends to do anything in Madison County."

"Then what does he want here?"

"Probably," Selby said, "just what he says he wants—a place to get away, where he's close enough to the city to be called in case anything important breaks, yet far enough away so he isn't too accessible. He wants to take life easier, wants a place where he can rest and relax, and enjoy some leisure."

Brandon said, "I don't think he knows what it's like out here. Here, everyone of importance knows everyone else of importance. He's moved into an exclusive residential district. The neighbors will snub him."

"I don't think he gives a damn about the neighbors," Selby said.

"Neither do I, now that I think of it," Brandon admitted. "But Rita is all burned up about it."

"How well do you know her?" Selby asked.

"Quite well," Brandon said. "I've known her ever since she was a kid."

Selby said, "She told me she was thinking of selling her place. Her folks wouldn't come to live with her."

"Of course they wouldn't," Brandon replied. "I could have told her that before she bought the place. When she ran away and married that gambler, she broke their hearts. When he was killed and she came into the dough, she thought she could come back to Madison City, move up on Knob Hill, let her dad quit work, and—well, it just didn't work out that way. Abner Hendrix figures that it's gambler's

8

money no matter whether it came from an estate, an insurance company, or where."

"She living in that house alone?" Selby asked.

"No. She has her father-in-law with her, Frank Artrim. His spine was injured in the automobile accident that killed the boy. He'll be a cripple all his life. Listen, Doug, if A. B. Carr starts using that place as a country home for gangsters, can't we do something about it?"

Selby said, "Let's see what he does before we decide what we're going to do, Rex."

Brandon said, "Okay, son. We will."

CHAPTER II

It was a week after Doug Selby's meeting with A. B. Carr that Sylvia Martin of the *Clarion,* looking fresh and cool in a plaid skirt, green silk blouse, and trim-fitting jacket, entered Doug Selby's office. Amorette Standish had just placed the morning mail on the district attorney's desk. "Hi, Doug," Sylvia said.

"Looking for news?" he asked.

"With an eagle eye," she admitted. "Business is slack, and we need some local dynamite."

Selby said, "I can't give you so much as a firecracker, Sylvia."

"How about this forgery case?"

"The man's decided to plead guilty and throw himself on the mercy of the court."

"What decided him, Doug?"

Selby said, "Rex Brandon had a talk with him. When he found out what he was up against, he decided to save lawyer's fees."

"Well," she said, "that's something," and her 6-B lead

pencil scribbled a hasty note on a sheet of newsprint. "Doug, what do you know about A. B. Carr?"

"Nothing," he said, picking up the pile of envelopes which Amorette Standish had placed in front of him.

"You do too, Doug."

"Well," he admitted, "I know what I read in the papers."

"You've met him?"

"Yes. That's all. Why?"

"He's going to sue us for libel."

"Why so?"

"He thought that our editorial a couple of days ago was aimed directly at him."

Selby smiled. "Wasn't it?" he asked.

"I wouldn't know," she said demurely. "I didn't write it."

"What does the editor say?"

"You wouldn't want to know, Doug—not from me. Such language ill becomes a young lady who has her reputation to consider."

Selby said, "I wish they'd leave him alone."

"Why, Doug?"

"It makes us look like a bunch of hicks. Good Lord, the man has to live somewhere. In the city he's a prominent man. Doubtless, there are a good many rather exclusive neighborhoods that would have welcomed him. He's famous."

"I know, Doug, but it's a cheap sort of notoriety like that achieved by gangsters and public enemies."

"But," Selby pointed out, "there's nothing we can do about it. Therefore, why leave ourselves wide open?"

"Do you," she asked, "think the *Clarion* left itself wide open?"

Selby said, "Privately and unofficially, Sylvia, I don't think he'll sue. In order to collect damages in a libel action, he'll be placed in the position of showing damage to his reputation. He wouldn't like to have his reputation brought out in court and appraised by twelve disinterested citizens.

10

He may file suit, but I doubt if it ever comes to trial. All he's doing is growling and showing his teeth just to let you know that he can't be pushed around."

"Go ahead and open your mail, Doug."

Selby started opening and reading his letters. "What are you doing, Sylvia?" he asked. "On the track of anything special?"

"Lord, no. I wish I were. I'm just patrolling the court-house beat trying to scare up a live lead."

Selby picked up a letter and saw the imprint of the office of the district attorney of Los Angeles County. As he pulled out the missive, a photograph which had been enclosed with the paper in the envelope slithered to the floor and came to rest at Sylvia Martin's feet. She picked it up, started to hand it to him, looked at it sharply, then glanced at Selby.

Selby, reading the letter, extended his hand mechanically and said, "Thanks."

She handed him the photograph, and Selby, engrossed in the letter, creased his forehead in a frown as he read:

DEAR SIR:

We are trying to enlist your aid in securing information as to the whereabouts of Peter C. Ribber, alias Peter Drumick, alias Alvin Catone.

This man is five feet seven and a half inches tall, weighs a hundred and fifty-five pounds, aged thirty-three, dark hair, partially bald, dark brown eyes, has a star tattooed in blue on his left forearm. Photograph is enclosed herewith, also fingerprints.

He was arrested on February 24 last on suspicion of larceny. Bail was fixed in an amount of two thousand dollars, and the defendant released. On March 7, when the case came up for trial, the defendant had disappeared and bail was declared forfeit.

Under ordinary circumstances, the matter would have ended at that point, but because of certain other circumstances our office is particularly anxious to apprehend Ribber. We note from your local press that A. B. Carr, an attorney who has appeared in a large number of criminal trials, has recently made his residence in your county. We have reason to believe that Peter Ribber has been in touch with Mr. A. B. Carr and may wish to get in touch with him again. Carr's city office has been under surveillance for some time without producing any results. We are not prepared to go so far as to keep his residence in Madison City under surveillance, but if you can take the necessary steps to see that the sheriff's office and the local police are instructed to keep a sharp eye out for anyone answering the description of Peter Ribber, the courtesy will be greatly appreciated.

Needless to say, Mr. Carr has no idea that we are investigating the matter, nor do we wish such knowledge to come to his attention.

Selby placed the letter face down on his desk and studied the photograph, a front view and profile view of a man with a bullet-shaped head, a long nose, close-set eyes, and a thin, cruel mouth. He slid the photograph under the letter and picked up the next envelope.

Sylvia Martin said, very carelessly, "Who's your friend, Doug?"

"Just another crook," he said.

"What's he wanted for?"

"Larceny, I believe."

"Who wants him?"

He grinned. "The long arm of the law."

"Why so cagey, Doug?"

"It's just routine," he said.

"There might be something in it for me."

"No. It's very *sub rosa*."

"Doug," she said, "I could find him for you."

Selby raised his eyebrows. "You could?"

"Uh huh."

"Where is he?"

She said, "That's confidential. If we found him for you, could you give us a story?"

"I don't think so," he said, "nothing that you could publish."

"Well, let me in on the inside, Doug. You know you can trust me."

He shook his head.

"Meaning you won't?"

"Another county is involved," he said, "and another official."

"Now you look here, Doug Selby," she said, "the *Clarion* has been boosting for you ever since you first started your campaign. We've boosted for you just as consistently as the *Blade* has been knocking you and plugging for Sam Roper and the old régime."

"Well," Selby said, "you get the breaks, don't you?"

"Yes, and I want to keep on getting them. I'm not talking through my hat on this, Doug. I think I can help you."

"The man's wanted for larceny," he said. "That's all."

"That may be all he's wanted for, but that isn't the whole story, Doug Selby, and you know it. If that had been a routine matter, it would have come in the form of a post card sent to the office of the sheriff and the office of the chief of police. Listen, Doug, I can put my finger on him in ten minutes. Surely, after he's arrested, there won't be any great secrecy. You know as well as I do that if the city police force makes the arrest, the *Blade* will be printing everything about it."

Selby thought for a moment, then handed her the letter. Sylvia Martin read it through, then pursed her lips into a little whistle.

"Well?" Selby asked.

Her laughing, reddish brown eyes were serious. "Doug," she said, "what's back of it?"

"I don't know," he told her. "There's the letter and the photograph. Now you know as much as I do—more, I hope."

"I do," she said. "The city police picked him up as a prowler last night and ran him in."

"You're certain?"

"Certain," she said. "I saw him in the line-up this morning. I went down to the jail before I came up here. I'm certain it's the same man."

Selby picked up the telephone and said to Amorette Standish, "Get me Otto Larkin, the chief of police. I'll wait on the line. Rush the call through. It's urgent."

A few moments later, he heard Larkin's cautious voice at the other end of the line, saying, "This is Larkin speaking."

"Doug Selby, Larkin," the district attorney said. "I believe you have a man we want, Peter Ribber, alias Peter Drumick, alias Alvin Catone, five foot seven and a half, weight one fifty-five, age thirty-three, with a star tattooed on his left forearm."

Larkin hesitated for a moment, then said, "What's he wanted for, Selby?"

"Larceny."

"Where?"

"Los Angeles."

"We picked him up last night," Larkin said. "Just hold the phone a minute."

Over the telephone, Selby could hear the thud . . . thud . . . thud . . . thud made by hurrying steps. There followed an interval of silence, broken only by the buzzing on the wire, and at length by Sylvia Martin's low voice saying, "What's he doing, Doug?"

Selby covered the mouthpiece with his palm. "Looking up the case," he said, "and stalling for time. If there's to be any credit for apprehending a dangerous criminal, Larkin wants to see that the city police get it. He . . . Yes, hello, Larkin."

Larkin said, "He's been discharged, Selby. We didn't

really have anything against him. The boys went out on a prowler call last night. They picked up this chap walking along the sidewalk, out in the residential district. He said he was a stranger in town, afflicted with sleeplessness, and was taking a walk to get good and tired before he got a room in a hotel. He had a roll of dough on him, five hundred bucks. The boys got suspicious and threw him in overnight to see if there were any complaints of robbery or burglary. When none showed up, we gave him a floater."

"Take his fingerprints?" Selby asked.

"Yes. When he was brought in, they took his fingerprints. Why?"

Selby said, "He seems to be wanted in Los Angeles. He was arrested on a larceny count and jumped bail. Better communicate with the police there, Larkin."

Larkin said, "They'll razz me for letting him slip through my fingers. Why didn't you let me know sooner, Selby?"

"I didn't know it myself," Selby said.

"How did you know we had him here?"

Selby said, "Someone in the city recorder's office told Brandon. He was speaking to me about it. I happened to remember I'd seen something about this chap. Where did you pick him up, Larkin?"

"Out at Orange Heights."

"I see," Selby said. "Better notify Los Angeles."

Larkin's voice was surly. "You notify them," he said. "Tell them that the sheriff's office didn't let me know in time, that the delay was up there. Well, maybe I'd better call them myself."

"Okay," Selby said, and had started to hang up when Larkin's voice came rapidly over the wire, "How did you know it was the same . . ."

Selby eased the receiver onto the hook, ran to the door which led to the outer office, and said to Amorette Standish, "Get Sheriff Brandon on the line right away. See that Larkin doesn't get to call me back for a minute. Tell the downstairs operator to give him a busy signal and put me on with Brandon."

Selby came back to the telephone, waited a second or two until he heard the tinkle of a quick ring and picked up the receiver. Rex Brandon said, "Hello, Doug. What is it?"

Selby said, "Get this, Rex. One of your men happened to check up on the city line-up, and told you about a prowler who had been picked up in Orange Heights. He gave the description, and I happened to connect the description with that of a man named Ribber who's wanted in Los Angeles for jumping bail on a larceny charge. Better look up your postals. You'll find one somewhere in your files. Make the story stick with Larkin.

"What's it all about?" Brandon asked.

Selby said, "He's connected with A. B. Carr in some way. The Los Angeles district attorney's office is anxious to get Ribber. I think they're more anxious to establish a connection with Carr, if you get what I mean. They might have him for being an accessory after the fact or harboring a fugitive or something. I don't know all the details, but I think it's a case that's a little too delicate for Larkin's blundering touch. Stall the thing along, make it casual, and be sure to back my play. Larkin is certain to ask you why we were interested in a prowler in Orange Heights. Kid him along a bit. He'll be sore and think we're holding out on him, but there's nothing else we can do."

Sheriff Brandon said, "Okay, Doug. Be seeing you. G'by."

He hung up. Selby dropped the receiver back into place, and said to Sylvia Martin, "I'll bet you dollars to doughnuts that this Ribber chap is connected with something big. They didn't dare to let him get sent up for fear he'd squeal. The big shots probably hired Carr to get him out on bail and then see that he kept out of circulation."

"What are you going to do, Doug?" she asked.

16

"Get in touch with the district attorney's office in Los Angeles and make a report."

He called his secretary, handed her the letter, and said, "Get me the deputy in Los Angeles who wrote that letter, and if anyone calls during the next fifteen minutes, tell them I'm out."

The Los Angeles call came through almost at once. Selby made a brief report to the deputy who had written the letter, and received nothing more specific than an acknowledgment and a request that the sheriff's office put out a couple of prowl cars to cover the through highway and see if it was possible to pick Ribber up.

Selby again rang the sheriff's office and transferred the request. Brandon said, "I've already put 'em out, Doug. Larkin telephoned, and I handed him a little salve. He's already called both police cars to concentrate on a search within the city limits. The chap only has a fifteen-minute start. We may pick him up.

Selby said musingly, "Somehow I don't think we will, Rex. There's more to this than we think. I held out on Larkin because I didn't trust his judgment, and the D.A.'s office in Los Angeles is holding out on me for the same reason. You'll probably get a call from the sheriff's office within the next few minutes." Selby hung up and turned to Sylvia Martin. "Well," he said, "there you are, Sylvia. Nothing you can print."

She said indignantly, "Well, I'll certainly print the story that the city had a man who was wanted and let him slip through their fingers."

Selby shook his head. "Not now," he said. "Save it, Sylvia. There may be a good story come from it later."

She said, "Larkin will tell his side of it to the *Blade*."

"Let him."

She said, "Okay, Doug, on one condition, that you let me in on this if a big story starts to break."

"You promise you won't publish it until I give you a release?"

"Sure."

"It's a deal."

She got to her feet. "Well, I'll be on my way, and see if the bureau of marriage licenses can give me anything new. . . . So you don't think Carr's going to sue us, Doug?"

Selby smiled. "That was my original opinion, and there has been nothing in this morning's mail to contradict it."

"I get you," she said, starting for the door. "Give me something I can quote sometime, will you, Doug?"

"I may at that," he told her.

CHAPTER III

IT WAS ON FRIDAY MORNING, JUST AS AMORETTE STANDISH was starting to leave Selby's office with a telegram he had dictated, that a little, round-shouldered man came rushing into Selby's office with a suit of clothes over his arm. He was breathless with exertion and excitement.

"What is it?" Selby asked.

The man said, "You don't know me, Selby. I'm Bill Horton, with the Acme Cleaners & Dyers. We had a run-in with the city police over double parking, and I don't want to go to them unless I have to. I know you and Brandon are running this place on the square. Brandon isn't in, and I decided to come to you."

"What is it?" Selby asked.

Horton unfolded the suit of clothes which was on his arm and laid them out on Selby's desk.

Selby stared at the coat and vest. It was a light brown suit on which the sinister red stain had incrusted into stiffness. Near the center of the red stain was a hole surrounded

18

by a slightly burnt area pitted into little holes. "Where," Selby asked, "did you get this?"

"Out of my truck," Horton said.

"And how did it get there?"

"I'm darned if I know," Horton admitted. "I was out getting pick-ups this morning. I made my regular run and came back to put the clothes in the sorting room. While we were sorting them, we found this."

"But don't you know where you got it?"

"I didn't get it," Horton said. "It was put in my truck."

"When?"

"I wish I knew."

"You don't know when or where or how it was put in your truck?"

"That's right."

Selby picked up the receiver on his desk telephone and said, "Locate Rex Brandon. No matter where he is, get him at once. Tell him to come up here. It's important." He dropped the telephone into place and turned back to face Horton. "How," Selby asked, "do you mark your suits— when you pick them up?"

Horton said, "That depends. If they're regular customers, we have our regular cleaning marks indelibly printed on the inside of the inside pocket of the coat. All I have to do is to look and see if the mark is still there. If it's a new customer, I pin a slip on the suit, and we obliterate the other cleaning marks and substitute our own."

Selby said, "How about this suit?"

"It has a strange mark. That is, it's an outside mark. It isn't one used by any of the cleaners here in Madison City."

"How do you know that?"

"We have a general system. We've divided up letters of the alphabet. For instance, the Acme Cleaners & Dyers have the first five letters of the alphabet. We can use them in any combination we want with any number we want. The Night

& Day Cleaning Company has the next five letters, and so on. Now the number on this suit starts out with AG. The A's our number, and the G belongs to the Night & Day outfit. If it was our number, we'd have it AB or AC—get me?"

"I get you," Selby said.

The telephone rang, and Amorette Standish said, "Here's Sheriff Brandon for you."

Selby said, "Hello, Rex. Where are you?"

"Just finishing up a session at the barber shop," Brandon said. "I thought my hair was getting so long people might think I was in disguise."

Selby said, "Come up as quick as you can, Rex. We may have either a murder or a suicide on our hands."

"Where's the body?" Brandon asked.

Selby said, "That's what I don't know."

"Coming right up," Brandon promised, and hung up.

Selby turned to a contemplation of the suit. He said, "I guess we can leave suicide out of it. It looks as though he'd been shot on the right side by someone who was standing slightly behind him."

Horton said, "Yeah, that's the way it looks all right."

Selby said, "Can't you give me any clue as to where you picked this suit up?"

"No, I can't."

"You can't tell from its position in the clothes?"

"Well, now, wait a minute," Horton said. "There might be something to that. Yes, I believe it was out in the Tenth Avenue district somewhere. I remember I turned in the clothes I got from Orange Heights and . . ."

"It couldn't have come from Orange Heights?" Selby asked.

"No. I'd turned in all that cleaning, and we'd listed it. We make a list of every garment that comes in. I turn over the stuff to the person who does the checking. He checks

20

them, and then looks through the pockets to see if anything's been left in them."

"Go ahead," Selby said.

"Well, I'd completely finished with the Orange Heights layout, and from there I swing down to Tenth Avenue. I was . . ."

"What garment did you check just before you found this suit?" Selby asked.

"I can call up the checker and find out, but I think it was a suit from Arthur Peel. Yes, yes, I'm pretty certain it was."

"And then you came to this?"

"Uh huh."

"Now where did you stop after leaving Arthur Peel's? Where did you go next?"

"Sidney Trace's place."

"Did you pick up anything there?"

"Yes. I had a couple of dresses and a blouse and two suits."

"How do you take things out of the car, in the order in which you put them in, or the inverse order?"

"I don't get you."

"When you take clothes in, do you push them toward the front of the car so that when you start taking them out, the last suit you put in is the last one out and . . ."

"Oh, I get you now. No. They come out the same way they go in. The stuff goes in a box that slides out of the delivery truck. It goes into the checker's office, and we start from the front end instead of the back end. That makes 'em come out the same way they went in."

"You don't think there's any chance this suit was in the Peel delivery or the Trace's?"

"Not a chance."

"Then it must have been put in the box by someone just

after you'd passed Peel's house and before you made the pick-up from Trace's residence."

"Maybe."

"You were alone in the car?"

"Sure."

"You parked it at the curb in front of Trace's house?"

"That's right."

"And went in to ask for the cleaning?"

"Uh huh."

"How long were you in there?"

Horton shifted his eyes and said sullenly, "Just a second or two."

Selby, watching him searchingly, said, "Who gives you the cleaning generally?"

"Sometimes Mrs. Trace. Sometimes the maid."

"Who gave it to you this morning?"

"The maid."

Selby said musingly, "I think I've seen her. Isn't she tall and thin with crossed eyes, a woman about forty-eight or fifty who . . ."

"Naw. That ain't it at all," Horton said hastily. "Eve ain't a day over thirty, and she sure has class stamped all over her."

"During the ten minutes that you were in there," Selby asked casually, "did you think anyone could have opened the back of the car and slipped the suit in?"

"Who told you I was in there ten minutes?"

Selby frowned. "Where was it I got that impression? Didn't you say there'd been a ten-minute interval?"

"Naw. Shucks, it wasn't any ten minutes. It was nearer to five."

"What were you and Eve talking about?" Selby asked.

"Oh, about the horse races and—well, you know, just kidding a little bit. I told her she was looking pretty swell, and she said it was a wonder a girl never got a break giving clothes to the Acme outfit, and she thought she'd try one of the other places for a while, that some of the other drivers would at least take her to a show on her night out."

"That was all?" Selby asked.

"That's about all of it, just kidding."

"And how long did that kidding continue?"

"Oh, maybe a minute or two."

"Perhaps ten minutes?"

"I don't think so."

Selby said, "Well, we'll take this suit and check up on it. Be around so I can reach you in case it's necessary. By the way, do you have any plans for this evening?"

Horton said, "Gee, Mr. Selby, I'd like to go to the movies this evening."

"Well, I can reach you there," Selby said carelessly. "You'll be alone?"

"No . . . Well . . . Well, you see, Eve's going to be with me."

Selby said, "Oh, I see. I think, Horton, we'd better make that time a good ten minutes. Even a fast worker like you couldn't have accomplished all that in one or two minutes."

Horton grinned and said, "Well, don't tell the boss, Mr. Selby."

" I won't," Selby assured him. "You can't give me any clue as to this cleaner's mark in the suit, can you?"

"No. But I think it's Los Angeles. It's a ready-made suit, and it was sold in Los Angeles."

"Quite a few of the ready-made suits worn in Madison City are sold in Los Angeles, aren't they?"

"That's right."

Selby said, "All right, Horton. No, wait a minute. While you were talking with Eve, where was Mrs. Trace?"

"I wouldn't know."

"Do you know whether she was in the house?"

"No, I don't."

23

"You didn't hear anyone moving around?"

"No."

"And what time were you there?"

"Oh, around ten o'clock, I guess. I left the shop a little before nine."

Selby said, "All right, Horton, I'll get in touch with you later."

Less than sixty seconds after Horton left, Sheriff Brandon walked rapidly down the corridor and tapped on the door of Selby's private office. The district attorney let him in, showed him the suit of clothes, and told him the story. Brandon rolled a cigarette and smoked it while Selby was giving him the details. "I suppose," he said at length, "we've got to let Otto Larkin in on this."

"I suppose so," Selby admitted. "I wonder if we can tell anything about those bloodstains—how old they are, or anything of that sort?"

Brandon said, "They look fresh to me, Doug. The blood has dried, but I think it's only a few hours old. I think the stain would get more brownish after a day or so."

Selby pushed tobacco into his pipe." Why should anyone want to send this suit to the cleaners?" he asked. "They certainly didn't want it back."

Brandon said, "Now, *that's* an idea."

Selby said, "The man who wore that suit was shot. The wound was undoubtedly fatal. The clothes were taken from the body. Those clothes were placed in the pick-up wagon of a cleaning and dyeing establishment. The person who placed those clothes in that wagon must have realized they would be discovered within an hour, and taken at once to the authorities. Now why did he do it?"

Brandon squinted his eyes, and said, "By gosh, Doug, if you want to look at it that way, why *did* he?"

"There were," Selby said, "two possible reasons. One of them was that the murderer didn't want to have the murder

24

remain undiscovered, and took this means of letting the authorities know."

"But why on earth should anyone take such a roundabout way of tipping us off to a murder, and why should he be so anxious that we find out about it?"

Selby shook his head and said, "It's the best answer I can give. However, let's go get Otto Larkin. He'll be sore if we don't call him in on it. It's probably something within the city limits. Then we'll go out and talk with the maid at Trace's place. Somehow I don't trust that chap Horton too much. I think he's trying to protect himself, and is more interested in seeing that he isn't accused of carelessness and negligence than in helping us out."

Brandon said, "I know him. He's a little runt, nuts on the horse races, spends anything he can get on playing the ponies."

The telephone rang. Selby picked it up, and his secretary said, "The Acme Cleaners & Dyers on the line."

Selby said, "Hello," and a man's voice said, "Mr. Selby, this is Bill Atwood at the Acme Cleaners & Dyers."

"Hello, Atwood," Selby said. "I was just talking with your driver."

"Yes," Atwood said, "and I'm not certain but what he gave you a wrong steer."

"How?"

"Well, while he was gone, I'd been working with the checker trying to figure how that suit got in the pile. Horton says he told you it was between suits from Peel's and Trace's and the Tenth Avenue district. He thinks it was, but the checker feels almost certain that it came from some stuff in the Orange Heights district, and he *thinks* it fell out of the stuff that came from A. B. Carr's place."

"Don't your records show?" Selby asked.

"Well, not exactly. The stuff that comes in from that district is on hangers, and the checker thinks this suit fell out

25

and dropped on the floor. He let it lie for a minute, looking for the vacant hanger from which it had dropped. It was a suit that had been stuffed in with some other suits."

Selby said, "Horton tells me that he checks the numbers on all of those suits that . . ."

"Well, he doesn't," Atwood said. "He's supposed to, but he doesn't. I doubt if any driver does. When they pick up suits from a regular customer, they just dump them in the truck—regardless of what they tell you."

Selby said, "All right. Thanks, Atwood. Now I want you to keep this under your hat. Say nothing to anyone about it until you get an okay from me. Can you do that?"

"I can," Atwood said, "but I'm not absolutely certain about the help. We may keep it quiet for a few hours, but someone's going to talk, and things like that get around like wildfire."

"I know," Selby said. "Just do the best you can."

"I will," Atwood said.

"And," Selby told him, "try and pound some sense into Horton's head. I don't want to go into a court on a case where your checker will swear to one thing, and Horton will swear to another, and we'll be left out on a limb."

"The checker's a lot more responsible than Horton," Atwood said.

Selby said, "You talk to Horton—and I'll talk to him later on. Give him a chance to talk with the checker, and see if they can't straighten the thing out between them." He hung up and nodded to Brandon. "Okay," he said, "let's go see Larkin."

CHAPTER IV

OTTO LARKIN, A PAUNCHY MAN IN THE EARLY FIFTIES, LIStened to Selby's story with interest, his little, glittering eyes shifting from time to time to Selby's face, then to Brandon's, then away to stare out of the window. He said, "I think Horton's more apt to be right than Atwood. Horton's the driver. He knows where he picked it up."

"The point is," Selby explained patiently, "that Horton apparently didn't pick it up at all. It was pushed in the wagon."

Larkin hesitated for a moment as though debating whether to speak or keep silent. At length, he said, "I don't suppose it means anything, but there was another prowler out in the Orange Heights district last night, and the man in the radio car heard a pistol shot."

Selby and Brandon exchanged glances. "Near Carr's place?" Brandon asked.

Larkin nodded and said, "That's why I don't like what Atwood says. It looks to me as though he's trying to take the facts we have and fit this suit business into them."

"How does he know those facts?" Selby asked.

"Oh, he knows them all right," Larkin said easily. "His brother-in-law's running the cigar stand in the corner of the poolroom where most of my men hang out when they're off duty."

Brandon said significantly, "I didn't hear anything about the revolver shot, Larkin."

Larkin said hastily, "Well, I don't think it was a shot, just some kind of an explosion, probably someone taking a shot at a cat or a rabbit. I didn't notify you because I didn't think it amounted to anything."

Selby said, "Suppose you tell us about it now, Larkin."

"Well," Larkin said, his eyes studiously avoiding those of the sheriff and district attorney, "we got another call from Mrs. Artrim."

"*Another* call?" Selby interrupted significantly.

"Yeah, she was the one who called in the first time about

that prowler, the one that was wanted by the people in Los Angeles."

"I see," Selby said. "Go ahead."

"Well, she called in last night along about two o'clock in the morning and said there was another prowler around her place—only she said it was the same one. Well, I remembered that this guy was wanted in Los Angeles and figured it was a swell chance to pick him up, so the radio dispatcher got in touch with the car that was out in that neck of the woods, and the boys beat it out there."

"Did they go directly to Mrs. Artrim's residence?" Selby asked.

"No. The technique on handling a prowler call is to run out to the neighborhood and go around the block a couple of times, then turn on the spotlight, and take a look through the vicinity, and *then* go up to the house that reported the prowler. Usually when the prowler hears the car coming, he figures it's a police car, and nine times out of ten, he goes back to the sidewalk and starts walking rapidly away from the place, looking neither to the right nor the left, trying to pretend that he's just an innocent citizen going some place in a hurry. That's the way we picked up that guy the other night."

"Go ahead," Selby said.

"Well, just as the boys got up to Mrs. Artrim's place for the first time, they saw a flash a little ways off from the road, and heard the sound of a shot. Well, naturally, they turned the spotlight on the place and went over and looked around. They didn't find anything."

"Where," Selby asked, "was this shot fired?"

"Well, it was right on the edge of that deep barranca between Artrim's place and Carr's house. You probably remember that deep canyon. Some subterranean water-flow must have dissolved the earth, and a section of the hill caved in. Originally they intended to terrace it, but the city engineer warned them not to. He said that the sagebrush and scrub oak in there were keeping the thing from all washing down, that if they tried to do anything with it, it would start caving back and ruin that much more property. They cemented the bottom some to keep it from getting deeper and . . ."

"I know the place," Selby said.

"Well, the shot was on that side of the barranca."

"What do you mean by that side?"

"The north side, the one nearest A. B. Carr's place."

"That barranca," Selby said, "is fifty or seventy-five feet deep at that point."

"That's right."

"Did anyone else hear the shot?"

"Oh, yes, the Artrims heard it. Mrs. Artrim was frightened to death. The old man's a cripple, you know, and he's a little goofy. They keep a nurse with him all the time. He heard the shot, and called to the nurse, but the nurse had run upstairs to Mrs. Artrim. After the officers started prowling around the vicinity, making an investigation, he banged on the floor and started cussing. The officers could hear him swearing clean across the barranca."

"And the officers found no one?"

"No one," Larkin admitted, "but you know how it is out there, Doug. A man could fire a shot and then drop down in that barranca, and if he only had sense enough to lie absolutely still. the officers could never find him—not at night. There are lots of little feeders running into that barranca."

Selby nodded.

"To tell you the truth," Larkin said, "when my boys got out there and got the dope on it, they figured it was some goofy guy wandering around and shooting up the town. Mrs. Artrim said he didn't have any clothes on."

"Didn't have any clothes on?" Sheriff Brandon said, with a significant glance at Selby.

"That's right, the man was naked as the day he was born, according to what she says. There was no moon, but she claims there was enough starlight so she could see him as a vague blur walking around on the lawn."

Selby glanced inquiringly at Brandon. Brandon nodded. "Let's go out there," he said, "and check up on it."

"Okay," Larkin said, "but I don't think that's connected with the suit of clothes. The man who was wearing that suit of clothes was shot when he had them on. This chap was wandering around without any clothes on."

"I know," Selby said, "but I think we can investigate that shot a little more."

"Okay," Larkin said, reaching for his hat. "We can run out there."

Sheriff Brandon said, "I've already telephoned Los Angeles. They're going to make an effort to chase down that cleaner's mark and find out who the suit belongs to."

"You got your car here?" Larkin asked.

Brandon nodded.

"Well, let's go in that."

The trio had started down the corridor toward the exit from the city hall when an officer from the radio dispatcher's room came running toward them. He nodded to Doug Selby and Rex Brandon, but made his report directly to Otto Larkin. "A party of boys playing out in the Orange Heights district found the nude body of a man jammed down into a barranca," he said." I've ordered the radio car out there. It's the barranca right at the top of the hill adjoining that place the lawyer bought."

Selby said, "Notify the coroner. . . . Come on, let's go— before footprints and clues get obliterated."

Otto Larkin said, "My boys will be on the job. They know how to handle it."

"Yeah, we know," Sheriff Brandon said and started running down the corridor toward the car. Brandon kicked the siren into action. The car lurched away from the city hall, swung into a wide, skidding turn on Main Street, and went flashing past the frozen traffic, the sheriff's red spotlight and screaming siren calling for the right of way. They left Main Street near the west end of town, and followed the winding contour driveway which led up to Orange Heights, one of the city's most recent and exclusive subdivisions.

None of the men talked as the car swung around the turns, climbing rapidly. Behind them, the valley opened into a panorama. Madison City showed in the clear, dry air of Southern California as a city modeled in miniature. Up on Orange Heights, the more expensive residences flashed by, houses of Spanish architecture with big white stucco walls, red tile roofs, patios, and landscaped grounds.

The barranca was on the western slope near the highest point of the subdivision. Here was an air of expensive luxury. The buildings became veritable castles. Over on the left, Mrs. Artrim's residence flashed dazzlingly white as the bright sunlight reflected back from the stucco walls. Just beyond was the barranca, and on the other side of that the big residence so recently purchased by A. B. Carr sprawled in spacious, indolent grandeur. A police car was parked almost directly in front of the building. Three very frightened small boys were being interrogated by two uniformed officers from the radio car. The men were looking down at a brush-covered cleft in the barranca.

Selby, Rex Brandon, and Otto Larkin joined the group. One of the officers led the way. The three men stood on the edge of the cleft and looked down at a nude figure, jammed down deep in the barranca.

Selby said, "All right, boys. Let's keep everyone back until we can check the ground for footprints. There are some over here—going down that spur and . . ."

One of the radio officers said, "That's where I went down." Selby frowned and looked over at the other side. The second radio officer said, "I went down there." One of the boys, a frightened lad of nine, said, "We ran down here. We were going down to shoot our air guns, and we walked right on him. Gee whiz, we . . ." His voice choked up, and he became silent.

Selby said dryly, "It doesn't look as though we were going to do much with footprints. We're going to want some photographs of this, Rex."

Brandon said, "The coroner carries a camera with him. He should be here any minute. I'll go over and telephone Bob Terry. He'll come up and bring the office camera."

Otto Larkin said significantly, "This is within the city limits, you know."

Brandon met his eyes steadily and said, "Yes, I know," then walked away.

Selby called to him, "Don't go in Carr's place, Rex. Better telephone from the Artrim house."

Brandon nodded.

The sound of a car became audible as it climbed the steeply sloping road in second gear. Otto Larkin, puffing importantly, slid down the steep sides of the cleft to bend over the body. "All right, boys," he said to the radio officers. "Let's lift him up and . . ."

"Don't move that body until the coroner gets here," Selby said.

Larkin flashed him a glance. His eyes glittered. He seemed on the point of saying something, but contented himself with a mere nod. They waited, silent, the air filled with tension.

The coroner's car came into view, roared up along the last slope, and slid to a stop behind the county car. Harry Perkins, tall, thin, and bony, descended from the car with unhurried efficiency. He walked over to where the men were standing, and said, "Hello, boys. What have we got?"

Rex Brandon emerged from the Artrim residence, walked

rapidly back to join the group. The coroner slid down to join Otto Larkin in an inspection of the body.

"Got a camera?" Selby asked.

The coroner nodded.

Selby, moving around the edges of the barranca, kicking aside clumps of tall grass and stunted sage, suddenly said, "Here's a revolver."

The other climbed up out of the barranca to join him in looking down at the blued steel of a thirty-eight caliber Colt police-positive. Larkin stooped to pick it up. Selby placed a restraining hand on Larkin's arm. "Just a minute," he said. "There may be fingerprints. We'd better take care to preserve them."

Brandon joined the group, broke off a short bit of dried sage.

Larkin said, "I'll take it. This is within the city limits." Once more he stooped for the gun.

Brandon said, "I'll take it, Larkin. I want to look it over for fingerprints."

Larkin's eyes glittered. This time he flared into speech. "Look here," he said, "this is within the city limits."

Rex Brandon nodded casually. "And I'm taking charge of the gun, Larkin," he said.

"But it's within the city limits. It's *my* case."

Brandon, hooking a fork of the sage through the trigger guard of the revolver, raised it carefully, and said, "I don't give a damn if it's in your backyard."

Selby said, "Take it easy, Larkin. This is a murder case. I'm going to have to prosecute it. I want to preserve the evidence."

Larkin said, "It's in my jurisdiction."

Brandon, holding the gun in front of him, looked it over. He said, "Bob Terry's on his way up. He'll have his fingerprint outfit with him, also a camera."

Perkins, the coroner, said, "I'll get my camera. We'll both take pictures."

Larkin, biting savagely into a cigar, said, "I can handle this. If you fellows get it all balled up, you'll take the responsibility."

"We will," Brandon said.

The coroner returned with his camera, shot several pictures. Bob Terry appeared on the scene, took more pictures, and dusted the gun with powder.

"Any latents, Bob?" the sheriff asked.

"Two or three," Terry said. "I'll photograph them right here. Then we'll put the gun in a box."

Brandon said, "As nearly as I can see, without pushing out the cylinder, there's only one shell fired."

Terry said, "I'll get those fingerprints photographed, then we can make an examination."

Larkin nodded toward the eight-foot wall which surrounded the patio of Carr's residence. "Almost in the guy's backyard," he said.

Brandon nodded.

"I'll go in and talk with him," Larkin said.

"We'll all go," Selby told him. "Let's wait until they bring the body up, and see if we haven't some definite questions to ask."

Larkin, biting down on his cigar, said, "I'm going now," and started for the house.

Sheriff Brandon glanced at Selby. "Think you'd better go along, Doug," he said quietly. "I'll stay here."

Selby nodded and joined Larkin.

Larkin, without turning his head, said, "This is going to be a big case. There'll be a lot of newspaper notoriety. Finding a body within fifty feet of Carr's patio is going to make a lot of news. I don't want you guys to hog all the credit."

Selby said quietly, "We're not going to."

In silence the two men walked around to the front of the

house. Larkin took the lead, climbed up the stairs to the tiled porch and rang the bell.

After several moments of silence, a broad, muscular woman in the early fifties opened the door.

"Who are you?" Larkin asked.

She met his eyes with a calm scrutiny. Her face didn't change expression. "Who are you?" she asked.

Larkin pulled back his coat, showed her his badge. "The chief of police," he said.

"Oh."

"Where's Carr?" Larkin asked, starting forward.

The woman in the door didn't give an inch. "In Los Angeles in his office," she said.

Larkin said, "We're coming in. We want to look around."

"What for?" she asked, still without budging.

"A body's been discovered out here in the barranca."

"Well," she asked, "what about it? It isn't Carr, is it?"

Larkin frowned and said, "We're coming in and look around."

The woman said, "I don't know anything about you. Mr. Carr said that if any officers came snooping around and wanted to look the place over, to ask them if they had a search warrant. If they had a search warrant, I was to let them in. If they didn't I wasn't."

Larkin said, "Oh, so he was expecting we'd be here to make a search, was he?"

"I guess so," she said.

Larkin said significantly, "That's very incriminating. That shows he knew a murder had been committed.

Selby said, "*When* did he tell you this?"

She shifted her eyes from Larkin to Selby, and said, "A week ago when he hired me. You're Mr. Selby, the district attorney, aren't you?"

Selby nodded.

She said, "You don't remember me. I'm Mrs. Fermal.

My boy was in some trouble about a year ago, and you made things easy for him."

Selby said, "Roy Fermal?"

"That's right."

Selby said, "I remember him. How's he doing?"

"He's doing fine. He's got a steady job, and he's quit chasing around with that wild bunch."

Selby said, "That's fine. I'm glad to hear it."

"I'm sorry I can't let you in, Mr. Selby. I'd like to do it, but a job is a job these days, and orders are orders."

"I understand," Selby said.

Larkin, frowning, said, "Well, no shyster lawyer is going to tell me where to get off. I'm coming in, do you understand?"

Mrs. Fermal said simply, "If you can handle me, you can come in. If you try to come in without a search warrant, there's going to be a fight. I've got my orders."

Selby said, "Better take it easy, Larkin. You aren't looking for anything in particular, you know."

Larkin chewed on his cigar and said abruptly, "I don't like it."

Selby said, "I don't like it either."

Mrs. Fermal said, "Those were the orders he gave me. Maybe he's right, maybe he's wrong, but as long as I'm working for him, he's right."

Selby said, "Come on, Larkin. They probably have the body moved by this time."

Larkin hesitated a moment, then turned and followed Selby off the porch.

Mrs. Fermal closed the front door with that degree of force which lent emphasis to her action—a force which stopped just short of being a slam.

Larkin said, as they walked off the porch, "That business isn't going to get him anywhere. I'll have him brought into my office for questioning."

Selby said, dryly, "I suppose it's occurred to you, Larkin, that A. B. Carr is pretty well versed in his legal rights."

"He may be able to get away with some of that stuff in the city," Larkin said, "but that's no sign he can do it here."

As they approached the little group gathered about the body, Rex Brandon detached himself and walked over to take Selby's arm. Larkin pushed importantly forward, and Brandon manipulated the district attorney to one side of the little group. "It's darn funny," he said. "The man has shoes, socks, and garters, and not another stitch on. He's been shot twice. Both bullets were evidently fired at close range, and they both went in the same place."

"In the same place!" Selby repeated in surprise.

"That's right," Brandon said.

"But how could that have happened?" Selby asked. "After the man was shot the first time, he'd certainly fall over. It's hardly conceivable that an assailant could bend over and place the gun at such an angle that the second shot would follow the same path as the other."

Brandon said, "What's more, Doug, there's only one shell fired out of this thirty-eight police-positive. I've got a hunch we're tackling a tough proposition here."

Selby frowned. "Anything to identify the body?" he asked.

"We've taken his fingerprints. And here's something funny, Doug. There's a star tattooed on his left forearm."

Selby said, "Why, that's an identifying mark on that man who's wanted in Los Angeles, Pete Ribber."

"I know," Brandon said.

"Any chance that this is the same man? He . . ."

"None at all," the sheriff said. "This man looks as though he was tubercular. Either that, or a dope fiend. He doesn't weigh over a hundred and fifteen pounds. He has a small-boned frame, but he's wasted away until he's just skin and bones."

"And he's been shot twice in exactly the same place?" Selby asked.

"Yes."

"Either bullet come through?"

"No. They're both in there."

Selby said, "All right. We'll have a post-mortem, and see what we find."

Brandon gave a word of warning. "Watch Otto Larkin," he said. "As long as he thinks there's a chance for some publicity, he'll hog the limelight."

"I know," Selby said, "but I'd rather let him do that than take a chance on having the murderer escape."

Larkin turned away from the group and came toward them. "Well," he said, "it's a gangster killing. They took this guy for a ride, took his clothes away from him so he couldn't get away, and were going to shoot him. He jumped out of the car, and started to run. The boys took after him. Mrs. Artrim saw him wandering around naked, and telephoned for us. Just before our car got here, the gang spotted him. They pumped a couple of bullets into him, pushed him down into the canyon, and then ducked for cover themselves. They waited until after the police had given up the search, and then beat it."

Selby turned to Rex Brandon. "How can you tell he was shot twice," he asked, "if the bullets both entered at the same place?"

The sheriff said, "It's *almost* the same hole, not quite. It looks to me as though he was shot once when he had his clothes on. That's a guess from what we already know and the way the powder burns appear in the skin."

Otto Larkin creased his forehead in a frown. "Well," he said, "I'll tell you what happened. They took him for a ride. He jumped out of the car. They shot him once as he jumped out. Then they caught him and took his clothes away, and shot him again."

"He was wandering around the Artrim yard without any clothes on," Brandon pointed out.

Larkin said doggedly, "Well, it's a gang killing anyway. Ten to one the guy's a crook."

CHAPTER V

SYLVIA MARTIN FOUND DOUG SELBY IN HIS OFFICE SHORTLY after five o'clock. She had a copy of the *Blade* under her arm. "Seen it, Doug?" she asked.

He shook his head.

"You should read it, and learn how fortunate it is that Madison City has a thoroughly efficient chief of police. The town is so well policed that officers all but caught the gangsters who were taking an unfortunate victim for a ride in the act of committing the murder."

Selby grinned and said, "And having the flash of the gun to guide them, they failed to see the body, and must have walked right past the gangsters who were hiding in the barranca."

Sylvia laughed and said, "I don't think they looked very hard, Doug. It's one thing to pick up a prowler. It's another to go gumshoeing around in the darkness where someone is waiting with a loaded gun."

"It is at that," Selby admitted. "What else does the *Blade* have to say?"

"Oh, lots of things," she said. "It even mentions your name. Yes, it does too. Right down at the very end of the account. It says that after Chief of Police Larkin had the case well in hand, he turned the proof over to Prosecutor Doug Selby with instructions as to how the case should be handled."

Selby grinned.

Sylvia Martin waxed suddenly indignant. "Now you listen to me, Doug Selby. Don't you sit there and grin and think it's a joke. It isn't. It's serious. Otto Larkin will work through the *Blade*, which hates you, and take every bit of credit he can. He'll belittle you all the way along the line, and if the case is solved, it'll be the brave and astute chief of police who apprehended the criminals. If anything goes wrong with it, the *Blade* will say that, because of interference by the district attorney and the failure to follow Larkin's instructions, the murderers have slipped through the net which Larkin was tightening about them."

Selby let his grin fade into a tolerant smile. He pushed tobacco into the bowl of his pipe, struck a match, and puffed complacently at his pipe.

"You can't let him get away with that, Doug," she said.

"What," he asked, "can I do to stop it?"

"You can give us some ammunition," she said. "We'll fire right back at 'em."

"What sort of ammunition?"

"Facts that you've discovered, things that Larkin knows nothing about."

"In other words," Selby said, "you'd like to have the absolute low-down and be given a nice little scoop?"

"How did you guess it?" she asked.

"I'm quite a mind-reader," Selby said. "My family were all psychic."

"Come on, Doug. Kick through like a good little boy."

Selby opened a drawer in his desk and took out some photographs, showing three somewhat blurred smudges of ridges etched in white against a dark background. "Do these mean anything to you, Sylvia?" he asked.

"No. What are they, Doug, fingerprints?"

"Yes, on the murder gun."

"Do you know whose fingerprints they are?"

"Yes."

40

"Whose?"

"Pete Ribber's, our friend from Los Angeles," Selby said. "As soon as we got the fingerprints, I had Bob Terry check them against Ribber's prints."

She said, "Then he's been back there."

Selby said, "Evidently."

Sylvia asked excitedly, "Does Larkin know this?"

"Not yet," Selby said. "It never occurred to him to check those fingerprints. As a matter of fact, if we hadn't stepped in, there wouldn't have been any fingerprints to take."

"That's swell, Doug. That'll give me a peach of an angle. Have you found out anything more about Ribber?"

Selby said, "Nothing new, but we should find out something shortly after the story gets around that his fingerprints are on the gun."

"And I can use that, Doug?"

"Go as far as you like. The more advertisement the better."

"That's swell."

Selby went on, "Also, we found out the identity of the dead man."

"Who is it, Doug?"

"A man by the name of Taleman."

"How did you locate him, Doug?"

"In two ways," he said. "We found that his fingerprints were on file in Washington, and we located the cleaner in Los Angeles whose number appears in the label of the clothes. His record shows that the suit belongs to a Mervin Sprague. The description checks, and we've established conclusively that Sprague is an alias of Taleman."

"That," she said, "is fast work. What else could you find out about him?"

"Nothing yet," Selby said. "We're trying to show a connection between Taleman and Pete Ribber. They both had stars tattooed on their forearms. It looks as though it had been done at the same time by the same person. You know, a couple of chaps travel together in a foreign country and come to the conclusion that it would be a good idea to have some tattooing."

Sylvia Martin thought for a moment, then said slowly, "Isn't that going to drag Carr into this thing pretty deeply?"

"Probably," Selby said.

"Has anyone secured a statement from him?"

"No. He wasn't at his office in Los Angeles. They hadn't seen him all day. The housekeeper said he wasn't home. He'd told her he was going to the office."

"Doug, is Otto Larkin going to interview him?"

"He says he is."

"Doug, don't let him. He'll simply be putty in that lawyer's hands. Larkin is just a stuffed shirt. A man like old A.B.C. will twist him and tie him into a knot. He'll squeeze Larkin dry of information, and then throw him out."

Selby nodded.

"Doug, you aren't going to let him do it, are you?"

Selby said, "I don't know as I can help it. I know that he's trying to get in touch with Carr, but he hasn't said anything to me about accompanying him on his visit."

"But why don't you go see Carr on your own, Doug?"

"I'm going to."

"Shouldn't you see him before Larkin does?"

Selby grinned. "Wouldn't it be too bad if Larkin tried to cross-examine Carr and didn't get anywhere, and I was able to set a trap which brought forth an incriminatory statement?"

"Doug, can you do that?"

"I don't know," he said. "There are a couple of things to be cleared up."

Sylvia Martin said, "Well, let me have that picture of Pete Ribber. We'll run it tomorrow. It's all right to state definitely that his fingerprints are on the murder gun?"

"On the gun," Selby said. "Don't refer to it as the murder gun as yet."

"Why, Doug?"

Selby said, "The post-mortem shows there were two bullets in the body. Both of the bullets followed almost exactly the same path. They were lying in the tissues almost side by side. The bullets were different. They were different in make, different in weight, and they were fired from different guns."

"Well?" she asked.

Selby said, "They weren't fired at the same time. One was fired later than the other. Either one would have produced death."

"Well?" she asked, puzzled.

"Because they were fired by two different guns," Selby said, "the shots were quite probably fired by two different persons. Now figure that out."

"What do you mean, Doug?"

"Whichever bullet was first," Selby said, "would have killed him instantly."

"Well?"

"According to the testimony of the medical experts, the man must have been dead by the time the second bullet was fired into his body. We don't know whether the gun we have with Ribber's fingerprints fired the first bullet or the second."

"But they both must have *intended* to kill him, Doug."

"That doesn't make any great deal of difference," Selby said, "not for the present purpose. It's murder to fire a bullet into the body of a living man—if the wound is fatal. But there's no particular law against firing a bullet into a corpse if a man is so minded. Therefore, Ribber may be guilty of murder, or he may be guilty only of violating a city ordinance by discharging a firearm within the city limits."

"But, Doug, couldn't you get him for assault with a deadly weapon with intent to commit murder because . . ."

Selby shook his head and said, "An assault with an intent to commit murder must be committed upon a human being. After a man is dead, he ceases to be a human being and becomes a corpse."

Sylvia stared incredulously at Selby. "Well, of all the mix-ups," she said. "But look here, Doug, you have one thing in your favor. It's a cinch that the shot which was fired through the clothes must have been fired first. Therefore, the fatal shot must have been fired when the man had his clothes on."

Selby grinned. "All right, and which gun fired that shot?" he asked.

"Why . . . why—can't you tell from the size of the hole, Doug?"

"They're both the same caliber."

"Look here, Doug. Do you mean to tell me that you can prove that Ribber fired a shot into this body and then can't do anything about it?"

Selby said, "It depends. But I'm commenting on some complicating factors."

"Look here, Doug. You know as well as I do that this is some of A. B. Carr's work. He's the only one who would have the ingenuity to think out something like that and the only one who knows enough law to figure how he could mix you up."

"It looks that way," Selby admitted, "although that's distinctly confidential."

"What are you going to do, Doug?"

"Let Larkin go off half-cocked if he wants to. I'll wait and interview Carr myself after I get more dope."

"Gee, Doug, this fingerprint stuff is swell. No one else knows about it, do they?"

"The sheriff," Selby said.

"He's all right. Could you manage to keep it from Larkin

for a couple of hours? The *Blade* will get out an extra if it has the chance. They'd like to make this a big boost for Larkin."

"We don't need to tell him for two or three hours," Selby said.

"That'll be long enough. Thanks, Doug. I'm on my way."

She flashed him a quick smile, walked rapidly to the door, and Doug Selby, sitting at his desk, listened to the sound of her feet on the flagged floor of the corridor. He heard her steps pause, heard her engage in low-voiced conversation with a man, then heard the steps of two people approaching his office.

Selby got up and opened the door when he recognized the quick drumming of fingertips which Sylvia usually used in place of a knock. The man who was with Sylvia was crowding sixty. His hair was sprinkled with gray. His eyebrows were bushy and white, the eyes steady and severe. Lines of self-discipline had stamped themselves upon the features.

Selby said, "Why, good evening, Mr. Hendrix. Won't you come in?"

Sylvia said, "I told him the offices were closed, but I thought I could get you by tapping on the door of your private office. Will you give me a ring later on if anything turns up, Doug?"

He nodded, and said to Hendrix, "Come in and sit down."

Abner Hendrix, the father of Mrs. Artrim, walked slowly over to the chair which Selby had indicated.

"What," Selby asked, "can I do for you?"

Hendrix said, "It's about my daughter."

Selby nodded sympathetically.

"I don't know how much of the family history you know," Hendrix said.

"Not very much," Selby admitted.

"Rita," Abner Hendrix said, "was one of those wild young

women who wanted to go modern in a big way. She was a great trial to her mother and me."

Selby inclined his head in sympathetic attention, giving the impression that he had nodded, without however quite committing himself by anything so definite as a distinct sign of affirmation.

"Rita married when she was twenty-two. It wasn't a match of which we approved, but we thought marriage would steady her down. It had quite the opposite effect. She got in with a wild young crowd in Hollywood. There was a lot of drinking and carryings on."

"Wasn't she divorced?" Selby asked.

"Yes. And two months after the divorce decree became final, she married James Artrim, a big-time gambler."

"He was killed in an automobile accident?" Selby asked.

"Yes. His father, Frank Artrim, was driving the car. From all I can hear, Frank Artrim shouldn't have been operating any automobile, but the son was intoxicated at the time. The car turned over, and caught fire. The father was thrown clear. James Artrim was caught—pinned underneath the car, and burned to a crisp. The father had a spinal injury which will keep him from ever walking again, and he's had a complete loss of memory."

"You mean amnesia?" Selby asked.

"That's what the doctors call it. He can't recall anything that happened prior to the accident. He doesn't know his name, doesn't know anything about himself."

Selby said, "This is all very interesting, Mr. Hendrix, and I know you wouldn't come here unless you felt it was important, but I could understand it better if you'd tell me in advance just what you're driving at."

Hendrix said, "As far as my daughter, Rita, is concerned, I don't consider her one of the family any longer—but"— and his voice choked slightly—"she's still my daughter, my only child."

Selby waited for him to go on.

"The money that she has is gambler's money," Hendrix said. "She tells me that it came from the insurance company, but I tell her that the premiums were paid with gambling money. In many ways, she's a good girl. She's lost a lot of that wild streak, and has steadied down. She bought that big house up in Orange Heights thinking that her mother and I would come and live with her and her father-in-law."

Selby said, "I still don't see what you're getting at."

"Well," Hendrix blurted, "I think the old man's crazy."

"Who?"

"Frank Artrim, her father-in-law."

Selby said, "Amnesia is not unusual following a shock. The fact that the memory cells are impaired doesn't have anything to do with a man's mentality."

Hendrix said, "It isn't that. You see, after the accident he didn't know anything about who he was or anything. Rita had to tell him all about his own family. James—that was Rita's husband—was intoxicated. He was going to meet some gamblers at a country club. The road ran along a steep bank over the river. Rita told him he was too drunk to risk money gambling and wouldn't drive the car. He got his father to drive. Well, they didn't show up at the gambling place, so one of the men telephoned to find out what had happened. Rita got frightened and drove clean out to the place without finding any sign of the car. She drove back going very slowly, and kept her eyes peeled. She smelled burning rubber, and then found where the car had gone over a cliff and caught fire. She managed to get down to the place and found that her husband had been trapped inside the car. Her father-in-law was hurt pretty bad. She called for help and got him up to the road and into a doctor's office. The point is, that when Frank Artrim got conscious again, Rita was the one who had to tell him the whole tragedy, about how he'd been driving the car that had killed his son, who he was, who his son was, and all of that. I think he's hated her ever since."

"Specifically," Selby asked, with just a trace of impatience, "what does his hatred have to do with it?"

Hendrix said simply, "I think he intends to kill her."

Selby stared at the man in surprised silence. After a moment he said, "Why, the man's a cripple."

"I know," Hendrix said, "but he's a brooding, deadly, dangerous cripple, and he's gradually losing his mind."

"Can he walk?"

"No. He can't use his legs to walk with, but his arms and his body are strong. I don't understand just what it is; he can move his legs, but he can't balance with 'em. Co-ordination, I think, is what they call it."

"What gives you the impression he's dangerous?" Selby asked. "Something that Rita has said?"

Hendrix said, "Last Sunday my daughter came to visit us. We won't go near her house. Sometimes she comes to ours. She doesn't came to see me. She comes to see her mother. She and I barely speak."

"All right," Selby said crisply, trying to impress upon Hendrix that he was in a hurry. "What happened Sunday?"

Hendrix said, "There were bruise marks on her throat. Someone had tried to choke her."

"Do you know who?"

"Artrim."

"Did she say so?"

"No. She swore up and down that the bruises weren't caused by that at all. You could see that they were. She'd worn a high collar, but it was opened at the front, and her mother got a glimpse of the bruises and insisted on seeing her neck."

"How did you get the impression it was Artrim?"

"I know she's afraid of him. He's the only person who

could have done it and the only person who could have frightened her into keeping silent."

Selby thought rapidly. "Just what," he asked, "do you want me to do?"

"I want you to look into it," Hendrix said. "I felt that Rita had put herself out of the family, but, after all, she's my own flesh and blood. I can't sit by and see her murdered."

Selby said, "There's been a murder committed in that neighborhood, and I'm making an investigation now. I'm glad you told me, Mr. Hendrix, and I'll make it a point to check up on Frank Artrim while I'm investigating that other case."

Hendrix got to his feet. "I wish you would," he said, and then added, almost apologetically, "I haven't closed my eyes for the last twenty-four hours. Her mother's all worked up. . . . Well, you know how mothers are. I think women kinda stick together anyway. If it wasn't for me, Elizabeth—that's my wife—would go live up there in the house on Orange Heights with Rita. She says the money's already been won at gambling, that Rita didn't win it, and that it's too late to give it back. You certainly couldn't give it back to the people who had lost it, and it would be foolish to try and give it back to an insurance company, or refuse to accept the money that was in the estate."

Selby said, "There is much to be said for the logic in that reasoning."

Abner Hendrix said stubbornly, "I won't live on no gambler's money." He pushed back his chair and shook hands with Selby, the crushing strength of his handclasp betraying his emotion. "Do the best you can, will you?" he asked. "You know, Rita's the only child we ever had." He turned abruptly and marched from the office.

Selby watched him through the exit door, listened to the steady pound of his determined feet on the flagged corridor.

For half an hour, Selby sat smoking and thinking. At length, as the office grew dim with the coming of twilight, he tapped the ashes out of his pipe, and started to walk down the corridor. He had gone less than twenty steps when a shadowy figure stepped out from the doorway.

"Mr. Selby."

It was a feminine voice, so low that it was almost a whisper, and Selby whirled to confront the slender, frightened young woman who stood before him.

"What are you doing here?" he asked.

"Waiting for you," she said. "I knew you were in your office."

"Why didn't you knock on the door?"

"Because I must see you alone. No one must know of this, absolutely no one."

"Who are you?" he asked.

She looked over her shoulder, up and down the deserted courthouse corridor, then she said, "Ellen Saxe."

Selby frowned. "I've heard that name before. I . . . Oh, yes, I place it now. Come on," he said. He led the way back to his office, unlocked the door, and started to switch on the lights.

"If you please," his visitor said, "I'd prefer to have the lights off."

Selby said, "Have it your own way. I've seen your name on a report made by Sheriff Brandon. Aren't you employed as a nurse by Mrs. Artrim?"

"Yes."

"What do you want to see me about?" Selby asked.

She said, "I hardly know just where to begin."

Selby smiled. "Suppose you begin at the beginning, Miss Saxe."

"Well, you know, I'm employed out there as a nurse— not a trained nurse, a practical nurse. I never had the opportunity to get the training to make me a registered nurse."

Selby nodded gravely.

"Well," she said, "I have reason to believe—that is, I think . . . I suppose, Mr. Selby, that whenever persons uncover any evidence of any crime, they're supposed to report to the authorities, aren't they?"

"Yes."

"Well, it's hard for me to do. You see, I haven't anything really definite, nothing that I can point to and say, 'This is it,' but . . ."

As she hesitated, Selby said, "Why don't you just go ahead and tell me what you have in mind, Miss Saxe, then we'll discuss the proof afterwards."

Ellen Saxe took a deep breath. "She murdered him," she said abruptly.

"Who murdered him?" Selby asked.

"Mrs. Artrim."

Selby said, "You mean Mrs. Artrim murdered the man whose nude body . . ."

"No, no," she interrupted, "not him. She murdered her husband."

Watching the nurse with the hard-eyed appraisal of a man who is accustomed to see others under the stress of emotion, Selby said, "I thought he was killed in an automobile accident."

"That's what everyone thinks, but it wasn't an accident."

"She wasn't even there at the time, was she?"

"No, but she tampered with the automobile. She knew that her husband was drunk. She thought he was going to be the one who drove the car. Naturally, she wanted the insurance. No one is going to sneeze at half a million dollars. She knew how to put the steering gear out of commission. She loosened a bolt so that it was almost ready to drop out. The vibration of the car did the rest. The car was traveling over a mountain road, winding around on the edge of a canyon."

"Go ahead," Selby said.

She said, "But her husband wasn't driving. Her father-in-law took the wheel, and he was sober. Mrs. Artrim followed along behind to watch and make sure that the accident happened just the way she'd planned. I wouldn't even doubt but what she was the one who set fire to the car just to make certain she'd made a good job of it."

Selby said, "That's rather a strong assertion to make, Miss Saxe."

"I know it is."

"And, as a practical, well-balanced young woman, you wouldn't make such a statement unless you had proof to back it up."

She said, "That's just the trouble. I've got too much proof to keep still, but not enough to really—well, you know, prove it absolutely."

Selby said, "Suppose you tell me just what has aroused your suspicions."

"Well, it's a lot of things. Mr. Artrim—her father-in-law—was driving the car. He was very seriously injured. There was some spinal injury, and he had a fractured skull and some cuts around the face and neck."

Selby nodded.

"He can't walk," she said. "His back isn't exactly broken. I don't know just what it is, but it's something that affects the co-ordination. He can move his legs as individual units, but he can't stand on them and balance himself. It's just like a child who can raise himself up on his legs, but hasn't learned the mechanics of walking."

"And wasn't his memory affected also?" Selby asked.

"Yes. He can't remember anything about the accident. And it's a lucky thing for Mrs. Artrim that he can't."

"Then what you suspect hasn't been because of something he's told you?"

"Well, not directly," he said, "but I'll tell you what *I*

think. I think Mr. Artrim had amnesia. I think he had a spinal injury. I think he's gradually regaining his memory and recovering his co-ordination, but I think he's too smart to let on."

"Why?" Selby asked.

"Because he knows that she tampered with the car. He knows that she is the one who really killed his son, but he hasn't any proof. He's staying on there trying to get proof, and pretending to be a fool. The other day I came in the room suddenly, and he was practicing walking. He didn't see me because the door was open, and I was coming in from the bathroom. He was standing on his legs in front of a mirror with his hands held out in front of him—just like a baby trying to walk. He actually took one step before he lost his balance and fell over—that is, he would have fallen if he hadn't been where he could grab the bed post."

"What did you do?" Selby asked.

"I ran to him," she said, "and told him that he knew he mustn't walk. The doctor's orders were that he wasn't to try to walk at all until after the blood clot on his brain had cleared up. The doctor said it might be another year."

"And then what?" Selby asked.

She said, "Then was when I became suspicious. He let me lift his legs back on the bed and put pillows under his head. Then he called me over to him and said, 'Nurse, sit down there on the edge of the bed. I want to talk with you.' So I sat down, and he said, 'I want you to tell me the truth. What did the doctor say about whether I can ever walk again.'"

"What did you tell him?" Selby asked.

"I told him the truth. I'd never talked with the doctor. Mrs. Artrim had hired me. All I knew was what she told me, but she told me that the doctor said inside of one year or two years, he might regain the use of his legs, that when he did, his memory would probably clear. Well, he looked at me with the funniest, foxiest look in his eyes, and said,

'Here's something I want to know about. After my mind clears and I get my memory back, will I be able to walk?' "

"What did you say to that?"

"I told him that was the way I had understood it, and he asked me to be sure and find out definitely. He said it was very important, and then he said, 'Now listen, nurse, I'm going to give you a little bonus, and you must promise me that you'll never say anything to my daughter-in-law about having seen me trying to walk. I don't want her to know that I'm trying to cure myself. Let her think that I'm willing to stay in a wheel chair the rest of my life.'

"Well, naturally I was surprised and upset, but I promised him that I wouldn't say anything, and then he looked at me and said, 'Nurse, you seem to be a pretty smart girl. Hasn't it ever occurred to you that there was something funny about my son's death?' I told him of course not. I hadn't ever thought of it because it wasn't any of my business, and he said, 'Well, I just wanted to know if you'd thought about it at all,' and then he asked me if Mrs. Artrim ever was in the kitchen when I was preparing his food, and I said that occasionally she was, and he said, 'Don't ever let her around my food. Do you understand? Don't let her get near it, and don't ever leave her alone in the kitchen when you're cooking for me.' So I asked him right out. I said, 'Are you afraid of being poisoned?' And he said, 'I'm more afraid of being drugged than poisoned. If she ever drugged me at night, she and . . .' And then he broke off and wouldn't talk any more."

"That's all you have to go on?" Selby asked.

She nodded.

"But how about this business about the automobile and the steering mechanism?"

She said, "Oh, I thought of that myself. I have a boy friend who's a good automobile mechanic. I asked him very casually if it would be possible for someone to commit a murder by doctoring up an automobile so it would run off a road, and he said it would, and told me how it could be done. I've forgotten just what particular bolt it was that he said you could tamper with and cause an accident."

Selby said, "You have to admit that's rather sketchy proof, Miss Saxe."

"I know it is, but if you could just feel the tension in that house. Something's going to happen, and I know it. I think she's intending to kill him."

"You don't think he's intending to kill her?"

"No. He's nice. He wouldn't hurt a fly, but he isn't the fool that she takes him for, not by a long ways; and if he could ever get the use of his legs back, he'd be strong. He's a big, broad-shouldered man, and to see his body you wouldn't think he was any older than she is. His face shows his age, but physically he's remarkably well-preserved."

Selby said, "Well, I'm glad you told me. I'll keep it in mind. In the meantime, if you see anything else or hear anything that makes you suspicious, let me know. Now how about that nude prowler? Did you see him?"

"Yes."

"Where?"

"He was walking past my window. I would say he was about thirty-five or forty feet away from the window."

"Could you see him clearly?"

"No, not real clearly. But I could see that he didn't have a stitch of clothes on."

Selby said, "Now this is important. Was there anyone following him, anyone with him?"

"Not a soul," she said, "that I could see."

"What did you do?"

"I started to go to the telephone," she said, "to notify the police, but then Mrs. Artrim started ringing for me frantically. I threw on a robe and ran upstairs. It seems she'd been sitting at her window because she couldn't sleep. She saw the prowler, probably about the same time I did."

"What were you doing?" Selby asked. "Why weren't you sleeping?"

"I don't know," she said. "I think there'd been some noise in the house. I wakened with a start, and couldn't go back to sleep. I had the feeling of tension which a woman gets when she feels something is going to happen."

"Could you describe this noise in the house?"

"No. I just know that something woke me up."

"Your room's on the ground floor?"

"Yes."

"So immediately after you saw this prowler, Mrs. Artrim rang for you and told you to notify the police?"

"Yes."

"And where was Frank Artrim at that time? Do you know?"

"Yes. He was sleeping in his bedroom. His bedroom adjoins mine. He takes sleeping powders, but after the officers came, he woke up and started ringing his bell and pounding on the floor with a stick he always keeps by the side of his bed. Mrs. Artrim was almost hysterical. I had to try and calm her and rush back downstairs and assure Mr. Artrim that I hadn't answered him because I was busy with his daughter-in-law."

"How did he take that?" Selby asked.

"He didn't like it. He said that I was employed to wait on him. I told him that there'd been a prowler seen around the house, and someone had fired a shot, that officers were making an investigation, and that Mrs. Artrim was almost in hysterics."

"What did he say?

"He said to let her have hysterics and be damned, and then he started asking me questions about the prowler. I told him I didn't know anything about him, that I'd seen a

56

man walking past the window, that apparently he didn't have any clothes on. And for some strange reason, that seemed to reassure him. He thought for a moment, then quieted right down. He said, 'You're certain he didn't have any clothes on?' And I said I was virtually certain, and he smiled and said, 'Well, go on up to Rita and take care of her.' And after that, I didn't have any more trouble with him."

"You heard the shot?"

"Yes, of course."

"How long was that before the officers arrived?"

"I think they were driving up when the shot was fired."

"Where were you at the time?"

"I was in my room," she said. "It was right after the shot was fired that Mrs. Artrim called for me, and I ran up and found her hysterical—well, not exactly hysterical, but exceedingly nervous and on the verge of hysterics."

"And then the father-in-law woke up?"

"Yes, and started pounding."

Selby said, "All right, Miss Saxe. Now get this straight. I don't want to belittle your information. I appreciate the fact that you came to me, but persons who are sick mentally usually have queer ideas. Mr. Artrim probably has no grounds for his belief that Mrs. Artrim might drug or poison him."

Ellen Saxe said nothing, and her tight-lipped silence furnished its own contradiction of Selby's statement.

"Now then," Selby went on, "you've come to me with this. That's all you can do. You've done your duty. I'll investigate it, but, in the meantime, you mustn't say anything to anyone. Do you understand?"

"Yes, of course."

"It's a very serious matter," Selby said, "accusing anyone of murder."

"Of course it is, but I feel so positive about it. Oh, there are lots of little things that show the strain, the tension, the hostility . . ."

"I understand," Selby said, "and I'll look into it. And in the meantime, don't do anything which would make them think you were suspicious. Just forget about having said anything to me. Return to your job, and now that you have this off your mind, you can relax and give your nerves a rest."

She said, "It's hard to do that when you're living in a house where people are planning to murder each other. You mark my words, Mr. Selby, she's going to kill him. She killed her husband, and she's going to kill him."

Selby said, "If you run into anything queer, let me know right away. In the meantime, take it easy. We'll be working on things." When she had gone, Selby called Rex Brandon on the phone. "Rex," he said, "what did you find out at the Artrims'?"

"Nothing much," Brandon said. "The nurse and Mrs. Artrim had seen this man wandering around. They called the police. It was about ten minutes after the call came in before the police arrived."

"Where was the nurse when the police arrived?"

"Up with Mrs. Artrim who was having hysterics."

"Where was Artrim?"

"Downstairs pounding on the floor, mad as a wet hen because he couldn't get some attention. He claims that the nurse was hired to wait on him and not on his daughter-in-law. Incidentally, Doug, he never refers to her as his daughter-in-law. He lost his memory in that accident and is dependent on what others tell him. Apparently he is inclined to take some of the relationship with a grain of salt."

Doug said, "I'm wondering if there's some connection between that prowler, Carr's purchase of the property, and Rita Artrim."

"What could she possibly have to do with A. B. Carr?" Sheriff Brandon asked.

"I don't know," Selby said, "but it's a possibility to keep in mind."

Brandon said, in his slow drawl, "Otto Larkin went out to call on Carr tonight."

"What did he get?" Selby asked.

"From all I can gather, he got back," Brandon said. "He looked about the smallest I've ever seen him. What makes it so funny is that he went out there breathing fire and boasting about what he was going to do to that big city criminal lawyer. He sure came back with his tail between his legs."

Selby thought for a moment, then said, "Listen, Rex, I wonder if you can arrange to have Carr kept under surveillance for a while?"

"Why?" Brandon asked.

"Because," Selby said, "I think Pete Ribber is going to get in touch with him."

Brandon said, "Sure, I can cover him here, and we can arrange with the Los Angeles authorities to handle their end. They're after Ribber too."

Selby said, "That's fine, Rex. Fix it up right away if you can."

"Okay. I will."

"Have you," Selby asked, "tried the clothes on the corpse?"

"Yes. We did that down at the coroner's office. The clothes fit perfectly. The bloodstain and bullet hole in the cloth matched the bullet hole in the corpse. Here's something to remember though, Doug. They can't tell at the post-mortem which bullet is the fatal bullet. The second bullet almost paralleled the course of the first bullet. Either bullet would have been instantly fatal. The coroner can't tell which bullet was the first bullet.

"That's why the testimony of Mrs. Artrim and that nurse

of hers becomes important. They saw the man wandering around without any clothes on shortly before the shot was fired. Therefore, the fatal shot was the one which was fired while the man was naked. Afterwards, someone put the clothes back on the body and fired another shot into the corpse, then took the clothes off and planted them where they'd be sure to come to the attention of the authorities.

"It looks to me as though it was a clever scheme to confuse things so we'd jump at the conclusion that the fatal bullet was the one that was fired while the man was dressed. And if you're asking my opinion, there's only one man connected with the entire case who could have schemed that out. Do you get me?"

Selby said, "I get you, and there's a chance it's going to be a bigger headache for us than we contemplate. I'm going to think that over a bit before I call on Carr."

"Okay," Brandon said, "but let's not allow any slick city lawyer to ride us with the spurs. You can see where it's going to leave us, Doug, if he's worked out some legal complication which will tie our hands."

Selby said, "I'll do a little thinking and a little studying. Let me know if there's anything new."

"Try and get a good sleep, Doug," the sheriff advised. "We can dig up the evidence, such as it is. You're going to need a clear head to untwist the legal red tape."

Selby said, "Okay, and, Rex, I wish you'd look up the death of James Artrim. Find out anything you can about it."

"Right now?" Brandon asked.

"Yes," Selby said. "It might be important. It looks as though Rita Artrim and Ellen Saxe, that nurse, are going to be our two most important witnesses. If Carr can get at them, and find something which he can use as a lever, he might keep us from playing the only trump card we seem to have in the deck."

Brandon said, "Okay, Doug. I'll get busy. Get a good night's sleep."

Selby said, "I'll try," and hung up.

CHAPTER VI

OTTO LARKIN SAT IN CONFERENCE WITH FRANK GRIERSON, editor of the *Blade.* Grierson, a big man in the early sixties whose shoulders had stooped until it seemed that his big head with its bushy, iron-gray hair was growing out of his chest, fastened his black, glittering eyes on the chief of police, and said, "Larkin, you're a damn fool." An affliction of the throat gave Grierson a peculiar, husky, whispering voice, made his utterances seem to have the finality of judicial decision.

Larkin flushed and started to blurt out some comment.

Grierson held up one of his big hands, moving with the slow patience of a man who has learned to conserve his time and energy. "Listen to me," he said, "then talk."

Larkin took a cigar from his pocket, ripped off the end by clamping his teeth together and giving the cigar a savage twist. "Go ahead," he said.

Grierson, speaking slowly in that husky, half whisper, said, "A. B. Carr has more brains than all the lawyers in this county put together. He sells those brains for big money. If Selby had half his brains, he'd be in the big time getting big fees."

"So what?" Larkin asked.

Grierson said, "He's in this case. No one but Carr would have had brains enough to figure out the dodge of firing that second shot into the corpse. Remember, Larkin, the people have to prove a case beyond all reasonable doubt. The people have to take one of those bullets and say, 'This is the fatal bullet. It was fired from such and such a gun, and that gun at the time it was discharged was in the hands of such and such a person.' All Carr has to do is to introduce a reasonable doubt. It isn't enough that the prosecution get it so that it's better than fifty-fifty, even get it so it's a hundred to one. That one chance in a hundred, if it's reasonable, is enough to upset their apple cart."

"Well?" Larkin asked. "What's that got to do with me?"

"Just this," Grierson said. "You're a publicity hound. You're vain, you're stupid, and you're stubborn. Selby and Rex Brandon have been doing some good work. In the paper we've claimed it was luck. Don't kid yourself. It's good work. Now then, here's a murder that breaks within the city limits. You're so damned anxious to show that you can do good work too that you've climbed right out in the center of the stage and hogged all the limelight."

Larkin said angrily, "Just because you're running the newspaper don't make you own the damn town, and don't kid yourself that we couldn't get along without your rag. There's another newspaper wants to come in here and . . ."

"Shut up, you fool," Grierson said without raising his voice. "I'm trying to save you from yourself."

"Thanks. I'm able to take care of myself."

"You," Grierson said, "are a babe in the woods. Carr has ten times as much brains as Selby and Brandon put together. Selby has ten times as much brains as you have. You listen to me, and you'll be all right. Keep on the way you're going, and you'll be in hot water within forty-eight hours. And that hot water is gradually going to get hotter. It's going to keep on getting hotter until it comes to a boil. It will cook the political goose of anyone who happens to be in it."

Larkin said sarcastically, "I presume you have ten times as many brains as Carr."

Grierson said, "Don't kid yourself, Larkin. I'm smart enough to know my own limitations. That's why I'm smarter than you. You don't know your limitations. You try to kid yourself into believing you haven't any. You went out to see Carr. What did it get you?"

Larkin said, "Not very much, but I'm not done yet."

Grierson said, "Listen. I'm on the inside. My paper's on the inside. We have a political organization which ran this county directly and indirectly for fifteen years. Then Sam Roper, the district attorney, got careless. The sheriff was crooked. The town got too wide open. I called them in and told them we were going to take a beating unless they laid off. You couldn't talk to them. They wouldn't listen. What happened? Selby and Brandon furnished the spearhead of a political ticket that swept the machine aside. They're in power."

Grierson paused impressively. His glittering eyes held the eyes of the chief of police. Then he said slowly and impressively, "But they're not going to *stay* in power. They're not politicians. They haven't a political machine back of them. They're still making capital out of fighting the old machine and out of giving the people a clean, efficient administration. The rest of the newcomers aren't doing so well. As long as Selby and Brandon stay in power, the rest of the outfit's going to ride along, and it isn't going to do us a damn bit of good to have part of the county machinery under our control unless we can control the sheriff's office and the district attorney's office. You know that. That's practical politics."

"What's all that got to do with me?" Larkin asked.

Grierson said, "You try to be a diplomat. You try to carry water on both shoulders. You try to ride along with Selby and Brandon. It doesn't fool them any. It doesn't fool anyone any. You're affiliated with the other political machine. You're a part of our gang."

"Well, I never claimed I wasn't," Larkin said. "But as long as they're popular, I'm pretending to co-operate with them."

"Sure," Grierson said, "that's smart. But it doesn't fool anyone. It doesn't fool them. It doesn't fool their friends, and it doesn't fool the voters."

"What do you want me to do? Sit down here and refuse to co-operate with them, let them hand me a package every time they get a chance and have people say it serves me right?"

"Of course not."

"Well, it sounds like it," Larkin said, raising his voice angrily. "The way things are now, I co-operate with them. If they hand me a lemon, I can walk up and down the streets cussing them out for letting politics interfere with the administration of justice."

Grierson said wearily, in his husky half whisper, "You don't need to dot the i's and cross the t's with me, Larkin. Now, listen. In this case, you're going up against brains. You can't beat it. Selby and Rex Brandon can't beat it. No one can beat it. It isn't in the cards. Carr couldn't do it himself."

"Why not, if he's so smart?" Larkin asked.

"Don't you see," Grierson said. "It's the thing I've been trying to explain to you. It's the law. The prosecution has to prove a man guilty beyond all reasonable doubt. All the defense has to do is introduce that reasonable doubt. Carr's already done it."

"You mean with that second bullet?"

"With that second bullet," Grierson said.

There was a long interval of silence. Larkin puffed with nervous rapidity at his cigar. Grierson, whose throat affliction prevented his smoking, stared at the chief of police with unblinking concentration. "What do you want me to do?" Larkin asked at length.

Grierson said, "We're going to pull a fast one. We're going to let *you* catch the criminal, and turn him over to the district attorney. You'll get credit for catching the man.

Then it will be up to the district attorney to convict him. You're going to step out of the picture. We're going to quit panning the district attorney. We're going to start boosting for him. We're going to minimize the difficulties of the case. We're going to act on the assumption that, of course, Selby will get a conviction. We're going to talk about how brave he is, what a good record he's making. We're going to back up on some of the mud we've been slinging."

"What good is that going to do?" Larkin asked.

Grierson smiled, a slow, ominous smile. "The effect of that propaganda we're going to release," he said, "is to concentrate the minds of the voters on the fact that *after* you have arrested the man, the rest of it is entirely in Selby's department. He's going to be the one to get a conviction. If he gets it, we're going to act on the assumption that it was a routine case, that the evidence had been worked out so carefully that all Selby had to do was to walk into court and present that evidence. If he doesn't get a conviction, we're going to . . ."

"I get it," Larkin said, his eyes gleaming, "then you're going to pan the pants off of him."

Grierson shook his head and said, "You don't get the sketch at all, Larkin. If he doesn't get a conviction, we're going to try to stick up for him. We're going to make excuses for him, and the excuses we make are going to be so lame and our argument for him is going to be so full of holes that the simplest, dumbest subscriber on our list can see those holes. Do you get me? Carr is going to be in this case. He may be out in front, or he may be behind the scenes, but he's going to be in it. Circumstances over which he has no control dragged him into it. He can't get out of it. Selby is our local boy. We're going to bury the hatchet in favor of boosting the local product against the outsiders. Our attitude will be that while we fight among ourselves, when someone seeks to cast a slur on our community, we fight for our community.

Selby isn't of our political party. We worked against him, and we voted against him. He's our district attorney, and as such he's the pride of Madison County. He's more than a match for any slick, city lawyer, no matter if it is old A.B.C. himself, the highest-priced mouthpiece in the city.

"And then when Selby comes a cropper—and you mark my words, this is one case where he's going to come a cropper—we'll spread alibis all over our editorial column. They'll run like this: 'Those persons who say that Carr's client was acquitted because of the lack of experience on the part of Doug Selby, Madison County's young district attorney, are not very patriotic to say the least. Madison County is a progressive, up-and-coming county. Doug Selby represents one of our officials. It is true that he is perhaps lacking in experience. It is doubtless true that he is young, but he is a man of unquestioned honesty, and while his ability will doubtless increase with the passing of years, and the maturity of judgment which will come with those years, he put up a good fight. The reason he didn't get a conviction was because of circumstances beyond his control. How was he to know that Carr, clever criminal lawyer that he is, would raise the doctrine of reasonable doubt? How was he to know that Carr's shrewd cross-examination would confuse the autopsy surgeon into admitting that he couldn't tell which was the fatal bullet?' Do you get me now, Larkin?"

Otto Larkin heaved a great sigh. "I get you," he said.

"All right," Grierson said. "Then that's settled. You catch the murderer and dump the case in Selby's lap."

"Yes," Larkin said, "that's easy. I catch the murderer. It sounds simple when you say it like that."

"Listen," Grierson said, "a man whose fingerprints were on that gun is the man they're looking for."

"Well?"

"That man is Peter Ribber, who was picked up by you and turned loose before you found out he was wanted."

Larkin said, "I'm not a mind-reader. Of course he was fingerprinted, and if he'd been held on a felony charge, I'd have checked his prints and then we'd have found out. But when he's simply picked up on . . ."

"Shut up," Grierson said. "I'm not blaming you. I'm simply telling you. He's the man they want. Carr has represented him before. Carr will represent him again. When Pete Ribber gets in a jam, he'll want the best mouthpiece he can get. He'll want Carr."

"That doesn't mean Carr will want him," Larkin said.

Grierson shook his head sadly. "You underestimate the ability of A. B. Carr," he said.

"How do you mean?"

Grierson said, "Carr's mixed up in this thing himself. Carr wants to get out. Pete Ribber is his out. Remember this. You can't prosecute a man for murder a second time. After he's once been tried and acquitted, he's been once in jeopardy."

"What's that got to do with it?" Larkin asked. "Who wants to prosecute him a second time?"

Grierson said, "You watch what Carr is going to do. Carr is going to rush their hand. They want Ribber. I'll bet you ten to one that Carr sees they get Ribber within twenty-four hours. After they get him, he'll be rushed to trial. Before they've had a chance to fully work up the case, Carr will spring a slick, legal loophole for Ribber to crawl through. Ribber will be acquitted. After he's acquitted, he'll disappear, and Carr will let some additional evidence come out which will show absolutely that Ribber was guilty—and then he'll laugh at them. They can't prosecute Ribber again because he's already been acquitted. I wouldn't doubt but what Ribber might even confess."

Larkin said, "You give Carr credit for a hell of a lot of brains."

Grierson said huskily, "I do."

Again there was an interval of silence, then Larkin, thinking back over the conversation, said, "You think Carr will be anxious to have them catch Ribber?"

"Yes."

"Where do I get in on that?" Larkin asked.

Grierson said, "They tried to cover up about those fingerprints. I found out about it. We're getting out an extra. That extra is going to have headlines reading: 'Otto Larkin identifies fingerprints on gun.' Shortly after that extra hits the streets, A. B. Carr is going to make a telephone call, and then jump in a car and drive into the city. He'll go direct to his office or direct to Ribber. I don't know which. I think he'll go direct to his office and let Ribber come to him. It will look better that way."

"How do you know all this?" Larkin asked.

Grierson said, "I know it because I have an ordinary amount of intelligence, because I know something of A. B. Carr's ability, and—" he paused to grin—"because there's been a leak on telephone conversations."

Larkin matched Grierson's grin. "Go ahead," he said.

Grierson said, "Rex Brandon has telephoned to the Los Angeles police asking them to keep a watch on A. B. Carr in case he shows up at his office. They have a photograph and description of Pete Ribber. If Ribber shows up, they'll arrest him."

"Well," Larkin asked, "what good is it going to do us if *they* arrest him?"

"Don't you see?" Grierson said. "They'll take Ribber down to jail. They want him on a larceny charge. Madison County wants him on a murder charge. They'll telephone the sheriff. The sheriff and the district attorney will pick up Sylvia Martin. The three of them will dash into the city, pick up Ribber, and bring him back. You'll read all about it in the *Clarion*."

Larkin blinked his eyes several times rapidly. His forehead creased into a frown.

Grierson said, "You keep a watch on Carr's house. Don't let Brandon or Selby know what you're up to. The minute Carr gets in his automobile and starts for the city, you beat it into the city. You go directly to headquarters and tell them that you're from Madison City, that you want a man to help you pick up a murderer who is going to call on Carr at his office. They'll tell you they're already acting under instructions, that Carr is under surveillance. You'll sit there and smoke. As soon as they pick up Ribber, they'll tell you that they have him. You'll tell him that you're there to take him back to Madison City. You'll arrest him for murder and bring him back. The *Blade* will have an extra on the streets tomorrow morning. There'll be headlines all over the front page: 'Otto Larkin catches murderer—Chief of Police turns murderer over to District Attorney Selby' . . . and then you'll be done. You identified the fingerprints. You caught the murderer. You turned him over to the district attorney. You'll walk up and down Main Street accepting congratulations. You won't have anything to do with the trial or the efforts to convict him. You caught him. That's all you're supposed to do. There was a murder in the city. You located the murderer, and apprehended him within thirty-six hours. What more do you want?"

Again Larkin thought for a moment, then he got to his feet and flicked ashes from the end of his cigar. "Nothing," he said.

CHAPTER VII

DOUG SELBY STUDIED UNTIL AFTER TEN O'CLOCK, THEN HE switched off his lights, tapped ashes out of his pipe, raised the shades, closed the windows of his office, and prepared to go home. He was just switching out the light when the telephone rang. The courthouse had a private switchboard, but at night the district attorney's and sheriff's offices were left plugged in on an open line. Selby discouraged night calls by the simple expedient of refusing to answer his office telephone at night. There was always someone on duty in the sheriff's office, and he felt certain that on important matters the sheriff would relay the information to him.

He stood by the light switch, frowning at the telephone. Then, reaching a decision, he walked across to the desk, picked up the receiver and said, "Hello."

A woman's voice said, "Is this Mr. Selby, the district attorney?"

"Yes."

"Mr. Selby, I wonder if I could see you right away?"

"Who is this talking?"

"Mrs. Fermal—Mr. Carr's housekeeper."

"Oh, yes, Mrs. Fermal. Where are you now?"

"I'm downtown," she said, "in a candy store. If you're in your office, I could come up right away. I called two or three places trying to locate you. Someone said you were at your office, so I called there."

Selby said, "Come on up, Mrs. Fermal. The courthouse door will be locked, but I'll be waiting there to let you in." He hung up the telephone, took the precaution of drawing the shades, then walked rapidly down the corridor and down the marble stairs to wait at the iron-grilled, glass door of the courthouse.

Mrs. Fermal drove up in a rattling car of ancient vintage. Selby watched her park the car and ease her ample bulk through the narrow door. She groped for and found the curb with her right foot, then slammed the car door, turned, and marched toward the courthouse with the grim rectitude of one who is performing a duty. As she climbed the stairs to the front door, Selby unlatched and opened it. "Good evening, Mrs. Fermal," he said.

She was somewhat out of breath. "Can we talk here?" she asked.

"Better come to the office," Selby said. He slowed his pace to accommodate hers. Together they climbed the stairs and walked through the echoing corridors down to Selby's office. When she was seated across the desk from him, Selby said, "What is it, Mrs. Fermal? Take your time and get your breath."

"I'm all right. . . . You'd forgotten all about me. . . . I hadn't forgotten all about you."

Selby waited.

She smiled and said, "Those stairs . . . sort of get one."

Selby nodded.

She was silent for a moment, then asked abruptly, "What time is it?"

Selby consulted his wrist watch. "Quarter past ten."

She said, "I'll have to hurry. . . . You're honest. You're sincere. You gave me a fair deal. . . . You gave my boy a fair deal. . . . I figure it's up to me to do something in return."

Selby said, "I try to be square, Mrs. Fermal. I did what I thought was best for your boy and best for the community."

She said, "It was. It was best all around."

"What," Selby asked, "was it you wished to tell me?"

She said, "If this gets out, I'll lose my job."

"It won't get out," Selby assured her.

She said, "Carr has had someone concealed in the house."

"A prisoner?" Selby asked.

"I don't think so."

"How do you know he's had someone concealed?"

"He fixed up a suite of rooms as a den and office. No one is allowed to go there."

"I see," Selby commented.

71

She said, "Sometimes when he'd be working, I'd take meals up to him. I think that was just a stall."

"You mean the meals were for someone else?"

"Yes."

"Who?" Selby asked.

"I don't know," she said, "but the last few days, he's had all of his meals served in the study. He said he was very hungry. I'll say he was hungry. He ate enough food to keep two men going."

"But don't you go into the study to clean up?" Selby asked.

"Two of the rooms I clean up. One room on the other side of the bath is kept locked. That is, it was kept locked. He told me I couldn't go in there. That didn't keep me from sort of listening when I would go in to take dishes away or clean up around his desk. A couple of times I've heard something moving in there."

"That person is still there?" Selby asked.

"No. The room's open."

"Open?" Selby repeated, using the question to prompt her and open the way for further comment.

"Yes. That chief of police came back tonight to call on him. The chief wanted to go through the house. Carr laughed at him, told him to go get a warrant and be careful in getting it because he'd sue for defamation of character."

"What did the chief do?" Selby inquired.

"He tried to bluff. He didn't get very far. Carr laughed at him, treated him like he'd treat a little child, and then the chief went out."

"And after that Carr went up and opened the door?"

"Not exactly like that," she said. "He said he had some work to do in his office, then a little while ago the telephone rang, and he did a lot of listening. He didn't say much. Then he hung up and told me he was going into the city and probably wouldn't be back until after midnight. He said he might stay overnight in the city."

"But the door's unlocked now?"

"Yes. I went up in the study to empty ash trays and straighten up after he'd gone."

"Isn't it rather late to do that work?"

She said, "He spends a lot of time in there. I have to clean it up whenever I can. Sometimes he'll work until one or two o'clock in the morning. Usually he's up at five or six o'clock."

"Did you hear the shot early this morning?" Selby asked.

"No. I didn't. But that's nothing. I sleep pretty sound."

"Did Carr hear it?"

"He *says* he didn't."

"You don't believe that?"

"I don't know. I'm telling you what he said."

"So you went up to the study to straighten up, and found this other door unlocked?"

"Yes, unlocked and opened."

"Did you go inside?"

"I looked around a bit. Someone had been living in there. There's a couch, and some blankets are stacked up in the closet. The place had a musty smell as though someone had been in there with the windows closed. There were three or four safety razor blades in the wastebasket."

"How about ash trays?" Selby asked.

"The ash trays were clean—but Carr smokes cigars most of the time. Lately I've noticed that the ash trays in his study were pretty well filled with cigarette stubs as well as cigar butts. There wasn't any lipstick on the cigarette papers, so I figure it was a man."

"You've never seen this man?"

"No."

"Did he stay in there all the time?"

"Yes."

"There's a bath in connection with that room?"

"No. Well, it opens on a bath. The door from the bathroom to the room was always locked whenever I did my cleaning, but that doesn't mean it was locked all the time."

"Did you," Selby asked, "touch anything?"

"Not a thing."

"The razor blades?"

"No. They're still there in the wastebasket."

"Does Carr use a safety razor?"

"Yes, but not that kind. He uses a double-edged blade. These were heavier blades. They only had one edge."

Selby said, "That is very interesting. You don't expect Carr back before midnight?"

"No," she said.

"Could you let me in that room?" Selby asked.

"I could, but I'd hate to have it come out afterwards."

"It wouldn't come out."

"Suppose you found something you wanted to use?"

Selby thought for a few seconds, then said, "I get your point. I think we'll get a search warrant."

"He's told me that if officers came with a search warrant, I'd have to let them in, but not to let anyone in while he was gone unless they had a warrant."

Selby picked up the receiver and dialed the sheriff's office. The deputy sheriff who answered him said that Brandon had started home about half an hour ago.

Selby called Brandon's residence and got the sheriff on the line. "Had you gone to bed, Rex?" he asked.

"No, but I was just getting ready for bed."

Selby said, "I think you'd better come up to the office right away, Rex, and get the justice of peace out of bed, bring him along with you. I'll have some papers for him to sign by the time he gets here."

Mrs. Fermal looked at Selby anxiously. "Will there be anything else for me to do?" she asked.

"No," Selby said. "I'm going to get out some papers asking for a search warrant. You go out to the house and wait until we get there."

"It would be a lot better if you could do it before he got back," she said, "and then you could leave me a copy of something."

Selby nodded.

She placed her hands on the arms of the chair, pushed herself up, and got to her feet. "I just wanted you to know that I appreciated what you did for my boy," she said.

"And your co-operation is certainly appreciated here," Selby assured her.

"All right," she said quietly. "I'm going back." She walked across the office, opened the door, and Selby could hear the pound of her short steps as she walked down the long corridor.

Selby went to the outer office, fed some paper into a typewriter, and proceeded to hammer away with two fingers of each hand. By the time the sheriff and the justice of the peace arrived, Selby had the papers ready for filing. "We'll want your fingerprint man," he said to the sheriff. "We're going to search Carr's residence."

"Isn't that loaded with dynamite, son?" Brandon asked solicitously.

"Probably," Selby agreed, "but we're going to do it anyway."

While the justice of the peace was filing the affidavits and issuing the search warrant, Brandon, at Selby's suggestion, routed Bob Terry, the sheriff's fingerprint expert, out of bed and had him hurry to the courthouse. Then, armed with the search warrant, Selby, Brandon, and Terry drove out to Orange Heights, brought the county car to a stop in front of Carr's residence, and Selby led the way up to the porch.

His ring was answered promptly by Agnes Fermal. "What do you want?" she asked truculently.

Selby said, "I'm the district attorney."

"Oh, yes, I know you."

"This is Sheriff Brandon."

"I've seen him."

"And this is Bob Terry, a deputy in the sheriff's office."

"What do you want?"

"We want to look through the house."

She made as though to slam the door. "Got a search warrant?" she asked.

"Yes," Selby said. "Are you in charge here?"

"I guess so. I'm the only one home."

Selby said, "We'll make a service on you then. Here's the original search warrant, and a copy."

"What," she asked, "are you looking for?"

Selby said, "Do you happen to know if a Pete Ribber is concealed somewhere in the building?"

"No, I don't."

"He's wanted on a felony charge," Selby said.

"I don't know nothing about it."

Selby said, "Very well, we're coming in."

She glanced at the search warrant, then said dubiously, "Well, if it's the law, I guess that's all there is to it." She stood to one side, and the officers entered.

"I think," Selby said, "you'd better show us through the building. We're primarily interested in the room where Mr. Carr has his office."

Mrs. Fermal said, "He isn't going to like this."

"I know he isn't," Selby said.

Silently, she led the way across the Spanish-style living-room, up a sweeping flight of stairs flanked by a wrought-iron banister, and down a corridor. "This," she said, "is the place."

The officers entered, looked around quietly. Selby said, "What's that room?"

"I don't know. It's part of this suite."

Selby nodded to Brandon. They entered the room, and Selby said to Terry, "Let's try a few fingerprints, Bob. Try the doorknob. Get the shaving mirror in the bathroom. . . . Here are some old safety-razor blades in the wastebasket. Let's take a look at those. You stay here and develop latents. If you find anything that looks promising, photograph it. Brandon and I are going to look over the house. Will you please show us the way, Mrs. . . ."

"Fermal," she said. "Mrs. Fermal."

"All right, show us the way."

The officers followed the housekeeper through the spacious structure out into the patio enclosed by a high stucco wall, back up the stairs, and finally to a balcony which opened from Carr's bedroom.

"What's this?" Selby asked.

"A telescope."

Selby studied the five-inch refractor mounted on a sturdy tripod. "What," he asked, "does he use it for?"

"Astronomy," she said curtly.

"Is that the only telescope?"

"No. He's got some big binoculars. They're in his desk drawer, I think. Do you want to go through the desk?"

Selby said, "No, I'm just looking through the house."

"All right," she said, "you've seen it."

Selby nodded to Brandon. They returned to the room where Bob Terry had brought out a tripod and a fingerprint camera.

"Find anything?" Brandon asked in a low voice.

Terry said, "Yes. Half a dozen latents."

"Do they check with those on the card I gave you?" Selby asked quietly.

Terry nodded.

Selby heaved an audible sigh of relief.

"There's a fingerprint on this old razor blade which has been set with rust. It's a print of the right index finger. Over on the other side is a smudge print which I think is the thumb."

Selby said, "We'll identify this razor blade. Seal it up in an envelope and write your name across the seal of the envelope, then give it to Brandon."

Terry produced an envelope and dropped the blade in, sealed it up, and signed his name across the flap. He handed it to the sheriff.

"You have photographs of these?" Selby asked, indicating the fingerprints.

"I'm getting photographs," Terry said.

"All right. Go ahead."

They stood and watched Terry place the fingerprint camera into position, click the switch which turned on an electric light, watched him consult the second hand of his watch for exposure. When he had finished, Selby said, "All right. Let's try this next one. We . . ."

He broke off as the sound of a car turning in the driveway reached his ears.

Mrs. Fermal, quite apparently frightened, said, "That will be Mr. Carr."

Selby said quietly, "Go right ahead, Terry."

Terry continued taking his photographs. Sheriff Brandon nervously spilled tobacco into a brown cigarette paper, twisted the cigarette into a cylinder, snapped a match into flame, and lit it.

There were steps on the stairs, the sound of a door opening and closing, then quick steps in the corridor, and Alphonse Carr stood in the doorway, his face set into grim lines. "What the hell's going on here?" he asked.

Selby said, "We're photographing fingerprints."

"The hell you are!"

Selby said, "Exactly."

"How did these people get in?" Carr asked of Mrs. Fermal.

"They said they were the law," she said. "They gave me

a paper." She handed him the copy of the search warrant.

Carr took the folded paper, but didn't look at it for a few moments. His eyes, cold, hard, and angry, surveyed the trio. Then he quietly crossed over to his desk, sat down, and studied the search warrant. He folded it methodically placed it in his pocket, took a cigar from his waistcoat pocket, clipped off the end, lit it, and then turned to Selby. "Getting rather officious, aren't you, Selby?" he asked.

"Perhaps," Selby said. "It depends on what you mean by the term."

"You know what I mean by it."

Selby said, "I'm an official. I'm here in the discharge of my official duties. If you consider that being officious, then I'm officious."

Abruptly Carr's face broke into a smile. He settled back in the swivel chair, crossed his long legs, and said, "Go right ahead, boys. Make yourselves at home."

Selby said, "We'll be done in a moment."

"Find anything?" Carr asked.

"Some fingerprints," Selby said.

Bob Terry clicked off the switch on his fingerprint camera and said to Selby, "All finished."

Carr said, "Just what good do you expect all this is going to do you, Selby?"

"I don't know," the district attorney said.

Carr said, "I suppose you know that you've laid yourself wide open to a suit for damages."

Selby shrugged his shoulders.

Carr said, "You rustic amateurs get quite tiresome. However, I suppose I should have expected it."

Rex Brandon came forward a couple of steps. "Allright," he said, "we're rustic, and we're amateurs, but *we're* honest. Don't think you're going to put us on the defensive while you get time to think. How does it happen that the fingerprints of a man who is wanted for felony are found in this room?"

Carr said, "I'm sure I couldn't tell you, Sheriff."

Brandon said, "Harboring a fugitive from crime is something we don't overlook—not in this county."

"I'm glad of it," Carr said.

"I notice," Selby went on, "that you have a telescope out there on the balcony."

"Did you indeed?" Carr inquired blandly.

Selby said, "I'd like to have you tell us when you last saw Peter Ribber, alias Peter Drumick, alias Alvin Catone."

Carr puffed quietly at his cigar. "Would you indeed?" he said.

"I would."

"Ask me the questions at the proper time and in the proper manner, and I'll consider answering them."

Selby said, "Very well, Mr. Carr. In order to keep the record clear, I'll here and now accuse you of having harbored Peter C. Ribber in this room for an indefinite period, knowing full well that Ribber was a fugitive from justice."

Carr yawned.

"Do you deny the accusation?" Selby asked.

Carr said, "I deny that I have violated any law. Does that satisfy you?"

"No."

Carr grinned. "Remain unsatisfied, then," he said.

Sheriff Brandon said impulsively, "We've got enough evidence to arrest you and throw you in jail for the night. How would you like that?"

"I wouldn't like it," Carr said. "I would be inclined to express my dislike by adding to the amount of damages I intended to ask for in my complaint against you three yokels."

Brandon stretched out a hand toward Carr's shoulder. "All right," he said. "We'll just give you a chance . . ."

"Take it easy, Rex," Selby cautioned. "Let me do the talking."

Brandon hesitated a moment, then reluctantly lowered his hand and stepped back from Carr's chair.

Carr laughed and said, "Well, well, you comic-opera enforcement officials may have some glimmerings of intelligence, after all. Anyway, we've discharged the official amenities. You've entered my house with a search warrant, a search warrant which I have every reason to believe is issued on a perjured affidavit. You think you have evidence connecting me with a crime. I think I can stick you plenty for filing false charges, exposing me to ridicule and contempt in my profession, and violating my privacy. You've made a direct accusation against me, and I've denied that accusation."

Selby said, "My accusation was specific. Your denial was general."

"And I think you'll find it quite sufficient under the law," Carr said. "Anyhow, boys, we've each of us done the things that are necessary to protect our positions. How about a little drink?"

Selby said, "No, thanks. These men are on duty."

"Chemically pure, eh?" Carr asked.

"Exactly," Selby said with a smile.

"Well," Carr said, "I'm not an officer. I have no taxpayers to consider, and *I'm* going to have a drink." He opened the drawer in his desk, took out a bottle of Napoleon brandy, took a glass goblet from another drawer, poured in a generous helping of brandy, and sniffed it appreciatively. Then he took a small sip.

"Nice stuff," he said.

"It looks like it," Selby agreed.

"Won't you sit down, boys?"

Brandon started to shake his head, but Selby said, "Certainly."

"Have one of my cigars?"

Brandon said shortly, "I'm smoking."

Selby said, "I'll have a pipe if you don't mind," and took his briar from his pocket.

"How about you?" Carr asked Terry.

"No, thanks," Terry said.

"Well, boys, there's no need to sit here and growl at each other. What do you think of my place?"

"A nice house," Selby said.

"Isn't it? You have a nice climate here, and you get some wonderful views of the stars."

Selby said, "I'm very much interested in astronomy, although I know but little about it. Could you tell us something about the stars?"

Carr laughed and said, "Thought you'd trap me with that one, didn't you, Selby? All right, come on out here, and I'll show you some stars." He led them out to the balcony, trained the telescope on one of the stars in the handle of the Big Dipper, focused it, and said, "There you are. There isn't a driving clock on it, but I have a fairly low-power eyepiece. Look in there, and I'll tell you about it."

Selby adjusted his eye to the eyepiece.

"You'll see a bright star and a fainter star a little above it with another star between them and slightly to one side."

"I see them," Selby said.

"That's the star in the bend in the handle of the Dipper," Carr said, obviously quite well pleased with himself. "The star is an optical double for the unaided eye. It was known to the ancients as Mizar and Alcor, the horse and the rider. The little star in between them was, at one time, mistaken for a planet. Now if you'll notice closely, you'll see that that bright star is a double. The component parts are so close together that you see them almost as one star."

"I see them," Selby said.

"Interesting, isn't it?"

"Yes."

"All done?" Carr asked.

Selby said, "Do you know any more about the stars? Do you know any other astronomical facts?"

Carr laughed and said, "That's enough, isn't it?"

"It depends," Selby said, "on what you call enough. It doesn't satisfy my interest."

"It will satisfy a jury," Carr said. "I've had a hard day, and I don't want to start in delivering a lecture on amateur astronomy. I intended to show you some other stars, but I find I'm very tired. After all, gentlemen, it's getting toward my bedtime."

"I hope we aren't keeping you up," Selby said.

"You are," Carr observed pointedly.

Selby said, "In that event, we'll wish you good night."

Carr abruptly thrust forward his hand. His face twisted into a magnetic smile. His eyes, no longer angry, twinkled humorously. "Well, Selby," he said, "you measure up—a lot different from that hick chief of police who tried to browbeat me."

Selby shook hands.

"Good night, Sheriff," Carr said.

Brandon hesitated momentarily, but then shook hands.

"And what's your name?" Carr asked.

"Bob Terry," the deputy said.

Carr shook hands with him. "Glad to know you," he said. "You look like an efficient and intelligent chap."

Terry flushed, but said nothing.

Selby said, "Before we go, I'd like to ask you some questions about the murder, Carr."

"I believe I told you that I'm somewhat tired," Carr said.

"Did you," Selby asked, "hear the shot?"

"I heard nothing, saw nothing, know nothing, and can tell you nothing."

"Are you acquainted with Peter Ribber?"

Carr frowned, and said, "After all, gentlemen, I hardly know how to answer that question. I have a business acquaintanceship with the man you mention."

"You know where he is now?"

"No."

"When did you see him last?"

Carr said, "I'm afraid I'm too tired to discuss that matter, Mr. Selby."

Selby said, "You refuse to answer that question?"

"I said that I was too tired to discuss the matter. At a later date, I'll be glad to take it up with you under more appropriate circumstances. And now, if you'll excuse me, gentlemen, I'll return to my brandy—too bad you wouldn't join me in a drink. It's really excellent stuff. Well, good night, boys. Come and see me again some time. Drop in any time when you have a search warrant."

Selby said sarcastically, "Thank you. We will."

Carr nodded to Mrs. Fermal. "You can show the gentlemen out," he said.

Mrs. Fermal silently led the way down the long corridor and down the stairs to the front door. The three men filed out. The door banged shut behind them.

Rex Brandon said, "The damn crook."

"Take it easy, Rex," Selby warned.

"What," the sheriff asked, "are we going to do now?"

Selby said, "Do you know, Rex, I have an idea the next move may come from Carr."

"What the devil can he do?" Brandon asked. "We've caught him red-handed. Ribber is a felon. He's wanted for larceny. He's a fugitive from justice. Carr has been concealing him in that room. We can prove it."

Selby said, almost musingly, "My estimate of Carr is that he's very intelligent and very resourceful. I wish very much we'd been able to photograph those fingerprints, then erased them, and have left the place without his knowing what we had."

"Shucks," Brandon said, "we've got the goods on him. What can he do now?"

Selby said, "I don't know, but I have an idea he's going to do something. . . . Let's go to the office and telephone Los Angeles. If they had him under surveillance while he was at his office, we may learn something."

Brandon said, "Okay. Of course, he may not have gone to his office."

"I know," Selby said, "but we can at least find out."

They returned to the courthouse. The sheriff called Los Angeles headquarters, and after a moment, got the man he wanted on the line. He said, "This is Brandon at Madison City. A. B. Carr was at his office tonight. Did you get a line on . . ." He broke off and sat listening to the noises which the receiver made, noises which sounded as harsh, metallic sounds in the silent confines of the sheriff's office. At length, he said, "Okay, Thanks. . . . No, I guess that's all right. Anyhow, it's done now." He hung up and turned to Doug Selby. "Pete Ribber," he said, "called on Carr at his office. The boys let him go in all right. When he came out, they quietly nabbed him and took him to headquarters. Carr didn't know anything about it."

"How long ago?" Selby asked.

"Something over an hour ago."

"Why the devil didn't they notify us?"

Brandon smiled wearily. "Because," he said, "Otto Larkin, the chief of police of Madison City, was sitting in police headquarters, waiting for the prisoner on a murder charge. As soon as they brought him in, the Los Angeles authorities turned him over to Larkin, and Larkin started back for Madison City."

Selby stared blankly at the sheriff. "Who," he asked, "tipped Larkin off?"

Brandon shrugged his shoulders.

Selby stood for a moment in thoughtful contemplation of the sheriff's profile, then stepped to the telephone, and dialed the *Clarion*. "Miss Martin, please," he said, and then after a moment when he heard Sylvia Martin's voice, said, "This is Doug, Sylvia. Just thought I'd let you know that Otto Larkin captured Pete Ribber in Los Angeles. You'll read all about it in an extra that the *Blade's* going to put on the street to-morrow morning. I thought you might like to know."

"Doug!" she exclaimed.

"That's a fact."

"How did it happen?"

"I don't know," Selby said. "I can make a guess, but that's all."

"Where is he now?"

Selby said, "Unless I'm mistaken, Larkin will have some engine trouble on the road home. He won't show up until the small hours of the morning, just in time to put the prisoner in the city jail where a representative of the *Blade* will be waiting to interview him. I thought perhaps you'd like to keep a weather eye on the city jail so that you could ask for press courtesies."

"Oh, Doug," she said, her voice showing her feeling, "I'm so sorry."

"You don't need to be," he told her. "By the way, Sylvia, I wish you'd do something for me."

"What?"

"See that Otto Larkin gets plenty of credit for making the arrest," he said. "Get a story from him, and play it up big."

"But, Doug . . ."

"I think it will be better that way," he said.

"Why, Doug?"

"Oh, I don't know. Just a hunch perhaps."

"We'll do it if you say so."

"I think it would be a good idea," he said. "See you in the morning, Sylvia."

"Okay. Thanks for letting me know, Doug. G'by."

"G'by," he said, and hung up. He grinned across at Sheriff Brandon. "All right, Rex," he said. "Let's go get some sleep."

CHAPTER VIII

Morning found Doug Selby lying in that condition of delicious drowsiness which is half sleeping and half waking, a warm, lazy languor. Birds were hopping through the eucalyptus tree which shaded his window. Down the slope were the fronds of palm trees, and below them Madison City, glinting in the early morning sunlight, seemingly freshly washed and sparkling in its cleanliness. Overhead the blue-black of the California sky showed as a vast depth of cloudless azure. The morning sunlight, splashing through the window to glint on the counterpane of Selby's bed, made crime seem distant and remote, a hideous, man-made nightmare superimposed upon a universe which was attuned to the singing of birds and the rustling of leaves. The telephone by Selby's bedside jarred him out of his half drowsy relaxation into a world of waking realities.

Selby picked up the receiver, said, "Hello," and heard Sheriff Brandon's voice, the good-natured, slow drawl which usually characterized his utterances entirely lacking.

"Doug," he said, "there's some trouble out at Artrim's place. Mrs. Artrim telephoned into the office and said she wanted me to come out right away. She said something terrible had happened. She's hysterical. How quickly can you get dressed?"

"About three minutes," Selby said, "if you think it's that important."

Brandon said, "From the way she talked, Doug, I think it is. I'll get the county car and be around in four or five minutes. Don't come down until I honk the horn. That'll give you a little more time."

Selby said, "Okay," hung up the receiver, and jumped out of bed. He stripped off his pajamas, then he climbed into underwear, hurriedly cleaned his teeth, combed his hair, neglected his shaving, and was just finishing knotting his necktie when he heard Sheriff Brandon tap lightly on the horn button of the county car. Selby ran down the stairs and into the freshness of early morning. "Have any idea what it is, Rex?" he asked the sheriff as he slid in beside him in the front seat.

"She just said that something terrible had happened," Brandon said. "When she said that, she was through. She was laughing, crying, and screaming all at once."

"Has anyone notified the city authorities?"

"I don't think so."

"Isn't it rather strange the call came through to your office?"

"I don't know," Brandon said. "You see, Otto Larkin's been messing around there in connection with that murder, and I've noticed that after Larkin gets one of his officious spells, people usually call my office for a while . . . I suppose we'll have to notify Larkin if it's anything serious. Ordinarily, we'd have referred the call to his office, but the way things are now . . . Well, you know, Doug."

"Heard anything from him about that prisoner?" Selby asked.

"Not a thing. He'll be notifying us pretty soon though. I'll bet he hates to face the music on that. He'll have to do some tall lying to make it appear he wasn't trying to give us the double-cross."

"If he gets the credit," Selby said, "he won't care much about what *we* think, although it's his nature to try to straddle the fence."

The sheriff swung the county car up the winding boulevard which led to Orange Heights. For the moment, Selby gave himself up to a contemplation of the panorama which was spreading out below. Then abruptly he was jerked back to reality by the application of the brakes, and he found that the car was coasting to a stop before the Artrim residence.

The two county officials jumped out of the car and ran up to the porch. Selby had time to notice that a hundred yards away the house of A. B. Carr gave forth no visible sign of activity on the part of its occupants. Then the door opened, and Ellen Saxe, her eyes dark with fright, said, "Come in."

"What's happened?" Selby asked.

She said, in a loud voice, "Mrs. Artrim is waiting for you," and then, in a lower voice to Selby, "She's done it."

"Done what?" Selby whispered.

"Made away with him," she said, and then, raising her voice again, said, "This way, please. Mrs. Artrim is waiting in the living-room."

They passed through the reception hallway and into a living-room. Rita Artrim was standing by the fireplace. She said, "Oh, *there* you are, at last."

Sheriff Brandon said, "We came as fast as we could. What's happened?"

She said, "My father-in-law," and stopped.

"Where is he?" Selby asked.

She shook her head. "I don't know."

"Isn't he a cripple?" Selby asked.

"Yes."

"Then he couldn't very well leave the house, could he?"

She shook her head.

Selby walked toward her. "Come, Mrs. Artrim, you can give us more information than that."

She took a deep breath as though bracing herself for some disagreeable duty which she had been anticipating and dreading. Selby noticed the strong odor of liquor on her breath, and glanced at Brandon. He could tell from the expression on the sheriff's face that he too had noticed the odor.

"He's gone," she said. "I thought I heard some peculiar noises during the night. I was frightened, but I've been such a baby that I didn't want to call the police again. I just kept my door locked and huddled under the covers. Then early this morning I felt that I at least owed it to my father-in-law to make certain he was all right."

"What sort of noises did you hear?" Selby asked.

"Things moving around—as though someone were in the house."

"What time was this?"

"I don't know. It must have been quite early in the morning, perhaps two or three o'clock."

"And when did you come downstairs to look for your father-in-law?"

"Just before I called the sheriff's office, about five or ten minutes before."

"And what did you find?" Selby asked.

"I found that his bed had been slept in, but he wasn't in his bedroom. I went to the bathroom, and he wasn't there. Then I wakened Miss Saxe. I had some difficulty doing it."

Ellen Saxe said, very distinctly and definitely, "I was drugged."

"What?" Selby asked.

"I was drugged," she said. "I recognized the symptoms."

"That's absurd," Mrs. Artrim said quickly.

"It's not absurd," Ellen Saxe insisted. "I know."

"What makes you think you were drugged?" Selby asked her.

She said, "The doctor left a powerful hypnotic, sodium

amytal, for Mr. Artrim to take when he's bothered with extreme nervousness. There's a milder hypnotic which he can use more regularly. I have some capsules which I take at night, not sedatives, just a general tonic. I take them three times a day. They're vitamin capsules."

"Well?" Selby asked.

She said, "Someone deliberately put one of the sodium amytal capsules inside of one of the vitamin capsules."

"How do you know."

"I could tell by the way I felt," she said. "A little while after I took those capsules. I began to feel exceedingly drowsy. I asked Mr. Artrim if he wanted anything more, and he said, 'No.' He'd been taken from his wheel chair and put to bed, and he was reading. I went in and lay down, and almost immediately went to sleep. I remembered thinking just before I went to sleep that I was frightfully drowsy and relaxed. I'm not usually that way. During the night I heard noises. I tried to wake up enough to get up. After all, you know, I'm on duty twenty-four hours a day. I'm supposed to be on call during the night whenever Mr. Artrim needs anything."

"What kind of noises were these that you heard?"

"The same things I heard," Mrs. Artrim said quickly.

"Just a minute, please," Selby said. "I'd like to have Miss Saxe describe the noises to me."

"I don't know," she said. "They were peculiar noises as though someone were moving around on tiptoe. I thought I heard . . ." Her voice trailed away into silence.

"What?" Selby asked.

"Just noises," she finished lamely.

"Did you get up?" Selby asked.

"No. I'd wakened just enough to realize that I should get up, but I felt too warm and drowsy. I'd say to myself, 'I must get up,' and then I'd doze off. Then a noise would waken me, and I'd think, 'Someone's moving around. I wonder if Mr. Artrim wants something.' Then I'd lie there listening for him to pound on the floor which is the signal he usually uses, and I'd drift off to sleep again. The first thing I knew Mrs. Artrim was shaking me and telling me to wake up."

"I had a frightful time wakening her," Mrs. Artrim said, "but I don't think she was drugged. I think she was just sleepy."

Ellen Saxe clamped her lips together in an obstinate line. "I was drugged," she said.

"Can you," Selby asked Mrs. Artrim, "describe the noises you heard?"

"Just as Ellen said—just as she has described them."

"Noises of someone moving around?"

"Yes."

"Did you hear voices?"

"No."

"Hear anything that could have been related to violence, blows, shots, or the sounds of scuffling?"

"No, only . . . only . . ."

"Go ahead," Selby said.

Her voice rose to a half scream. "Someone was dragging something across the floor!" she cried. "Oh, it was terrible!"

Selby turned to Ellen Saxe. "Did you," he asked, "hear that dragging noise?"

"No," she said. "I thought I heard . . ."

"Thought you heard what?" Selby asked.

"A rustle," she said defiantly, chin tilting up in the air, "the rustle of feminine garments."

Rita Artrim said quickly, "That was the dragging noise. She was drugged, and she couldn't hear clearly."

"Have you," Selby asked, "searched the house carefully?"

"Yes," Ellen Saxe said, "we've gone through it, and we haven't been able to find anything."

Selby said, "Let's go through it again. Where are Mr. Artrim's clothes?"

"Hanging in his closet," Ellen Saxe said, "where I placed them when I undressed him."

"And he can't walk?"

"No."

"Then if he left the place he must either have been carried or used his wheel chair. Could he get in the wheel chair by himself?"

"Yes, he can. Usually he needs some help. He can move his body all right, but his legs refuse to track. However, he can get into it and out of it. That's why the wheel chair is left right by the side of the bed—and it's still there. If he had taken it and gone any place, he'd have had to come back in it—and there it is."

"Exactly as you left it last?" Selby asked.

"No," she said. "It's been moved."

Selby said, "Let's take a look around."

They went through the rooms on the ground floor first, the women following them, lagging a few steps behind as though fearful of what they might find. Ellen Saxe, grim and uncompromising, made no effort to make any conversation with Mrs. Artrim. Mrs. Artrim seemed as though she were ready to turn and run at the first sign of anything out of the ordinary.

Rex Brandon glanced significantly at Selby, cautiously lowered his right eyelid. Selby surreptitiously shook his head, and motioned for silence.

"Where does this door go?" Selby asked, indicating a door in the side corridor.

"It leads into the garage," Mrs. Artrim said.

"How many cars do you keep, one or two?"

"Just one," she said. "I'm the only one who drives."

"The servants sleep in the house?"

"No. We have a housekeeper who comes in by the day.

93

My father-in-law was very peculiar. He wanted his own food prepared by his own nurse."

Selby said quietly, "Has it occurred to you, Mrs. Artrim, that you're referring to him in the past tense?"

Mrs. Artrim placed a handkerchief to her eyes, and sobbed audibly.

Ellen Saxe, leaning toward Selby, whispered in his ear, "Ask her about her clothes?"

Rita Artrim abruptly dropped the handkerchief. "What's that?" she asked sharply.

Ellen Saxe said, "As a nurse, I was warning him that you're on the brink of a collapse."

For a moment, Rita Artrim's eyes flashed. There was no vestige of tears, then she again pressed the handkerchief to her face.

Selby said, "Well, let's take a look in the garage." They walked down a short flight of stairs, opened another door and entered the garage. "Dark in here," Selby said.

No one said anything.

Selby glanced at the sheriff, and walked over to the far side of the garage, peered in the car, came back, and stood in front of the car frowning thoughtfully. He placed his right foot on the bumper, casually rested his right hand on the radiator, and said, "I'm sorry to bother you so much when your nerves are upset, Mrs. Artrim. I'd like to take a look in the basement. You have a basement, don't you?"

"Yes."

"You say you're the only one who drives the car?"

"Yes."

"Are the keys in it, or is it locked?" Selby asked, and without waiting for her to answer the question, opened the door and peered inside.

Ellen Saxe said quickly, "She keeps it locked."

"Yes," Mrs. Artrim said shortly. "I have the keys."

"Where is your purse?" Selby asked. "With you?"

94

"I think I left it in my bedroom."

'You might look in there," Selby said, "and see if the keys are all right."

"I'm certain they are," she said. "I had men from the Madison Garage come up yesterday to take the car down for greasing and oiling. They brought it back about five o'clock last night and left it in the garage. They brought me the keys, and I haven't been out since."

Selby asked Ellen Saxe casually, "Do you drive?"

"Yes," she said.

"Have you ever driven this car?"

"Occasionally when Mrs. Artrim has sent me on errands."

Selby said, "Well, if you'll go take a look for those keys, Mrs. Artrim, the sheriff and I will look around. I guess Miss Saxe can act as guide."

"Where do you want to go?" she asked.

"Down in the basement."

"I'm quite certain there's nothing down there," she said.

"Have you looked down there?"

"No."

"Then why do you feel there's nothing there?"

She said, "It wasn't that kind of a noise."

She left them to go and get the keys. Selby turned to Ellen Saxe. "There hasn't been anything so far to indicate violence," he said.

"That wheel chair has been moved," she said. "He was put in there."

"He didn't call you during the night?"

"I don't think so. . . . But remember, I was drugged. He could have been drugged, too. They gave me one capsule. They could have given him two very easily."

Selby said, "Why do you use the word 'they'?"

"I don't know. She must have had an accomplice. Oh, please don't stand here and talk. Go to the basement."

"Lead the way," Selby said.

95

She led the way back to the hallway. A door, turning to the side, opened on a winding flight of stairs. They went down into a well-kept, concrete basement with a smooth cement floor. There was an oil-burning furnace, the usual miscellaneous stored articles and a workbench.

"Who does the carpenter work?" Selby asked.

"Mr. Artrim," she said.

There were quick steps on the stairs, and Rita Artrim joined them. "Yes," she said, "the keys were safe in my purse, just as I thought."

"And the purse was in your bedroom with you?"

"That's right."

"Then no one could have operated the car?"

"No, of course not. Why do you attach so much emphasis to the operation of the car, Mr. Selby?"

Selby said ingenuously, "Obviously, he had to leave the house in some way. He couldn't walk. The car is the only method of transportation available."

"Oh, I see," she said. "You thought that perhaps someone —someone might have used the car?" and she looked for a brief, flashing glance at Ellen Saxe.

"That's right," Selby said.

"No, the keys were in my purse."

"And the purse was with you?"

"Yes."

"All the time?"

"Yes."

Sheriff Brandon indicated the workbench. "We were just asking Miss Saxe about this workbench."

She said, "My father-in-law likes to make things."

"How," Selby asked, "did he get down here? In his chair?"

"You can come in the back way. The lot slopes down the hill. The door opens onto a lower level."

"Can you drive a car around here?"

"Yes."

"And that other door?" Selby asked. "Where does it go?"

"That's a wine closet. This house was built during prohibition, you know, and people took excellent care not to have their liquor stolen. That door is a foot thick, and the wine closet is really a concrete vault."

"What do you keep in there?"

"Nothing," she said. "It's dark. There are no windows. I don't think the door's been opened—well, hardly since I looked the house over when I bought it."

"We may as well look in there now," Brandon said, and crossed over to the door. He said, "It's locked. Do you have the key to it?"

She said, "There's a key somewhere. Ellen, I think it's in my bedroom in the little jewel case, that big long key. If you'll run up and get it, please?"

Ellen Saxe nodded and started climbing the stairs.

Mrs. Artrim said, "It's such a shock. I can't seem to adjust myself to it. I really need a drink. Would you care to join me?"

"Not this early in the morning. Thanks," Selby said.

"No, thanks." Brandon shook his head.

She said, "The whiskey's upstairs. We may as well go up. You can see this door is locked, and it's been locked. If Ellen finds the key in my bedroom, it means no one could have got in here."

Brandon tried the door and said, "Yes. It's firm all right."

Selby said, "Miss Saxe gets up in the night occasionally with her patient, doesn't she?"

"Oh, yes."

"And that makes some noise?"

"Yes, some."

"Then why didn't you assume that the noises you heard were made by Miss Saxe in waiting on your father-in-law?"

"I don't know. I guess because—because it wasn't that

kind of a noise. . . . Please, Mr. Selby, I feel I must have a drink?"

"Where do you keep your store of liquor?"

"In the sideboard, what there is of it. I don't keep much on hand. I can buy all I want from the liquor store, and they deliver."

The three climbed the stairs. In the lower hallway, they met Ellen Saxe returning. "Here's the key," she said.

Mrs. Artrim took it and said, "There's no need of looking in there. That door's been locked, and this is the only key to it. . . . I'm going to have a little drink. I feel very upset."

"Her clothes," Ellen Saxe again whispered to Selby.

Selby said, "How about your clothes, Mrs. Artrim? Were any of them missing?"

"Why, no," she said.

As she turned away, Ellen Saxe caught Selby's arm and shook it vigorously. When she had his attention, she made motions with her hands along her form, indicating clothes. Brandon frowned, but Selby suddenly nodded.

Mrs. Artrim led the way back to the dining-room. She opened a sideboard, took out a bottle of whiskey, and poured herself a generous drink.

Selby asked, "What time do you usually rise, Mrs. Artrim?"

"Oh, not before seven-thirty or eight."

"And it was because of what you had heard during the night that you got up so early this morning?"

"Yes."

"And hastily ran downstairs in order to see if everything was all right?"

"Yes."

"And, as soon as you found the bed empty, you went in and awakened Miss Saxe?"

"That's right."

"How were you dressed at that time?" Selby asked. "What were you wearing?"

"Why," she said, "what I have on now."

Selby said, "Pardon me. I don't want to seem inquisitive, and I know very little about women's dress, but wouldn't it have been more logical for you to have thrown on a robe and slippers rather than dress for the street?"

She put down the empty whiskey glass. His question seemed to have jolted her. She said, "Well . . . the truth of the matter is . . . Frankly, Mr. Selby, I thought I might have to jump in my car and rush uptown. So I . . . so I dressed."

She glared at Ellen Saxe. "That's what all *your* whispering has been about," she said. "I heard you use the word 'clothes.' You're an underhanded person, and I think it will be well for the officers to check up on you. You and your capsules! Drugged! Drugged, my eye! You were mixed up in what happened last night, and then you deliberately took some sodium amytal to give yourself an out."

Ellen Saxe said quietly, "You can't clear yourself by dragging me into it, Mrs. Artrim."

Rita Artrim took two steps toward the nurse; then stopped. She said, "I'm not going to brawl with you. Get your things, and get out."

"I can't get out any too fast to suit me," Ellen Saxe said, leaving the room.

Rita Artrim turned to Selby. "I'm sorry," she said. "I'm emotionally upset, and—well, she'll bear watching."

Sheriff Brandon said, "We'll take a look through the upstairs rooms, if you don't mind."

Selby said, "Go right ahead, Rex. I want to put in a call. Where's the telephone?"

Mrs. Artrim showed him the telephone, and escorted Sheriff Brandon upstairs. Selby looked up the number of the Madison City Motor Company, got the night man on the line, and said, "This is Selby, the district attorney. You serviced a car for Mrs. Rita Artrim of Orange Heights yesterday and delivered it."

"I can look it up," the night man said.

"You make it a point to note the mileage on the speedometer as you do a grease job?"

"Yes."

"Look it up quickly and let me have the mileage on the speedometer."

There was a delay of almost a minute, then the man said, "Okay, Mr. Selby, i've got it here. The mileage was 32,394."

Selby said, "Thanks," hung up, took a pencil from his pocket and jotted a series of figures on the back of an envelope. A few seconds later, he heard light steps on the stairs and Mrs. Artrim joined him.

She said, "The sheriff is looking over the upstairs rooms. I thought perhaps I could be of some further assistance to you, Mr. Selby."

"Look here, Mrs. Artrim. That automobile is still warm. The temperature gauge inside of the dash shows that the car is almost at normal driving temperature right now. The Madison Motor Company serviced that car and delivered it last night. At that time the mileage was 32,394. When I looked at the inside of the car this morning, I noticed the mileage on the speedometer. It's now 32,486."

Mrs. Artrim stared at him in blank consternation for a moment. "Ellen Saxe must have driven him somewhere. I didn't drive it at all."

"You have the only keys?"

"As far as I know, yes."

Sheriff Brandon came down the stairs. "All clear upstairs, Doug," he said.

Selby said, "Rex, telephone Bob Terry. Ask him to come out here right away. Someone drove Mrs. Artrim's car over ninety miles last night. I want to take fingerprints from the steering wheel and find out who it was."

Brandon rang his office, told them to locate Terry, and have him make a rush trip out to Mrs. Artrim's residence. After he had hung up, Selby said to Mrs. Artrim, "We've covered all of the house now?"

"Yes," she said, "every bit of it."

Selby said, "With the exception of that liquor closet. The more I think of it, the more I think we should look in there."

"Very well, just as you say, Mr. Selby. I want to do everything I can to co-operate."

They trooped down the stairs in silence. Selby fitted the key to the lock, flung it back, and opened the door.

"I think there's a light switch somewhere just inside the door," Mrs. Artrim said.

Selby nodded, clicked on the light switch, and then stood perfectly still, staring at the interior of a thick, concrete room and at the sinister stains on the walls, at the dried, crusted pool on the floor.

Behind him, he heard Rita Artrim's scream.

CHAPTER IX

OTTO LARKIN WAS WAITING AT THE SHERIFF'S OFFICE WHEN Selby and Brandon drove up. His greeting was unduly effusive, and he followed up that greeting by saying, "Gosh, don't you folks ever sleep? I've been trying to get in touch with you on the telephone for the last half hour."

Brandon said, "What's the matter, Larkin? Did something develop?"

Larkin cleared his throat. "Well," he said, "I didn't know that you folks had telephoned the Los Angeles police about shadowing Carr so that he'd lead you to Ribber. You know, I felt rather cheap about letting Ribber slip through my fingers. I know I wasn't to blame, but just the same I'm sorry it happened."

"Oh, that's just one of those thing," Selby said.

"Well," Larkin explained, "I went into Los Angeles to do some work on my own, and found that the Los Angeles police had picked up Ribber, so I brought him back with me."

"When did they pick him up?" Selby asked.

"Shortly before midnight," Larkin said. "I had a few delays unwinding some red tape, then I put Ribber in the car and started back. I had a little motor trouble, nothing serious, but I had to get a garage man out of bed. I didn't fancy the idea of being stuck out in a lonely road some place with a broken-down automobile and a murderer on my hands."

"You brought him back with you?" Brandon asked.

"Yes."

"Where is he?"

"Well, he's down at the city jail. I thought I'd put him there, and then get in touch with you folks and see what you wanted."

"That isn't much of a place for a desperate prisoner," Selby said.

"I know it isn't. I figured it would be a good plan to bring him up to the county jail, but I thought you'd prefer to handle that yourself. I could turn him over to you, and you could bring him up and book him."

"What," Selby asked, "does he say?"

"Nothing very much. He's close-mouthed and wise—stir-wise."

"Won't he say anything at all?" Selby asked.

"Oh, he talks about the weather and about the war situation, and says I'm trying to frame something on him, but that I can't make it stick and that's about all."

Selby said, "I guess we'd better go see him. There's been some trouble out at the Artrim residence. We haven't made any arrests, but we've closed up the house, sealed everything up, and left Bob Terry in charge. We've asked Mrs.

Artrim to leave. There's some work out there which we aren't equipped to handle. It calls for an expert criminologist and laboratory equipment. I'm going to telephone Los Angeles to see if we can't get a criminologist from their Homicide Department."

"What is it?" Larkin asked. "What's happened?"

"It looks like murder," Selby said. "Apparently Frank Artrim was the victim, but we can't find the corpse."

"Any idea who did it?"

"No. Nothing definite."

"What's the idea of putting Mrs. Artrim out of her house?"

"She's taken a room in the hotel," Selby said. "It'll only be for a few hours. We drove her up with us. She's mad as a wet hen, but I don't think she'll skip out. I want to be certain that no one tampers with the evidence that's in that house."

"I'll go out and look it over," Larkin said.

Selby said, "I think the best thing to do is to keep the house closed tight as a drum until we can get an expert on the job. There are some bloodstains to be analyzed, and some fingerprint work to be done."

Larkin said sullenly, "It's within the city limits, ain't it?"

"That's right," Brandon said truculently, "and it's within the county."

"I should see what's there," Larkin said.

"We'll all see what's there when we can do it without obliterating clues," Selby observed.

Larkin said, 'I guess the Los Angeles fellows must have tipped 'the *Blade* off."

"To what?"

"About Ribber."

"Why?"

"One of the *Blade* reporters was waiting for me to show up."

"Did you give him an interview?"

103

"I couldn't help talking with him."

"How about the other paper?" Selby asked.

"Sylvia Martin was hanging around the jail, but I couldn't let her see the prisoner."

"How about the *Blade* man? Did he see him?"

"He wasn't waiting at the jail," Larkin said. "He was about a mile out of town. He recognized my car and drove alongside. I thought he had some message from you folks, so I stopped and asked him about it, and he talked with me and asked a few questions of the prisoner. As soon as I saw what he was up to, I told him I couldn't let him have an interview without your consent, and started my car and drove on in."

Selby and Brandon exchanged glances. "What," Selby asked, "do you intend to do now, Larkin?"

Larkin spread out his hands in a gesture of surrender. "Why," he said, "it's up to you boys. I just happened to be on the spot, and as chief of police I picked up the prisoner and brought him in, but he's all yours. I'll do anything I can to help, but I don't want to interfere in any way with your plans."

"That's nice," Brandon said sarcastically.

Selby said, "I think we'd better go down and pick him up, Rex, and put him in the county jail."

"Okay. Let's go."

"I'll ride down with you," Larkin said.

They drove down to the city jail. The turnkey on duty said, "You want Ribber?"

"Yes," Brandon said.

"He's talking with his lawyer right now," the turnkey observed.

"His lawyer?" Brandon asked.

"Yes."

"Who?"

"A. B. Carr."

"How did *he* get in?"

The turnkey seemed ill at ease. "Well," he said, "Carr showed up right after we'd booked him on suspicion of murder, and demanded that he see his client. I told him to wait until the chief got back, but he said he wasn't waiting for anyone. He showed me a section of the penal code which made it a misdemeanor for an officer not to allow an attorney to visit his client and showed me that as the officer who was in charge I'd be stuck for five hundred dollars in addition to fines if I didn't let him in. There's a law right there in the penal code."

"So you let him in?"

"I let him in."

Brandon said, "All right. We'll interrupt the conference. Where are they?"

"In the detention room."

The three men walked across the jail office and pushed open the door. Carr looked up and greeted them affably. "Good morning, gentlemen," he said. "We seem to all be working early this morning."

Selby said, "We want to question Ribber."

"Go right ahead," Carr invited.

"Thank you," Selby said. "I think we can dispense with your presence."

"I'm his attorney. I want to be present when any questions are asked."

"You can be present in court," Selby said.

Carr sighed. "I have a lot of trouble with you fellows," he said. "In case it makes any difference to you, Ribber will answer questions if I'm here. If I'm not here, he won't answer any questions. You have the right to see him without my presence. He has the right to refuse to answer any questions. Now then, what do you want to do?"

Selby said, "We want you to get out."

"Quite all right," Carr observed. "No hard feelings, boys. Have a cigar?"

Selby held the door open. "No," he said.

"How about you?" Carr asked Larkin. "You know, Chief, we had a difference of opinion, but that doesn't mean we can't be friendly. Better try that cigar. It's a fifty-cent Perfecto specially made to order. I think you'll like it."

Larkin stretched forth a tentative hand and took the proffered cigar.

"Okay, boys. Call me any time," Carr said. "Ribber will answer questions if I'm present. If I'm not, he won't."

"After this," Selby said ominously, "Mr. Ribber is going to be at the county jail. If you want to call on him as his attorney, you'll have to make an application to the sheriff."

Carr's grin was broad. "After this," he said, with just a trace of sarcasm in his voice, "I don't think it'll be necessary for me to call on the prisoner. In the event it is, I'll be only too glad to comply with all of the rules of your hostelry, Sheriff. Good morning." He closed the door behind him.

Ribber, looking rather sullen about the mouth, but with his eyes glittering with the cunning which comes to men and animals who are much hunted, said, "My name's Pete Ribber. My age is thirty-three. I'm a citizen of the United States—and that's all, boys."

Selby said, "Ribber, I'm going to show you a gun and ask you some questions about it."

"No comment," Ribber said.

"Where," Selby asked, "have you been since your release from this jail when you were picked up on suspicion of being a prowler?"

"No comment."

"Isn't it true that you were held by A. B. Carr, concealed in his house?"

"No."

"Better be careful, Ribber. We have some of your finger-prints."

Ribber laughed easily. "Well, now," he said, "I guess Carr wouldn't have any objections to my telling you folks the true facts about that. You see, Carr was my lawyer. After I was arrested here, and fingerprinted, I figured that there'd be an attempt to pick me up again. I went to Carr's office to try and see him. I didn't see him. I found that he was living here in Madison City—which I hadn't known when I was here. I came back last night and tried to find Carr. I was looking pretty seedy, hadn't shaved for a while, and needed a bath. Well, I rang the bell and knocked on the door, and nothing happened. Carr had told me that if I ever wanted to see him real badly, and he wasn't at home, to walk in and wait. So I walked right on in."

"Wasn't the door locked?" Brandon asked, ominously.

"Strange to say, it wasn't. The door had been pulled shut, but the spring lock hadn't quite slipped into place. All I had to do was to push the door, and it opened. I closed it behind me and locked it."

Selby said tonelessly, "Go ahead. Let's hear the rest of it."

"Well," Ribber went on reminiscently and with every evidence of enjoyment; "I looked around the house and found Carr's study all right. I decided I'd wait for him, but I certainly did look plenty tough. I knew it would be all right with Carr because he'd told me to make myself right at home any time when I was waiting for him. So I stripped off and took a bath, and found some shaving things and shaved myself. I sort of made headquarters in a little room which opened off of his den."

"You shaved yourself?" Selby asked.

"That's right."

"What kind of a razor did you use?"

"A single-edged safety razor."

"How many times did you shave?"

"Just once."

"How many blades did you use?"

Ribber grinned. "Oh, that," he said. "I don't know. I used quite a few. My beard was awfully tough, and I couldn't seem to get a blade that did the work. I kept changing blades in the razor."

"And you left fingerprints about the place?"

"Why, sure. Why shouldn't I?. I was Carr's guest. I had just as much of a right to be there as anyone that he'd invite to the place. Why, he was my lawyer. I'd taken a powder on him, but there were good reasons for that, and I wanted to explain those reasons to him."

"How long did you stay there?" Selby asked.

"Well," Ribber said, "my ideas of time are pretty hazy. I didn't have a watch that was worth a darn. . . ."

"Didn't you have a watch when you were booked here in jail?" Larkin asked.

"Sure. Sure," Ribber said, "but that was a watch which Carr gave me afterwards. Now just don't interrupt me, and I'll tell my story."

"Go ahead," Selby said.

"Well, I looked around Carr's place, and then got to thinking he'd gone into Los Angeles to work. He does that sometimes—spends almost all night at his office. So I went down and looked in the garage and sure enough his car was gone, so I figured I'd better go on into Los Angeles and see if he wasn't there. I thumbed rides into the city and found Carr at his office. I went in and told him what I'd done, and he said that was quite all right, that I'd done just the right thing. He told me that he couldn't represent me unless I gave myself up to the police. He said I was a fugitive from justice, and it was up to me to give myself up. So I told him I'd go right down to police headquarters and surrender. Well, I intended to do that too, but as soon as I got out of

Carr's office, a couple of dicks nabbed me and took me down."

"Did you tell them you were going to jail to surrender?" Selby asked.

"I didn't tell them anything. They were wise guys. They knew it all. There was no sense in getting into an argument with them. A lot of guys get teeth pushed down their throat arguing with smart dicks."

"And this," Brandon asked, "is the story that Carr fixed up for you to tell?"

Ribber was indignant. "Say, what do you mean?" he asked. "A story Carr fixed up? Nothing to it, brother, nothing to it. Somebody's been feeding you a lot of malarkey."

Selby said, "All right, we'll take you out of here and go up to the county jail. You'll like it better up there."

"This is a crummy joint," Ribber admitted.

"Have you read anything in the papers about a murder out in Orange Heights early yesterday morning?"

"No comment."

"Where were you from midnight until six o'clock in the morning yesterday?"

"No comment," Ribber said.

Selby nodded to Brandon. "All right, Rex. Let's take him up and book him up there."

"Suspicion of murder?" Larkin asked.

Selby nodded.

Ribber said easily, "That isn't going to get you anywhere, boys. I haven't committed any murder, and you can't pin one on me."

Selby said, "If you can convince us that you're innocent, Ribber, that'll be all there is to it."

Ribber grinned. "No comment," he said. "Incidentally I want bail."

"You've run out on one bail bond already," Selby pointed out.

"No comment," Ribber said.

Larkin said, "Well, there's no need of me going up with you boys. I'll go get some breakfast. Now if there's anything else I can do to help you fellows, you just call on me. I want to co-operate. I know that from now on it's your party, Selby, but if there's anything I can do, just let me know, and I'll do it."

Selby said, "Very well. We'll take him up to the county jail."

Ribber said, "I want to see a justice of the peace, and I want bail." Brandon said nothing. "How about that bail?" Ribber asked. "Do I get it?"

Selby smiled. "No comment," he said.

"How about the magistrate?"

"We'll take you before the magistrate within the time provided by law," Selby told him.

"Any time you want to find out anything from me," Ribber said, "Mr. Carr is my lawyer. He's going to represent me at all stages of the proceedings. Just call him, and he can answer any questions. There's no use bothering me."

"You mean you refuse to answer any questions?" Selby asked.

"Why, no. Certainly not. I'll answer all questions—except those that I think are connected with my case. On those I'll simply say, 'No comment.'"

The sheriff gave an audible exclamation of disgust, turned toward the door, and said, "Give me his stuff, Larkin. I'll sign for it. We're taking him up to the county jail."

Larkin followed Brandon, leaving Selby alone with Ribber. Ribber said, "You look like an intelligent guy."

"No comment," Selby said.

"You know, if you wanted to," Ribber went on, "you could get into the big-time stuff. You don't need to stick around a little burg all your life."

Selby said, "Listen, crook, I know your game. I'm not

open to bribery. You're in jail. You're going to stay there a while. If your lawyer is so smart, let him figure some way of getting you out."

The twinkle faded from Ribber's eyes. He said gruffly, "Don't worry. Old A.B.C. is going to get me out—the best mouthpiece in the country. He makes lots of dough. He's awfully busy, though. He's looking for a junior partner."

Selby turned on his heel and walked out. A few minutes later, he was back with the sheriff and Otto Larkin.

Larkin said, "Okay, Ribber. We're going up to the county jail. Put out your wrists."

Ribber's face showed bewildered surprise. "Why, say," he said, "you boys aren't going to put those things on me, are you?"

"Put out your wrists," Sheriff Brandon said grimly. "You're not going to slip out of this rap. You're going to wear bracelets, and you're going to have a leg iron."

For a moment Ribber's face twisted, then he said, "All right, you dumb hicks. Go ahead and see if you can dish out anything that I can't take."

CHAPTER X

Sylvia Martin found Doug Selby in his office, a large scale road map of Southern California in front of him with a ten-inch circle neatly compassed in red pencil. "What's the idea, Doug?" she asked.

He grinned and said, "A circle tour."

She walked over to study the map. The center of the circle was Madison City. "Be a sport, Doug," she said. "Give a working girl a break."

Selby said, "Working girls don't need breaks. Heaven is the traditional protector of the working girl."

"Well," she said, "suppose I appeal to you as a friend."

Doug made a great show of hesitating.

Sylvia Martin went on, "A friend, a constituent, a taxpayer, and *a voter!*"

Selby said, "That last does the trick. I'm going to need the support of the voters."

Sylvia Martin indicated the "Extra" edition of the *Blade* which reposed on Selby's desk. "If there's much more of this, you are," she said.

Selby grinned. "Oh, that was just an accident," he explained. "Otto Larkin has told me all about it. He's very much put out that the *Blade* should have made political capital out of it. It seems that he just happened to be in Los Angeles looking for Ribber when Ribber was apprehended. So, as our agent, he undertook to bring Ribber here. In doing that, he accidentally bumped into a reporter from the *Blade*, and then, having lodged Ribber in the city jail and made the mistake of booking him instead of holding him for questioning or as a material witness, he let A. B. Carr have a few minutes alone with the prisoner."

"And what happened then, Doug?"

"Oh, nothing," he said. "Carr just passed the time of day, but following that visit, Ribber told the most plausible story which explains away every bit of evidence we had against Carr."

"Does it explain the evidence against Ribber, Doug?"

"Not yet. He isn't commenting on that phase of the case, but in due time Carr will call on him again, and then Ribber will have another story which will fit into all the facts of the case. However, I doubt if we hear that story until after it's been very well rehearsed. We'll probably get our first inkling of what it's to be on the witness stand."

"At the preliminary, Doug?"

"No, not at the preliminary. Carr won't show his hand

there. He'll make me show mine, and then wait to spring his defense in front of a jury."

"What's the circle for, Doug?"

Selby said, "Somewhere along that circle a body has either been dumped or buried."

"Mr. Artrim?" she asked.

He nodded.

"How do you figure it, Doug? As I get the story, it's just a disappearance."

Selby said, "You should see the bloodstains in the wine cellar. It looks as though the place had been used for a butcher shop."

"Doesn't Mrs. Artrim claim that Ellen Saxe did it?"

Selby grinned. "You get around, don't you?"

"I try to. What about the circle, Doug?"

"Mrs. Artrim's car was driven ninety miles last night sometime after midnight."

"How do you know, Doug?"

"The car had just been serviced. The garage noted the speedometer reading."

"You think the car was used to transport Artrim's body?"

"That's the theory," he admitted.

"And this circle is forty-five miles?"

"Forty-five miles in an air line," Selby said. "I'll have to make some adjustments for turns and twists in the roads."

Sylvia thought for a minute, and then said, "If I suddenly found myself confronted with the job of disposing of a body, I'd drive around looking for a place to dump it. I might drive ninety miles, and never be more than ten miles from Madison City."

Selby said, "This wasn't that kind of a crime, Sylvia. It was deliberately planned down to the most minute detail, even to the drugging of the nurse."

"Was she really drugged, Doug?"

"I think so."

Sylvia bent over the desk, her head close to Doug's, as she studied the map. She said, "That circle takes in a lot of territory, Doug."

Selby took the red pencil and divided the circle into segments. "This part of the circle," he said, "just misses quite a few suburban cities. We can probably disregard that part of it. It runs directly through the center of one city—El Bocano, and just misses three other cities. This segment gets up into the mountain country. There's only two roads there we'd have to consider. This segment runs down to the desert."

"Would a person bury a body in the mountains, Doug?"

Selby said, "Probably not. If a person were going to *dump* a body, he could drive along a mountain road, stop on the edge of a sheer drop, and unload the remains. If a person were going to *bury* a body, he'd be inclined to pick the sandy desert country."

"A woman would be more apt to dump a body," Sylvia said.

"It depends on the woman," Selby replied. "Let's put ourselves in the position of the murderer with a body in the car. The crime has been carefully planned. The idea is to keep the police from ever finding the body. Dumping it in the canyon would gain a little time, perhaps two or three days. Digging a grave in the desert might gain a lot of time. The body might never be discovered."

"Go ahead, Doug."

Selby said, "A person wouldn't park a car by the side of a main desert highway, and dig a grave. A lot of people drive desert roads only at night to avoid the heat and glare. Relatively speaking, there's a lot of night traffic on a desert road."

"But they could turn off on a side road, Doug."

"That's what I'm getting at," he said. "Suppose we figure that a person would drive down a little-used side road for

114

a mile or two. That would account for three or four of the miles shown on the speedometer. Now figure another two or three miles for the difference between air-line distance and road distance, and that brings us right to here." Selby placed the point of his pencil at a side road which turned off from the main Indio highway.

There was excitement in Sylvia's voice. "Doug," she said, "that's the only side road which turns off anywhere within a distance of ten miles."

He nodded.

"What are you going to do?"

"Take a run out and investigate," he said.

"Doug, take me."

He pushed tobacco into his pipe and studied her gravely. "The taxpayers wouldn't like it if we took a newspaper reporter along," he said, "—some of them wouldn't."

"Oh, bosh. Those are the ones who wouldn't like anything you did. You can't please everybody, Doug. Don't be so conservative."

He grinned and went on calmly, as though there had been no interruption. "On the other hand, we should have some disinterested witness who would make a favorable impression on a jury—preferably a nice-looking girl who would know how to keep her mouth shut in case we *didn't* find anything."

She flashed him a smile. "When do we start, Doug?"

"In about an hour. If we find a grave and exhume a body, it probably won't be a pleasant experience."

"I can take it, Doug," she said confidently.

"Okay. We'll go in about an hour. Do you want us to pick you up at the *Clarion* office?"

"Yes. Incidentally, Doug, I've been commissioned to get the latest news from you on that murder case."

Selby grinned, and said, "The latest news is all in the *Blade*. It seems to have covered the situation very thoroughly."

"Doug, why did you let them do that to you?"

"I couldn't help it."

She said, "You make me sick. You always sit back and let people push you around, and never do anything about it. Why didn't you put a stop to that?"

"I didn't have the chance," he said.

"Otto Larkin's taken all the credit, and you're going to have all the responsibility."

"I know that," Selby said.

"Weren't you the one who rang up the Los Angeles police and told them to keep an eye out for Ribber at Carr's office?"

"The sheriff did that," he said.

"But you told him to."

"Yes."

"We're going to town on that, Doug. We'll show just what a contemptible trick it was."

Selby said, "Don't."

"Don't what?"

"Don't try to show them up. Just let it ride."

"But, Doug, you can't afford to. Larkin has taken all the credit. He's arrested the murderer and turned him over to you. He's done his duty. It's up to you to get a conviction. If you get one, it'll be because of Larkin's prompt action. If you don't get one, it'll be because you didn't have the ability to properly present the case after Larkin had it all worked up. I don't like it."

"I don't like it myself," Selby said, "but there's nothing we can do about it."

"That's what you think."

Selby said, "That's right, and nothing you've said changes my mind."

She said, "Doug, I wish I could take you and shake you."

"Don't do it," he said. "You might break my pipe. Here's something you might care to know. Morton Taleman, the man who was killed, was an associate of Pete Ribber. Both of them served a term in San Quentin for a larceny which they pulled together. They had both been sailors, and had stars tattooed on their forearms several years ago in Shanghai. About a year ago, they had a falling-out. They haven't been together since, and the Los Angeles police think there's been some bad blood between them."

She said, "Doug, that just makes Larkin's move look that much more brilliant."

He nodded carelessly. "Those are the facts," he said. "You want the facts, don't you?"

"Yes, but—I'd like to publish the real facts. I'd like to show up how Larkin double-crossed you."

"Readers aren't interested in that," he said. "They're interested in facts. They want the murderer apprehended. They don't care who does the apprehending."

"You just think they don't."

"And," Selby went on, "it's going to be a job building up a case against Ribber."

"Why, Doug?"

"A. B. Carr," he said.

"What do you mean?"

"Two bullets were fired into Taleman's body. One of them was fired through a suit of clothes. One of them was fired into the body. Either bullet would have been instantly fatal."

"But, Doug, I don't understand. Why would anyone want to fire a second bullet?"

"Probably," he said, "because of the clothes. If the man was naked when he was killed, someone wants us to believe he was wearing a suit of clothes at the time the shot was fired; or, looking at it the other way, if he was wearing a suit of clothes when he was shot, someone wants us to think he was murdered while he was naked."

"You think that Carr's mixed up in that?"

"It's rather a clever dodge," Selby said noncommittally.

"Doug, can attorneys get away with that kind of stuff?"

"They've been known to," he said.

"But why would they go to the trouble and risk of doing that just for the purpose of confusing you?"

"That," Doug said, "remains to be seen. Remember that a man can only be murdered once. Remember also that the district attorney has to prove his case beyond all reasonable doubt."

Her eyes showed her apprehension. "Doug, do you mean to say that Carr could use that other bullet to mix things up so you couldn't tell—that you couldn't prove . . ."

"Beyond all reasonable doubt," Selby reminded her.

"Doug, you can't let him get away with that. You simply can't."

Selby said, "There's not a great deal I can do. It's a peculiar case, and now this Artrim business comes along right on top of it."

"Do you think Carr's mixed up in that, Doug?"

"There's no indication that he is."

"Doug Selby, don't you let them leave you holding the sack."

"No, ma'am," Selby said.

"You'll pick me up in about an hour?"

"Uh huh—and you'd better wait to do your writing until after we get back. You might have more to write about."

When she had gone, Selby put through a call to the Los Angeles Homicide Detail. "I want to borrow a criminologist," he said, after he'd identified himself.

"We can't let our men go out of the city very well unless it's in connection with some city murder. What do you want, Selby?"

"I want some bloodstains analyzed. I want some fingerprints checked, and above all, I want someone who can go over an automobile with a magnifying glass and tell something about the roads over which it's been driven."

"Tell you what we can do. We can send down a chap who

118

helps us out once in a while. He's a consulting criminologist, name of Victor Hawlins. How soon do you want him?"

"Just as soon as he can get here," Selby said. "Have him report to the sheriff's office, and they'll tell him what to do."

"He'll be there by noon," the officer promised.

Selby hung up and called Rex Brandon. "How about having the county car ready for a drive out to the desert in about an hour, Rex?" he asked

"Okay, Doug. Got a tip?"

"Just a hunch," Selby said. "We'll probably be gone about four hours. A little after noon, a criminologist by the name of Victor Hawlins will call at your office. Arrange to have him taken out to the Artrim house."

"What's that name?"

"Victor Hawlins."

"Okay, Doug. And I meet you in an hour?"

"Uh huh. Can you do it?"

"Sure thing," Brandon said.

Selby had just hung up the telephone when Amorette Standish appeared in the door to announce that Sam Roper was waiting in the outer office and wanted to see him.

"Show him in," Selby said.

Sam Roper had been the former district attorney. Ever since Selby had displaced him in a bitter, hard-fought political campaign, there had been no love lost between the two men. Roper, retired to private practice, had taken an occasional criminal case, had been the instigator of much curbstone criticism of Selby's policies and the manner in which the office was conducted.

Roper, apparently wishing to preserve the semblance of social amenities, shook hands, wished the district attorney a good morning, and chatted for a moment about generalities.

Selby, very much on guard, matched the other's casual courtesy, gave him a chair, and sat back to listen.

Roper said, "Mrs. James B. Artrim telephoned me a short time ago, and asked me to come up to her room in the hotel for a brief chat."

"Indeed," Selby said.

Roper said, "Of course, Selby, we have our differences of opinion. I ran the office my way when I was here. Now that you're here, you're running it your way. That's all right. That's expected."

"Exactly," Selby agreed.

"But it's rather unusual for a woman to be evicted from her own house, deprived of her own automobile, held a prisoner in a hotel, all without any process of law."

"It is," Selby agreed.

"It's illegal," Roper pointed out.

"If," Selby said, "she were placed under formal arrest on suspicion of homicide or held as a material witness, the situation would be legal. It would, in effect, be the same, and Mrs. Artrim would be inconvenienced a great deal more."

"Is that," Roper asked, "a threat?"

"No," Selby said, "it's a statement—something for you to think over."

"I consider it as a threat," Roper said.

Selby shrugged his shoulders. He filled his pipe, calmly tamped the tobacco in the bowl, and struck a match.

Roper said, "I have advised Mrs. Artrim that the proceedings are highly irregular. She has asked me to do something about it."

Selby said, "And the reason you came here instead of going into court is that you don't want to force my hand, and have me take formal proceedings."

Roper said, "The reason I came here was to give you an opportunity to put yourself in the clear before I did anything."

Selby said, "Very well, you've come here. You've given

me that opportunity. Now go ahead and do whatever you want to."

"You refuse to alter the status of the situation?"

Selby said, "There's evidence in that house which I consider important. That evidence indicates a homicide has been committed on the premises. I've arranged for a consulting criminologist to go over the evidence. As soon as he has completed his inspection, the house will be restored to Mrs. Artrim. Until then, the situation remains in status quo."

Roper said, "I don't like that."

Selby said, "I hardly anticipated that you would."

"I don't like your attitude, Selby, and I don't like your way of handling this."

Selby said, "There's a man by the name of Ribber who's in jail. He's held on suspicion of homicide. He doesn't like my attitude either. In all probability, he likes it even less than Mrs. Artrim does."

Sam Roper placed the tips of his fingers together. His eyes met Selby's, wavered, shifted to a contemplative study of his shoes, then flashed back to meet Selby's. "There's certainly no reason why you should impound her automobile," he said.

"I think there is."

"Why?"

"I consider it's evidence."

"Evidence of what?"

"Evidence of a crime I'm investigating."

"What crime?"

"Homicide."

"In what possible way could that be evidence?"

"I don't care to discuss it."

Roper shifted his position in the chair, still keeping his fingertips together. "Surely," he said, "there's some limit to what you intend to do."

"Undoubtedly," Selby agreed.

"Perhaps the matter could be amicably adjusted if you could give me something definite which I could take to my client."

Selby said, "The criminologist will arrive between one and two o'clock this afternoon. He should be finished with his examination by five. At the end of that time, I see no reason why Mrs. Artrim can't have her automobile and return to her house—unless the evidence discovered by this criminologist makes it necessary for me to prefer more formal charges."

Roper thought for a moment, then pushed back his chair. "Very well," he said.

His entrance had been accompanied by an outward semblance of professional courtesy. His departure was with no word of farewell, an indignant striding across the office, a jerking open of the exit door, and an abrupt departure.

Selby got some things together, gave Amorette Standish a few instructions, and was on the point of leaving the office when the telephone rang. A. B. Carr was on the other end of the line.

"On that Ribber case, Selby," Carr said affably, "the defendant is entitled to a prompt hearing. I want it."

"How soon do you want it?"

"Just as soon as we can get it."

"We could arraign him on the complaint in the justice's court on Monday," Selby said, "and fix a date for a preliminary examination."

"All right by me," Carr said, "*if* the preliminary examination is held not later than ten o'clock on Tuesday morning."

Selby said, "Very well, I'll stipulate to that effect."

"This is Saturday, a half holiday," Carr pointed out, "but we could go into court this morning, and make the stipulation, fixing the time for the preliminary."

Selby said, "I'm going to be out of town this morning. We can do it Monday."

"Very well. Better take my advice, Selby, and dismiss that case. If you go ahead with it, you're going to get your fingers burned."

Selby said, "My fingers have been burned before. They've become calloused by this time."

Carr's laugh was friendly and magnetic. "Oh, well," he said, "it's all in a lifetime. By the way, Selby, I'm filing suit against you and the sheriff for defamation of character, misuse of legal process, unwarranted search, and false accusations. I'm asking for fifty thousand dollars damages."

"When are you filing?" Selby asked.

"Oh, sometime the first of the week. I thought you might be willing to accept the service of the papers and expedite matters somewhat."

Selby said, "Let me know when you've actually filed the suit, and we'll discuss that phase of the case."

Carr said, "All right, Selby. It's just a business matter. I can't let you fellows get away with this stuff, you know. I have my prestige and professional standing to consider. It's all in the game, you know."

Selby said, "Certainly, and if I should proceed against you for subornation of perjury, you'll understand that I have my own prestige to consider, and that it's purely a matter of business with no hard feelings on either side."

"Are you," Carr asked, "intending to proceed against me on that charge?"

Selby said, "I don't know. I merely said *if* I did, that I'd want you to appreciate my position."

Carr laughed heartily and said, "You know, Selby, I like you. I wish you were in the city where we could lock horns oftener. I think I'd find you a worthy foeman. Well, I'll be seeing you Monday morning in the justice's court then."

Selby hung up the telephone, told Amorette Standish he wouldn't be in until late afternoon, and joined Rex Brandon who was waiting in the county car in the official parking place in the rear of the courthouse. They picked up Sylvia Martin and, with a careful check of the speedometer, drove out toward the main highway which traversed the desert.

There was but little conversation. A general atmosphere of tension filled the automobile. The sheriff drove rapidly up over the grade, out of the orange lands into the apple country, and then down a gradual slope between snow-capped mountains to where the country abruptly changed from fertile soil to arid desert. The road was straighter here, and the sheriff pushed the car into speed.

Their speedometer showed exactly 41.6 miles at the turn of the desert road which led off the highway. Selby, making a note of the mileage, nodded his head in satisfaction. "Figure about a mile and a half from the courthouse to her house in Orange Heights," he said. The sheriff swung the car off the highway and onto the dirt road which ran to the left. Selby said, "Drive as slowly as you can in high gear. Sylvia, you watch one side of the road. I'll watch the other side."

Brandon said, "We can see if any automobile has turned off of the road or backed to turn around. Tracks would last for days in this soil—even if there's been a wind." The car crawled along. When it commenced to buck in high gear, Brandon shifted to second. He started calling out the readings on the speedometer. "One mile from the turn-off," he said, and a few moments later, "a mile and two-tenths; one and four-tenths."

The speedometer clicked over on two miles even. Brandon took his eyes from the road ahead to glance swiftly at Selby. The district attorney sat motionless. His eyes squinted against the glare of the desert sunlight, studying the ground along the side of the road. The sheriff turned his attention back to the speedometer. He no longer read off tenths of miles. He said, "Three miles," in a flat, toneless voice, and then a while later, "four miles." At five miles, he stopped the car. "How about it, son?" he asked.

"One more mile," Selby said.

They crawled along for another uneventful mile.

Selby said, "That looks like a crossroad ahead. We can go up there, turn around, and come back. Sylvia, you stand on one running board. I'll stand on the other. In that way, we can look directly down at the sides of the road."

Sylvia Martin seemed to be fighting back tears of disappointment. "Okay, Doug," she said.

The sheriff backed and turned the car at the crossroads. They started out slowly. Sylvia stepped out to stand on the left-hand running board. Doug Selby stood on the right.

The car crawled back along the road at a snail's pace. Hot, desert sunlight beat down upon it until the interior became like an oven. The dust, raised by the wheels, swirled about the car and into the nostrils of the disappointed trio. Selby seemed entirely oblivious of the physical discomfort. He stood on the running board, his arm crooked around the frame of the door for support. Brandon dropped the car into low gear, crawled along at a pace but little faster than a walk. After what seemed an interminable interval, the car crawled back up the slight slope to the main highway.

"Well?" Brandon asked.

Selby opened the car door, slid into the front seat, and nodded to Sylvia. "Okay, Rex," he said. "We're licked."

Sylvia Martin said, "Don't you suppose the automobile itself will furnish some clue, Doug?"

"I hope so," Selby said. "We'll stop at this town up here, get something to eat, and call Madison City. I left word for that criminologist to go over the car first."

Lunch was for the most part a silent, dejected meal. Sylvia Martin occasionally tried to make conversation, but the effort was wasted against Brandon's discouragement and Selby's concentration. After the meal, Selby called Madison City, using the number of the Artrim residence. Bob Terry answered the phone, and Selby had him put the criminologist on the line.

The district attorney said, "This is Selby speaking. We're out on the desert running down a possible clue. Can you tell us anything about that car?"

"Not very much," the criminologist said. "It's been driven over a road which has recently been oiled. There are particles of oiled earth clinging to the underside of the fenders. I haven't made a detailed analysis of the earth, but it looks more as though the car had been over an oiled detour than over a highway which was under construction. Aside from that, there's no indication that it's been driven off of paved road."

Selby said, "Thanks. I guess we're on a false trail. How about the blood?"

"Human blood," the criminologist said. "An attempt has been made to sluice the stains on the floor with water. Nothing had been done about the spatters on the wall. Looks as though someone had tried to remove the bloodstains on the floor, but had given it up as a bad job. The sheriff's deputy and I are working on fingerprints."

Selby said, "Okay, do the best you can. If you can think of any other test to make on that car . . ."

"I can't," the criminologist said. "I've gone over every inch of it very carefully."

"Had a body been transported in it?"

"I don't know. Something had been carried in the rear. It was wrapped in a woolen blanket. The blanket had green, red, and yellow stripes—a blanket such as is put out by the Hudson Bay Company."

"You can't tell whether it was a body?"

"No, but it was some bundle with a blanket of that description covering it. I feel quite certain it's a Hudson Bay blanket because I notice there are two Hudson Bay blankets on the bed in Mrs. Artrim's room."

Selby said, "Thanks. Do the best you can. I'll be seeing you in a little over an hour." He hung up the telephone and walked back to the table where Sheriff Brandon and Sylvia Martin sat anxiously waiting. "No dice," he said. "The car was operated over an oiled dirt detour. Apparently, it didn't leave pavement aside from that detour."

Brandon frowned thoughtfully. "I don't remember any detour," he said. "Not within forty . . ."

"The criminologist is making an analysis of the soil. Ring up the automobile clubs when we get back, Sheriff, and find out about roads. We'll try and get someone in the Highway Department to check up on every place within a radius of forty-five miles where there's an oiled detour. That should give it to us."

Sylvia Martin's hand slid across the table to rest on Selby's and give it a reassuring squeeze. "I'm sorry, Doug," she said.

He grinned. "You don't need to be," he said. "We're only beginning."

CHAPTER XI

An air of expectancy permeated the courtroom, which was crowded to capacity. Word had been whispered around Madison City that Selby had been caught in a trap by the resourceful criminal lawyer whose name was a byword in the metropolis.

Selby sat at one of the counsel tables. A few feet behind him, seated next to the rail which separated spectators from the space reserved for counsel, Sheriff Brandon sat motionless. A. B. Carr, the cynosure of all eyes, and seeming to enjoy the attention he was attracting, occupied the other counsel table with Peter Ribber, smirking in complacent self-satisfaction, at his side. Behind the lawyers, the crowded courtroom hissed with whispers.

Judge Faraday, the justice of the peace who was to conduct the preliminary and who gave every evidence of being greatly impressed by his own importance, entered the courtroom and took his seat behind the bench. The sounds of whispers, surreptitious titters, and the rustlings of motion in the courtroom died away to a tense, expectant silence.

Judge Faraday said, "This is the time fixed by yesterday's stipulation for the preliminary hearing in the Case of the People versus Peter Ribber."

Selby nodded and said, "Ready for the People."

Carr flung out his long right arm in an inclusive gesture, indicating the defendant and the courtroom. "Ready, Your Honor, for the Defense," he said, and contrived to make the mere statement sound dramatic and exciting.

Selby took up his duties with the feeling of a pugilist who goes out to the center of the ring to meet certain defeat. The time-honored procedure for a prosecuting attorney placed in his position was to establish the crime, produce just enough proof to create a reasonable probability that the defendant was guilty, and then to rest. To go farther would be to show his hand to the defense. As it was, the defendant's attorney would have an opportunity to cross-examine his witnesses twice, once at the preliminary, and again at the trial.

This procedure was established by custom, just as the course of the attorney for the defense had been mapped out by an equal array of impressing precedents. His tactics were to rip the prosecution's witnesses to pieces, dare the district attorney to produce evidence definitely linking the defendant with the crime, make it appear that the defendant would take the stand in his own behalf, and try to stampede the district attorney into producing all the evidence possible. Then, at the last minute, the defendant's lawyer would smile and say,

"Your Honor, the defendant has no evidence to present at this time."

It was all a part of a legal chess game which they were playing, and all of the rules, all of the advantages were on the side of the magnetic individual with a flair for the dramatic, "Old A.B.C."

"My first witness," Selby said, "will be Mrs. Rita Artrim."

She came forward because she knew she had to. She held up her hand and was sworn, her eyes glaring hostility at the district attorney as she took the oath. This was the man who was trying to pin a murder on her. At any time, now, she might find herself in the position of the defendant, held up to public ridicule and scorn, watching her aged father and mother sit stoically in the front row, their faces like graven images of expressionless detachment, their souls shriveling within them, their hearts breaking. . . .

"Take that witness chair," Judge Faraday instructed.

Selby began at once with crisp, businesslike questions. "You are Rita Artrim, the widow of James C. Artrim?"

"Yes."

"And where do you reside, Mrs. Artrim?"

"At 2332 Orange Heights Drive."

"On the seventh of this month, who was living in that house with you?"

"My father-in-law, Frank W. Artrim, and his nurse, a Miss Ellen Saxe."

"Directing your attention specifically to the early-morning hours of the seventh instant," Selby said, "did you notice anything unusual?"

"I did."

"What?"

"I heard mysterious sounds," she said.

"Can you tell me their nature?"

"Not specifically. They wakened me."

"Can you give us some general description of those sounds?"

"A rumbling sound as though something heavy had been moved on a roller."

"What did you do?"

"I arose and went to the window."

"What did you see?"

She said, "It was night, but it was bright starlight. I could see objects indistinctly. I leaned out of my window and looked down at the stretch of lawn between my residence and the edge of a barranca."

"What did you see?"

"I saw a naked figure."

"The figure was nude?"

"Yes."

"Do you know whether it was a man or a woman?"

"I could not see distinctly. I feel certain it was a man."

"What did the man do?"

"He wandered around the house. I watched him until he had disappeared toward the front door. I waited, half expecting that he would ring, then I saw him move back again. Then he passed toward the front of the house, and this time I heard a peculiar noise as though someone were drawing a stick sharply across a screen."

"What did you do?"

"I telephoned the police, and reported what I had seen."

"What time was this?"

"I don't know exactly."

"What happened after that?"

"I returned to the window to watch."

"Did you see the man again?"

"No."

"From your window, can you see the house which adjoins you on the north, that of Mr. A. B. Carr, the attorney who is representing the defendant in this case?"

"No, not from my window. My room is on the other side of the house."

"Did anything else happen that night which was unusual?"

"I heard the police car coming up the hill. That must have been about ten minutes after I called. Then I heard a shot."

"From what direction did this shot come?"

"From somewhere on the north, in the general vicinity of the barranca."

"Can you fix that time accurately?"

"It was somewhere between two and two-thirty in the morning."

Selby said to Carr, "You may inquire."

Carr said sympathetically, "You must have been quite badly frightened, Mrs. Artrim."

"I was," she admitted.

"Your room is on the second floor of the house?"

"Yes."

"You were looking down on this figure which you saw?"

"That's right."

"You're not certain that the figure was naked, are you?"

"Why—I thought it was the figure of a nude man. I could see the white blur of the flesh."

"That might have been a close-fitting Palm Beach suit, mightn't it?"

"Well," she said dubiously, "it might have been. But I don't think so."

"Now you say you heard the sound of a shot?"

"Yes."

"Just one shot?"

"That's right."

"And what makes you think it was a shot?"

"Why—why, I know it was a shot."

"Had you ever heard a similar sound made by a firecracker?"

"Not like that shot."

"Had you ever heard a similar sound made by a shotgun?"

"Not like that."

"Or a rifle?"

"No. It was a pistol shot."

"Have you heard the sound made by a truck when it backfires?"

"Yes."

"And you have heard torpedoes which are used on the Fourth of July?"

"Yes."

"And is there some subtle gradation of sound, some peculiar distinction which enables you to tell the difference between a revolver shot, the sound of a shotgun, the noise of a small caliber rifle, a torpedo, a firecracker, and the backfire of an exhaust?"

"I think there is, yes."

"And this was a revolver shot?"

"Yes."

"And you don't know where this nude figure was when the shot was fired?"

"No."

"You don't know who fired that shot?"

"No."

Carr smiled and said, "I think that's all, Mrs. Artrim. Thank you very much. Unless, on reflection, you could tell from the sound of the shot the exact make of the revolver from which it was fired. If you can, I think you should volunteer the information."

The laughter from the courtroom caught Mrs. Artrim by surprise. She seemed dazed for a moment, then, flushing, she flounced from her chair and marched angrily down the courtroom.

Selby next called Robert Peale, one of the radio officers, who testified as to the time the call was received, the length of time required to go to Mrs. Artrim's place on Orange

Heights Drive, and the exact time when the officers had seen the flash of a shot and heard the report. Carr had no questions by way of cross-examination.

Selby gave Otto Larkin a chance to enter the limelight by calling him as a witness to establish the location of the body, the time and manner of its discovery. Larkin, puffing with importance, made a positive witness, and as Selby turned him over to Carr for cross-examination, the police chief seemed eager to put the defense attorney in his place.

Carr looked at the paunchy police chief with a smile. "Chief," he said, "how was the body lying when you first discovered it?"

"It was sort of doubled up and on one side."

Carr pretended not to understand. "Doubled up and on one side," he echoed musingly. "That doesn't mean much to me, Chief. I wonder if you would illustrate the position of the corpse. Show me its exact position when you saw it."

Larkin took the bait. He stepped from the witness chair, said, "The corpse was lying on its side. The knees were pushed up like this . . . like . . . this."

It had quite probably been years since the chief of police had resorted to any calisthenics. He tried to illustrate the position of a thin corpse which had been doubled up and thrust into a small space, but his avoirdupois made the demonstration something which set the spectators howling with a glee that Judge Faraday himself could not silence, even on the threat of clearing the courtroom.

At length, A. B. Carr, smiling broadly and wiping his eyes with a handkerchief by way of mute evidence of his enjoyment, said, "Well, Chief, I think I understand now. Just take the stand again if you will, please."

Larkin, red with embarrassment, seething with rage, returned to his more dignified position.

Carr said, "Now when you first discovered this body, you

could see no indication of a bullet wound. Is that right, Mr. Larkin?"

Larkin said, "No, that's not right."

Carr seemed perplexed. "Mr. Larkin, I don't want to try to confuse you. I want to get your evidence into the records so that it's just the way you want to give it, but, as I understand it, the wound in the body—or perhaps I should say the wounds—were on the right side, slightly back of the median line, were they not?"

"That's right."

"Those bullet wounds, I believe, ranged forward, and there were no wounds of exit?"

"Yes, sir."

"And when you first saw this body it was lying in this barranca?"

"Yes, sir."

"And you were standing above it?"

"Yes, sir."

Carr's voice suddenly became triumphant. "Then kindly explain," he said, "how it happened you could see bullet holes looking down on the left side of the corpse."

Larkin also raised his voice. "You're not slipping anything over on me," he sputtered. "I wasn't looking down on the left side of the corpse. The corpse was lying with its right side exposed and partially raised."

An expression of sheer incredulity manifested itself upon the criminal lawyer's countenance, a facial reflex which would have done credit to the highest-priced talent on the screen. "Lying so the *right* side was elevated?" he asked.

"Yes, and you can't confuse me on it either."

"My *dear* man," Carr said, "I'm not trying to confuse you. I'm trying to get the records straight. I'm trying to get your testimony so it makes sense."

"Well, you listen to it, and it'll make sense," Larkin said truculently.

"But just a moment ago," Carr said, getting to his feet and raising a long, dramatic forefinger above his head, "when I asked you to demonstrate the position of the corpse, you got down on the floor right there"—Carr paused impressively to snap his forefinger down into a dramatic pointing gesture at the exact spot on the floor where Larkin had been lying—"and you tried to elevate your knees and to lie over on your *right* side so that the left side was elevated."

"I was trying to get my knees up," Larkin said indignantly.

"So I observed," Carr commented with a dry, detached humor which brought forth a ripple of laughter from the courtroom. When that laughter had subsided, he suddenly went on sternly, "But in addition to trying to get your knees up, you were endeavoring to illustrate the exact position of the corpse when you first saw it."

Larkin began to get a little rattled. "When you try to get your knees up, you get a bend in your back, and you have to kinda get over on one side."

"Well?" Carr demanded.

"Well, I wasn't trying to particularly get the side up that was up on the corpse. I was trying to get the knees the way they were and so I sort of rolled over on my right side."

"And yet you *now* say that the corpse was lying on its left side with its right side elevated?"

"Well, something that way."

"And it would have been just as easy for you to have lain on the floor partially on your left side with your right side elevated as for you to have lain on your right side with your left side elevated?"

"I guess so, yes."

"Then were you endeavoring to confuse me when you adopted a position which was exactly opposite to that of that corpse?"

"I was just trying to get my knees up.'

"But I asked you to get on the floor and assume exactly the position of the corpse."

"Well, I did," Larkin shouted.

Carr gave a somewhat exaggerated sigh of weariness. He sat down in the chair and said, in a voice which held a note of fatigue, "Well, Chief, there you are, testifying again that your position on the floor was correct. Then a moment ago, you said it was *not* correct. Now, which was it? Was it correct, or wasn't it correct?"

"It was correct as far as my knees were concerned."

"And you wish us to understand that the knees of the corpse were in the same position in which you got your knees?"

"Well, I couldn't get mine up as high as the dead man had his."

"Then the position of the knees was *not* correct. Is that right? And your position on the floor with reference to the side on which you were lying was not correct. Is that right?"

"Well . . . well . . . I don't know."

"You don't know!" Carr exclaimed incredulously. "You aren't hard of hearing, are you, Chief?"

"No."

"You can hear my questions?"

"Yes."

Carr said, in a tone of voice which indicated that he was mentally bewildered, "I asked you particularly to assume the position on the floor which was the position in which the corpse was lying when you first discovered it. Now, was your failure to do that due to any attempt to confuse me?"

"I didn't fail to do it. I did it."

"Your knees weren't in the correct position."

"I couldn't get them there."

"And you deliberately lay on the wrong side?"

"I did no such thing."

"The corpse was lying on its left side, was it not?"

"Yes."

"Then you failed to assume the position on the floor that was occupied by the corpse."

Larkin said, "I did the best I could. A man can't keep all those things in his mind at once."

"All of what things?"

"The manner in which a guy's lying."

Carr, as though he had made an interesting scientific discovery, but in a voice which seemed to contain only friendly concern, said, "Oh, I believe I begin to understand. When I ask you to assume a position in which a corpse is found, if you happen to be thinking of his knees, you concentrate everything on the position of the corpse's knees. If you happen to be thinking of the position in which the corpse lay on its side, you concentrate on that. But you can't grasp both of those things at once in your mind, and demonstrate both simultaneously. Is that right?"

"No, that's not right!" Larkin shouted.

"But I thought you just said that it was right. You said you couldn't keep all of those things—two, to be exact—in your mind, didn't you, Chief?"

Larkin thought for a while, and then said, "There were lots of things."

"Oh, pardon me," Carr said. "What other things were there, Chief?"

"Well, there's the position of the hands for one thing."

Carr said, "The corpse's hands were clasped very tightly about his knees. I understand that, Chief."

"Well, they weren't," Larkin said triumphantly. "The hands were clenched and were doubled up on the man's chest."

Once more Carr fought with an expression of utter incredulity. "Do I understand you to say that the man's hands were clenched and pressed against his chest?"

"That's what I said."

"A moment ago, when you were on the floor you'll remember that you had your hands clasped tightly around your knees."

"Well, I had to get 'em up, didn't I?"

"The knees?"

"Yes, certainly."

"But . . . Oh, I understand, Chief. You were just trying to pull your knees up. Is that right?"

"Yes."

"Then you weren't trying to put your hands in the same position as those of the corpse?"

"Well . . . well, no."

"Then it was necessary to keep *three* things in your mind instead of two? It was not only getting the knees up. There was the position of the side, and there was the position of the hands. Is that right?"

"Yes, that's right."

"Now you weren't able to get your knees up into the position of the corpse?"

"No, not quite. I couldn't do it."

"And your hands weren't in the right position?"

"No."

"And you weren't lying on the same side as the corpse? Is that right?"

"Well . . . well, all right."

"And your inability to assume the correct position was because you couldn't keep all of these things in your mind at once. Is that right?"

"Well, I wouldn't put it exactly that way."

"But, Chief, I'm only trying to quote your own words. I understood you a moment ago to say that that was the reason you hadn't been able to do it, that you couldn't keep all of those things in your mind at once. There were three things which you had to carry in your mind: the position of the knees, the position of the hands, and the position of the body as to lying on its side; and as I now understand your testimony you did all three of those things wrong. . . . I think that's all."

Larkin, his face darkened with anger, sought to think of some proper rejoinder, and could not. Judge Faraday said, "That's all the cross-examination, Chief. You may leave the witness stand."

"Call James Prague," Selby said.

James Prague, a tall, thin man, came forward and was sworn. Having heard the cross-examination of Otto Larkin, he glanced with vindictive, apprehensive eyes in the direction of the criminal attorney, who was seated apparently with only courteous curiosity as to what the testimony of this witness would be.

As Prague took the witness stand, Selby asked him, "Your name is James Prague. You live here in Madison City at the Crestview Rooms?"

"Yes, sir. That's right."

"What's your occupation, Mr. Prague?"

"I'm a member of the Madison City Police Force."

"In what capacity?"

"I drive a radio car nights."

"And you were so employed and in that capacity on the seventh of this month?"

"Yes."

"How old are you, Mr. Prague?"

"Twenty-eight."

"Now, directing your attention to a time around two o'clock in the morning of the seventh instant, did you have occasion to go to Orange Heights?"

"I did. Yes, sir."

"What was that occasion?"

"We received a call from the office—you know, over the radio. They called our car and said there was a prowler in the vicinity of 2332 Orange Heights Drive, to go and investigate."

"And what did you do?"

"We drove there at once."

"What time was that call received?"

"At seven minutes past two."

"Do you know what time you arrived at the address?"

"Yes, sir. At twelve minutes past two."

"Did you see or hear anything unusual?"

"We heard the sound of an explosion, and saw a flash such as could have been made by a gun."

"And what time was that?"

"At twelve minutes past two."

"And where was the direction of the flash?"

"Well, it was over on the north side of the barranca between the building numbered 2332 Orange Heights Drive and the one numbered 2419 Orange Heights Drive. It was on the side closest to 2419."

Selby said, "You may cross-examine."

"No questions," Carr said.

"Frank Carter will be the next witness," Selby said.

Carter came forward and was sworn. He gave his name, his address, stated his age to be twenty-six, and his occupation to be that of the policeman in charge of a radio car during the daytime.

"Did you have occasion to go to Orange Heights on the seventh instant?"

"Yes."

"At what time?"

"At eleven-forty-one—just nineteen minutes before noon."

"And what was the occasion which caused you to go there?"

"A statement made over the police radio that some boys playing there had discovered a body."

"And you drove there at once?"

"That's right."

"And found the body?"

"Yes."

"Where was this body?"

"On the north side of the barranca, not over fifty feet from the house of Mr. Carr there."

"That house is at 2419 Orange Heights Drive?"

"That's right."

"What was the position of the body?"

"It was lying down in the barranca sort of doubled up. The knees were up toward the chest. The hands were clenched on the chest, and the body was lying partially on the left side so the right side was up. You could see where the man had been shot."

"What else did you find?"

"Nothing right then, but a little later on, we found a gun."

"I show you a Colt thirty-eight revolver and ask you if this is the gun."

"That's right. That's the gun."

"And where was that gun lying?"

"In some little bush stuff up on the barranca."

"About how far from the corpse?"

"Oh, maybe fifteen feet. It was almost directly above where the corpse was lying."

"You may cross-examine," Selby said.

Carr's voice was courteous. "Could you," he asked, "take a position on the floor and demonstrate to us just exactly how the body was lying?"

The young man, thin-waisted, supple, promptly placed himself on the floor, lying on his left side, his hands clenched into fists and placed against his chest, his knees elevated until they all but touched his chest.

"Thank you," Carr said. "You may now resume the witness stand."

When the witness had again taken his position in the witness chair, Carr said, "That was exactly the position in which the body was lying?"

"Yes," the policeman said, in the tone of voice a man would use in saying, "Wanta make something of it?"

Carr inclined his head with grave courtesy. "I notice," he said, "that you clenched your fists and held them against your chest, that you doubled up your knees, and that you lay on the left side so that the right side was partially elevated."

"Well," the officer said, "that's just the way the body was found, and that's what you told me to do."

"Exactly," Carr said. "Now you didn't have any trouble keeping all of those things in your mind, did you?"

"No."

Carr said, conversationally, "I'm glad to hear that. I didn't *think* there was anything unfair in the questions I asked of the chief of police."

Selby said, "If the court please, we object to comments from counsel. He should confine himself to questions of the witness and statements to the court."

"That's right," Judge Faraday said.

"I beg the court's pardon," Carr announced courteously. "My violation was unintentional, caused merely because there had been something in the attitude of Chief Larkin which made me feel that it might have been unfair to ask a man of ordinary intelligence to do something which necessitated keeping his mind on three things, but I'm glad to learn that I really wasn't taking an unfair advantage."

Judge Faraday smiled.

Carr said, "That's all of my cross-examination," and then, turning to Selby, said, "A very intelligent witness, Mr. Selby."

Despite himself, Selby smiled at the clever manner in which Carr was adroitly pouring vinegar on the mental wounds of the chief of police.

His next witness was Bob Terry, who qualified as a finger-print expert, identified fingerprints on the gun, identified a card of fingerprints as containing those of the defendant in the case, and pointed out that the fingerprints of the defendant were found on the gun.

Because he had the Los Angeles criminologist available, Selby didn't seek to prove the identity of the bullet by the local man. Carr excused him with no cross-examination.

Victor Hawlins, the Los Angeles criminologist, was the next witness. Having given his name, age, occupation, and residence, Selby asked him concerning his qualifications, and a period of several minutes was taken up while the wit-ness, a small man with thick lips, a dark mustache, protrud-ing, watchful blue eyes, and horn-rimmed spectacles, recited a catalogue of achievements, starting with university work, followed by a course in fingerprinting, a study of ballistics, a course in photomicrography, a year of forensic medicine, a course in applied physics, followed by some additional post-graduate work in criminology in an eastern university, supplemented by five years of national experience in various cities, the last three years of which had been in Los Angeles.

By his first questions Selby showed that the witness was familiar with the gun which had been introduced in evidence, had fired what were known as test bullets from that gun, that he had checked the fingerprints on it, that he had ex-amined the body of Morton Taleman, that he had taken fingerprints from the body, that he had personally classified them and compared them with fingerprints on file in police archives.

In the precise, well-modulated, carefully considered words of an expert, Hawlins established that the body was that of Morton Taleman, a man with a police record whose finger-prints were on file and whose photographs were in the Rogues' Gallery, that the man had been shot twice with two different weapons, that one of the bullets had undoubtedly been fired from the weapon which had the fingerprints of Peter Ribber, the defendant, impressed upon them, that, from the nature of the powder burns, apparently both shots had been fired at close range, that both bullets had followed approximately the same course, that either bullet would have been fatal, that one bullet was manufactured by the Peters Company, another by the Winchester Company, that the gun which had been found and which bore the fingerprints of the defendant had fired the Winchester bullet, that the Winchester bullet had evidently been fired into a nude body since there were certain microscopic bits of wool cloth adhering to the bullet which he described as the Peters bullet, and undoubtedly one bullet had been fired at close range while the man had clothing on which had partially protected his skin, while the other bullet had been fired at equally close range while the man was nude.

Selby turned him over to Carr for cross-examination, and Carr's manner plainly said that here at last was a disinterested expert, one who had ordinary, human intelligence, and was not trying to slip anything over on the court. "Can you," he asked, in a manner which was almost deferential in its courtesy, "tell whether the bullet which you referred to in your testimony as the Winchester bullet was fired *before* the bullet which you have referred to as the Peters bullet?"

"No, I can't."

"It may have been fired afterwards?"

"It may have been."

"But the course of the bullet which you have referred to as the Peters bullet was such that it would, in your opinion, have been instantly fatal?"

"Speaking as a criminologist," Hawlins said cautiously, "and not as a doctor, but as one who made a careful postmortem examination, I would say that the Peters bullet would have been instantly fatal."

"That," Carr said, "is assuming that the Peters bullet had been fired first?"

"Exactly," Hawlins said, "and, on the other hand, if the Winchester bullet had been fired first, I would unhesitatingly say that that bullet would have been instantly fatal."

"I understand," Carr said courteously. "Now, your examination, Mr. Hawlins, did convince you that the Peters bullet was fired while the man was wearing clothes, is that right?"

"Yes."

"And the Winchester bullet was fired while the man was nude?"

"Yes."

"Now the body when it was found was nude?"

"So I understand."

"Therefore, you would naturally assume, would you not, that the Winchester bullet had been fired second and last?"

"Well," Hawlins said, "of course there's the testimony of Mrs. Artrim that when the shot was fired, the man was naked —that is, a naked man was wandering around in the immediate vicinity."

"Exactly," Carr said, "but for the Winchester bullet to have been the fatal bullet, it would have been necessary for that bullet to have been discharged into the body of the decedent. It would then have been necessary for the body to have been clothed, and another bullet fired which we will refer to as the Peters bullet, and thereafter it would have been necessary for the body to have again been stripped in order to have been found in the condition in which it was described by the various witnesses."

"Well," Hawlins said cautiously, "assuming all of those factors, I would say such was the case."

"That," Carr announced triumphantly, "is all."

"Just a moment," Selby said, "there is some re-direct examination. As I understand it, Mr. Hawlins, your testimony doesn't establish the fact that the body was clothed when the Peters bullet was fired. Your testimony is that you found bits of what you consider wool in the Peters bullet. I assume that what you mean is that the Peters bullet was fired through cloth."

"That's right, yes."

"And you have no way of knowing whether that cloth was the coat and vest of a suit or whether it was a fragment of cloth only three or four inches square which was held between the muzzle of the gun and the body. Is that right?"

Carr said, "Your Honor, I object to that question. It's leading and suggestive. It's an attempt on the part of counsel to cross-examine his own witness, and assuming facts not in evidence."

Selby said, "I am merely trying to clarify the evidence of this witness, Your Honor, in order to prevent a confusion of the issues because of the cross-examination of counsel."

"Objection overruled," Judge Faraday said.

Hawlins, who had seen the point as soon as Selby asked the question, said, "Of course that's right. I don't know whether the bullet was fired through a suit or through a piece of cloth only a few inches square. I only know that it was fired through cloth, and that the muzzle of the gun was held within a few inches of the body when the shot was fired."

"Thank you," Selby said. "That's all."

The criminologist was followed by Dr. Trueman, the autopsy surgeon who testified that the body on which he had performed a post-mortem examination contained two bullet holes. He described the course of the bullet holes and identified the bullets which he had taken from the body, and testified that, in his opinion, either bullet would have been instantly fatal.

"The prosecution rests," Selby announced. Carr arose to move that the judge dismiss the case and discharge the defendant on the ground that the prosecution had failed to establish any case, that every bit of evidence introduced by the prosecution was equally consistent with the theory that the defendant had done no more than discharge a bullet into a corpse. Certain it was that some person, either the one who had fired the Peters bullet or the one who had fired the Winchester bullet, had been guilty of no offense other than that of firing a gun within the city limits. There was, Carr said, to the best of his recollection, no law which prohibited the firing of a bullet into a dead body. It was, of course, a matter of poor taste, but it was not illegal. In any event, it was not homicide. The defendant in this case was being prosecuted on a charge of first degree murder, and Carr asked that the action be dismissed.

Judge Faraday glanced perplexedly down at Selby. "Any argument?" he asked.

Selby said simply, "I have no argument whatever, Your Honor, other than to call the court's attention to the fact that at this time it is not necessary to prove the defendant guilty beyond all reasonable doubt. It is only necessary to show that a crime has been committed and to introduce evidence which may reasonably tend to connect the defendant with the perpetration of the crime. This proof, of course, does so."

"It does nothing of the sort," Carr objected. "It only establishes a fifty-fifty chance. The law doesn't contemplate any such a procedure. A defendant isn't to be deprived of his life or liberty by the toss of a coin or the turn of a card."

Selby grinned. "You tossed the coin and turned the card," he said. "I'm talking about evidence. The evidence shows that the defendant in this case held the gun which shot a bullet into Morton Taleman, and that Morton Taleman is dead, that the course of that bullet would have produced instant death. That's my case. Now then, if you want to show that your client was playfully tossing slugs into dead bodies for the purpose of testing the penetration of his gun or making a premature Fourth of July celebration within the city limits, go ahead and establish that as a matter of defense."

Carr flushed. "You don't need to talk to me," he said angrily. "Address your remarks to the court."

Selby kept grinning. "You asked for it," he said, and sat down.

Carr turned to argue with the judge, but read in His Honor's smiling countenance that argument would be useless. The tide had turned against him.

"The motion to dismiss is denied," Judge Faraday said.

"In that event, Your Honor," Carr observed, "we will make no showing whatever. Go ahead and bind the defendant over."

Judge Faraday held the defendant to answer to the superior court on the charge of first degree murder and remanded him without bail into the custody of the sheriff. Court adjourned, and the corridor instantly became a hubbub of noise.

Gleeful citizens were recounting the discomfiture of Otto Larkin, and Larkin, pounding his way down the corridor with grim jaw and angry eyes, tried to keep well ahead of the chuckling spectators.

Selby walked over to talk with Sylvia Martin.

"Doug," she said, in a low voice, "you were grand! He didn't put anything over on you at all."

Selby laughed. "He didn't even try," he said. "He paid his respects to the chief of police just to give the crowd a show. All he was doing was making me show my hand. He was trying to find out whether I had any more evidence against Ribber."

"Have you, Doug?" she asked.

"No," he said. "Sylvia, I want you to do something."

"Anything you say, Doug."

"Mrs. Artrim is over there talking with Sam Roper. Roper is her lawyer. I'm going over and chat with them for a minute. I think I can hold her long enough for you to get down to her car and make a note of the speedometer reading."

"You can't hold them for two minutes, Doug. They'll insult you and walk away. Sam Roper is furious with you."

Selby grinned. "That's all right, but the thing I have to ask them will make them go into a huddle for four or five minutes."

"On my way, Doug," she said.

Selby walked across to where Mrs. Artrim was talking with Roper. "I'd like to ask you a question, Mrs. Artrim."

"What is it?"

"When we were checking the property at your house, we found that one of the Hudson Bay blankets was missing. Do you know where it is?"

Selby was watching her face. For a moment, the color drained from it. Her eyes seemed to show stark panic, but Selby was not the only one who was watching her face. Sam Roper, who had been staring with sullen hostility at the district attorney, suddenly shifted his gaze as he sensed his client's reaction to the question. One look at her face was enough.

"Don't answer that question," he said.

"Why not?" Selby asked.

"Because it's none of your business," Roper said.

"I think it is," Selby told him.

"Well, I don't. In the first place, you had no business taking possession of that house. In the second place, you had no business making an inventory of the contents, and, in the third place, my client can do anything she damn pleases with any of her belongings, and, in the fourth place, if you want to get technical, if you want to ask any further questions of this witness, you can call her to the witness stand or in front of the grand jury."

Selby said, "Do I understand that her father-in-law has disappeared under circumstances indicating a crime has been committed, that you advise her not to answer any questions pertaining to clearing up that crime or locating her father-in-law?"

Roper realized the position in which he was being placed. "Well," he said sullenly, "we'll answer any proper questions."

"But you can't tell me about the blanket, Mrs. Artrim?"

"Don't answer," Roper said.

She bit her lip and turned away.

Selby bowed affably. "Thank you," he said.

Carr came across to shake the district attorney's hand. "Done rather cleverly, Counselor," he said.

Selby smiled. "There was," he admitted, "nothing exactly amateurish about your performance."

Carr's broad mouth twisted into a grin. "I've been laying for that bird," he said, "ever since he came busting into my house with that officious, overbearing manner of his."

Selby said, "By the way, you've never told me very much about *your* whereabouts at the time of the murder."

Carr didn't bat an eyelash. His face remained twisted in that characteristic grin. "That's right, I haven't," he said, and turned and walked away.

Selby found the sheriff and together they sought the sheriff's office where they were presently joined by Sylvia Martin who was breathless from rushing up the stairs. "I got it," she said.

"What is it?" Selby asked.

"32,779."

Selby took a pencil from his pocket, took a sheet of paper from the sheriff's desk, and started figuring. "Let's see," he said. "When we last saw the car, the speedometer was 32,486. That's quite a few miles she's put on it since. Let's see how it figures—two hundred and ninety-three miles. I wonder where she's been."

"Los Angeles and back and some running around probably," Sylvia Martin said.

Selby stared down at the figures. "Listen, Sylvia," he said, "I wish you'd keep a check on that speedometer. Whenever you find the çar parked anywhere, make a note of the speedometer reading at the time."

"How do you figure the car enters into it, son?" Rex Brandon asked.

Selby said, "I want to know where that car went the night of the murder."

"Well, she wouldn't go back to the same place," the sheriff said.

"She might."

"I've got a report from the automobile clubs," the sheriff said, "and there isn't any place within a radius of forty-five miles of Madison City where there's any road construction which would get that type of oil on the fenders. There's some highway construction going on, and there are some detours, but those detours are all hard surface. Moreover, this isn't the ordinary kind of road material. There are pieces of gravel in here of various sizes which make the criminologist think it didn't come from an ordinary road at all. It must have been some detour which was freshly oiled."

"But," Selby said, "there isn't any detour."

"That's right," Brandon observed with a wry grin.

"What have you been able to find out about James Artrim's death?" Selby asked. "Any chance that she could have murdered him?"

"No chance. She wasn't even in the car at the time," Brandon said.

"Who was with him?"

"Just his father. Mrs. Artrim came along sometime later —perhaps as much as half an hour after the crash."

Selby said, "That amnesia business sounds fishy to me."

"It does to me too, Doug, but I'd be more inclined to figure she murdered her father-in-law than her husband."

"But," Selby said, "don't you see, Rex? It all ties in. The motivation for killing her father-in-law is that he had recovered his memory, or at least was showing signs of marked improvement, and she thought he would recover his memory. Therefore, she put him out of the way."

"You mean if there wasn't a murder in the background it wouldn't have made any difference whether he recovered his memory or not?"

"Exactly," Selby said.

Brandon scratched his head. "Hang it," he said. "We're almost on the trail of something."

"Almost isn't going to help us," Selby said. "We have a bear by the tail, and we're up against a dangerous antagonist."

"I hate to see those tactics used in this country," Brandon said. "Not that I care a hang about Otto Larkin, but it's the general setup that makes me mad. You could see that crowd in the back of the courtroom just eating that stuff up."

"I know," Selby agreed, "and it's going to be a lot worse in front of a jury."

"You know as well as I do that that business about the position of the body didn't mean a damn thing."

Selby said, "That's the way those big-shot criminal lawyers work, Rex. They inject their own personalities into the case, put on a free show for the courtroom audience. Pretty quick the jury loses sight of the fact that it's called on to try a case and considers it's witnessing a show—and a verdict of not guilty is simply the jury's way of showing applause for the actor it likes."

Sylvia Martin said, "Isn't there some way you can beat that, Doug?"

Selby said, "It's a tough combination to beat. They have to contend with it in the big cities all the time."

"But can't you fight the devil with fire? Can't you run a show of your own?"

"When you try to do that," Selby said, "the crowd turns against you. They feel that as the district attorney you should be above showmanship. No, the only way to beat that is to become one of these high-powered, crusading prosecutors, driving ahead, waving your hands, shouting, ranting, and shouting vilifications. That's showmanship, but it passes for the sincerity of zeal."

"Will that do the trick?" Brandon asked.

"Usually it will do the trick," Selby said, "if it's done cleverly."

"Then go ahead and do it, Doug."

Selby shook his head.

"There's too much chance of convicting an innocent man. What's more, I don't like it. I want to hit hard, but I want to know at what I'm hitting. I want to be certain that convictions are the result of logic rather than prejudice on the part of the jurors. In other words, I don't want to be a rabble-rouser."

Sylvia Martin said pleadingly, "Doug, you're on trial as well as the defendant."

Rex Brandon ·shook his head. "There's no use arguing with him, Sylvia," he said.

Sylvia Martin said indignantly, "It doesn't seem fair."

Selby grinned. "It isn't," he said. "I even went farther than I wanted to in this case with that business about the square of cloth. We know from the finding of that suit that the bullet wasn't fired through a square of cloth. It was fired through a double-breasted, brown coat and vest. From the extent of the bleeding . . . Well, I'm not going into that now. Carr evidently doesn't know anything about our finding that suit."

"Will it help his case if he finds out?" she asked.

"It will help his case a lot," Selby said, "and we've got to produce it in the superior court."

"Why, Doug?"

"Because it's part of the evidence."

"But it's evidence that will benefit the other side."

"I think so, yes. I'm going to have a talk with Victor Hawlins about it. I asked him to drop in here. . . . Here he comes now."

Hawlins knocked and entered the sheriff's office.

Selby said, "Come in, Hawlins. Sit down. This is Miss Martin of one of the local papers. I want to ask you some questions."

"Go ahead," Hawlins said.

Selby nodded to the sheriff. "Let's have that suit, Rex."

Brandon hesitated for a long moment before he reluctantly opened the safe and took out the brown, double-breasted coat and vest. Selby passed them across to Hawlins. "What do you make of these?" he asked.

The criminologist studied the garments carefully, took a small magnifying glass from his pocket, inspected both sides of the cloth, and said cautiously, "It looks as though the small fragments of wool which I found imbedded in the Peters bullet had come from this material. Do you think that this coat belonged to the dead man?"

"We're practically certain of it," Selby said.

"Then it was the suit he was wearing when he was shot." Selby nodded.

Hawlins lit a cigarette. He shifted his gaze to look out of the window. His slightly protruding blue eyes stared steadily at the section of blue sky which showed above the tops of the palm trees, through the window.

"Well?" Selby asked.

Hawlins said, "If I were you, Mr. Selby, I'd simply forget about this suit—unless it should be such an essential part of the case that you had to introduce it."

"What do you mean by that?" Brandon asked.

Hawlins said, "Well, if I have to come right out and say so in so many words, unless the other side knows about this. Do they?"

"I don't think so," Selby said.

"Then I'd forget it."

"Why?"

Hawlins said, "From the nature of the bloodstain, from the apparent extent of the hemorrhage, knowing what I do of the location of the wound and . . . Well, that makes me believe the Peters bullet was the fatal bullet."

"Even considering the testimony of Mrs. Artrim, that the man she saw was naked, and that she saw him only a few minutes before the shot was fired?"

Hawlins weighed his words carefully. "This suit," he said, "if it belonged to the dead man, is circumstantial evidence. Attorneys frequently like to belittle circumstantial evidence, but circumstances are frequently of much greater probative value than human testimony. In my opinion, the man who wore this suit was shot, and the shot which was fired through this suit was fatal. If that suit actually belonged to Morton Taleman, I would say that the bullet which was fired through this cloth was the fatal bullet."

"And," Selby asked quietly, "going a step farther, you would say that the Winchester bullet was then fired sometime subsequent and into a body that was already dead?"

"Yes."

There was a period of silence. Hawlins said, "If you'll take my advice, Mr. Selby, you'll let the defendant establish his own innocence. You haven't too robust a case as it is. As far as I'm concerned, I've finished my job here. I'm going back to the city. No one will know that I've seen this suit. Naturally, it won't occur to the defendant to subpoena *me* as a witness."

Selby shook his head doggedly. "No," he said, "I don't

do business that way. For the purpose of the preliminary and in order to get Peter Ribber bound over for trial, I was willing to put on only enough evidence to establish a *prima-facie case*. When I try that man for his life in the superior court, I'm going to introduce all of the evidence that I have."

Hawlins shrugged his shoulders. "Well," he said, "it's your funeral. I don't mind telling you, Selby, that district attorneys in the cities don't figure that way. They'd never get a conviction if they did. They present the evidence that points to the guilt of the defendant. They leave it up to the defendant to uncover evidence establishing his own innocence. Don't ever kid yourself, a skillful attorney for a defendant has everything his way, and old A.B.C. is one of the most skillful criminal attorneys I've ever seen in a courtroom."

"You've seen him in other cases?" Brandon asked.

"A dozen of them," Hawlins said. "Cases where I've been a witness. He's shrewd. He never strikes in cross-examination until he knows he has a weak point, and then he strikes like lightning."

Brandon got up, took the suit and significantly crossed over to the safe. He slammed the door and spun the dial. Selby said quietly to Sylvia Martin, "In tomorrow's issue of the paper, Sylvia, I want you to let it be known that with the discovery of a bloodstained suit in a local cleaning and dyeing establishment, the sheriff and district attorney think they have located the suit which was worn by Morton Taleman when the Peters bullet was fired."

Sylvia's eyes met Selby's for a long, steady gaze, then she nodded quietly. "I'll be glad to, Doug," she said.

Rex Brandon heaved a sigh. Hawlins said, "I admire your integrity, Mr. Selby," and the tone of his voice indicated that he couldn't say as much for the district attorney's judgment.

CHAPTER XII

IT WAS ON A FRIDAY MORNING THAT A. B. CARR TELEPHONED Selby long distance from Los Angeles. "I want that Ribber case set for immediate trial," he said. "I think we're entitled to it. Your court calendar isn't crowded, and my man is entitled to an acquittal—unless you want to dismiss the case."

Selby said, "I don't want to dismiss the case."

"Well, let's agree on a trial date then. In that way we can get one that's mutually satisfactory. Otherwise, I'll go into court and ask for an immediate hearing."

Selby said, "Suit yourself, Carr."

"How about next Tuesday?"

"That doesn't give me much time for preparation," Selby said.

Carr laughed. "You don't need any time for preparation. You haven't anything to prepare. You know it as well as I do. You haven't one bit of evidence right now you didn't have at the time of the preliminary."

Selby said, "I'm making progress."

Carr's laugh was jovial. "You know, Selby," he said, "you're a good scout. You're giving me a fair deal, which is more than I'd do if our situations were reversed. But I can get Ribber acquitted, and he's entitled to an acquittal."

"Then," Selby said, "I suppose he can turn around and confess to the murder, and there's nothing we can do about it."

Carr said, "You never heard of one of my clients confessing to anything, did you?"

Selby said, "Well, I'll speak to Judge White and see about Tuesday."

"The case shouldn't take over two days, should it?" Carr asked.

157

"It depends on how long it takes us to get a jury."

"I can have a jury in twenty minutes," Carr said confidently. "All I want are twelve persons who have eyes that can see, ears that can hear, and no prejudices.".

Selby said, "All right. I'll have it set for trial." He hung up the telephone and stared thoughtfully at the slip of paper on his desk, a slip which represented various speedometer readings taken from Mrs. Artrim's automobile. Abruptly he picked up the telephone and called A. B. Carr's residence. Mrs. Fermal answered the telephone.

Selby said, "This is the district attorney speaking, Mrs. Fermal. I want you to do one more thing for me."

"What is it?" she asked.

Selby said, "I want you to make it a point to take the speedometer readings on Mr. Carr's automobile. Whenever he comes home, take a speedometer reading. Can you do that?"

"Sure. Sure," she said. "That's easy. Anything else?"

Selby said, "I think that's all."

He hung up the telephone and picked up the copy of the *Blade* on his desk. A scorching editorial demanded that the sheriff and district attorney get busy and do something about the disappearance of Frank W. Artrim. The editorial was written in that highly impersonal manner which made its criticism the more blistering, and Selby was reading it through for the second time when Sylvia Martin was ushered into his office.

"Notice the dirt, Doug?" she asked.

He nodded.

She said, "Sam Roper's representing Mrs. Artrim. He's hand in glove with Frank Grierson, the editor of the *Blade*. The fact that they've started to ride you shows that Roper thinks his client is in the clear."

Selby said, "I notice that when Morton Taleman was killed, the arrest of Peter Ribber was due to the splendid detective work of Otto Larkin, our chief of police, and with the arrest of Ribber, Larkin apparently had nothing else to do except sit back and twiddle his thumbs. It was up to me to prosecute. On the other hand, as far as the Artrim case is concerned, you'd think that Orange Heights wasn't in the city limits at all. The *Blade* insists that Sheriff Brandon and District Attorney Selby should discover Artrim or his body, or else confess their complete inability to cope with the crime situation in this county."

Sylvia said, with a smile, "Newspapers sometimes are inconsistent. How about those speedometer readings, Doug? Do they mean anything?"

Selby said, "I think they do."

"Well, they don't to me."

Selby said, "When Mrs. Artrim first got the car back, she drove two hundred and ninety-three miles. Then, for a day or two, there was only a matter of ten or twelve miles a day registered on the speedometer. Then there was a jump of ninety-five miles. Then a couple of days more with routine mileage, and last night there was another jump of ninety-two miles."

"What are you getting at, Doug?" she asked.

Selby smiled and shook his head. He tamped tobacco in his pipe, lit it, settled back in his swivel chair, and frowned thoughtfully into the drifting smoke. He said, "I think I'm going to pull a fast one."

"What, Doug?"

"I'm going to resort to a third degree."

"You mean with Mrs. Artrim?"

"No, with Pete Ribber. Would you like to be there?"

"Do you think I should, Doug?"

"Yes," he said. "There's going to be an awful stink go up if I don't make it stick. The *Blade* will claim that I violated the law, beat a man into insensibility, and lied to him. I want to conduct a third degree, and I don't want to do any of those things. I'd like to have a representative of the press present."

"Can I use it, Doug?"

"You can if I get anything out of him."

"When are you going to do it?"

"As soon as I can set the stage," Selby said, "probably in about an hour."

"What are you working on, Doug?" she asked. "What's your theory?"

Selby said thoughtfully, "You published that story about the bloodstained suit of clothes. Carr certainly read that story, but he hasn't said a word about it. He's never said a word about those clothes."

"Well?" she asked.

"Under ordinary circumstances," Selby said, "the attorney representing a defendant would have called on me, asked to inspect the suit of clothes, asked to give his own criminologist an opportunity to examine them, stirred up a big stink, had a criminologist report that the Peters bullet was the fatal bullet, and demand that I dismiss the case against Ribber."

"And because Carr hasn't done that, you think it means something?"

"I'm certain it does."

She said, "Perhaps he underestimates you, Doug, and figures it would be a lot better for him personally to make a grandstand out of the whole business in a courtroom."

"Even so," Selby said, "he'd want to know his facts in advance. He'd want to have some expert examine those clothes."

"Then you think—Doug, do you think that . . ."

Selby nodded. "Yes," he said. "That suit of clothes could very well have been inadvertenly included in the cleaning which came from Carr's residence."

"And he knows all about it?"

"He must," Selby said. "I don't see any other logical explanation."

Sylvia Martin said, half under her breath, "Gosh, Doug, if you could involve *him* in the case in some way—that would be something."

Selby said positively, "He's mixed up in it. He isn't acting only as Pete Ribber's lawyer. There's something fishy about the whole thing, something that goes deeper than we know."

"Do you believe Ribber's guilty?"

Selby frowned for a minute, then said, "If he isn't guilty, he probably fired a bullet into a corpse. Now why would he do that?"

Sylvia said, "I hadn't figured it that way, Doug. I'd figured it more as a scheme on the part of Carr to get his man off."

"That's the way everyone's looked at it," Selby said. "It looks like a smart trick, but suppose Ribber actually fired a shot into the corpse. *Why* did he do it?"

"Why," she said, "to confuse the issues and put him out in front as a red herring."

"Exactly," Selby said, "to protect the person who did the killing."

"And that's what you're going to try to get out of him, Doug?"

"Yes. I'm going to quit trying to prove that he committed the murder. I'm going to try and make him tell whom he is trying to protect."

"And you think that's Carr, Doug?"

Selby said, "I don't know who it is. I'm going to set the stage."

"In an hour?" she asked.

He nodded.

She said, "I'll be there. Do you want me to take shorthand notes, Doug?"

"No, just listen and watch facial expressions. I'll have a court reporter called in if he starts talking."

"At the jail, Doug?"

"At the jail," he said, "in an hour."

"I'll be there."

She almost ran out of the office. Selby picked up the telephone, called Brandon's office, and asked the sheriff and Bob Terry to join him for a conference. When he had them seated in his office, Selby said, "Rex, I'm going to try something."

"What?"

"A third degree."

"What sort of a third degree, son?"

"A psychic third degree," Selby said. "I want to have certain stage properties."

Brandon rolled a cigarette. "I don't think you're going to get anywhere, Doug," he warned. "That man Ribber is a tough egg. He's a two-time loser. He's what is known as stir-wise, and he knows enough to keep his mouth shut."

"I know," Selby said, "but I'm going to try and make him talk. I have a scheme."

"I don't think he'll fall for schemes."

Selby said, "I want you to get me a thirty-eight caliber Smith & Wesson revolver and load it with Peters bullets, then discharge one chamber."

"Anything else?" Brandon asked.

"Yes," Selby said, turning to Bob Terry. "How about forging fingerprints?"

Terry said, "It can be done all right, but I'm not enough of a technician to do it."

"Do you know someone who is?"

"No. What do you want?"

"I want to put Pete Ribber's fingerprints on that Smith & Wesson gun."

Rex Brandon scowled. "Doug," he said, "I wouldn't do that."

"Why not?"

"It's going to have a bad effect. Sooner or later it will come out that those fingerprints were forged. If people figure that you're forging fingerprints for the purpose of trapping a criminal into a confession, it won't be long before they'll get to thinking you're forging fingerprints to get convictions. The *Blade* will always refer to you as the district attorney who makes a practice of forging fingerprints. It won't work."

Selby said, "I guess you're right—but, gosh, Rex, I think I'm on the track of something, and I want to find out."

"You're monkeying with dynamite," Brandon warned.

Selby thought for a minute, then suddenly said, "Look here. Fingerprints all look alike to a layman. Suppose I put *my* fingerprints on that gun? You could develop those latent prints and pretend to check them with Ribber's fingerprints, Terry, and then if you nodded your head very mysteriously, he'd think they were the same."

Terry said, "That end of it's okay. If he doesn't have the gun in his hand and study the fingerprints under a magnifying glass, he couldn't tell the difference. Even then, he'd have to know something about fingerprint classification."

Selby said, "Okay, get me the gun. I'll put the fingerprints on it. Then put the gun in a box, just as you would a gun that you'd picked up somewhere."

"You mean one we were holding so as to develop latents?"

"Yes. How do you handle that?"

"We usually put them in a box," Terry said. I've fixed a little wooden box with hooks in it, and I can suspend a gun right from the cover of the box."

"Okay," Selby said. "You get the gun, and I'll meet you at the jail in an hour. Sylvia Martin's going to be there. I'll put my fingerprints on the gun just before we go in to talk with Ribber."

"Where's Carr?" Brandon asked.

"In Los Angeles."

"Ribber won't say anything unless Carr's there."

Selby said, "I'm not so certain I want him to say anything. I just want him to start thinking. That's all."

An hour later, Selby, Rex Brandon, Sylvia Martin, and Bob Terry gathered in a little office at the county jail. Selby made something of a ceremony of putting his fingerprints on the gun which, by an ingenious arrangement of threads, was held suspended in the wooden box which Bob Terry carried.

"Want me to develop those latents now?" Terry asked.

"Not now," Selby said. "I want you to wait about five minutes, and then come in all out of breath. I'll ask you if you have it there, and you can say, 'Yes.'"

Brandon said dubiously, "I don't get the sketch, Doug. Aren't you apt to play right into Carr's hands?"

Selby nodded.

"Why do it then?"

Selby said, "Because there's no use going ahead with this thing the way we're doing it. I'd rather dismiss the case than go to trial the way it now stands."

Sylvia Martin gave a little exclamation of dismay. "Doug, if you dismiss that case, they'll say you were afraid of Carr, that you didn't dare to meet him in court, and that you let a murderer go free rather than jeopardize your own reputation. They'll fling it up at you as long as you live."

"I know that," he said, "but I'd rather take a chance on anything than sit in a game where the cards are all stacked against me."

"What do you mean?" she asked.

"Simply this," Selby said. "Pete Ribber is not an amateur. He's a professional criminal. It's absolutely inconceivable that he would kill a man and then leave a gun with his fingerprints on it in the neighborhood. To a man of Ribber's experience, that's just the same as pinning a calling card with his name on it to the man's body."

"Well?" Sylvia Martin asked.

"Therefore," Selby said, "the whole thing was framed up as bait for us to take. Thanks to Larkin's attempt to grab the limelight, we've walked right into it. I'd a darn sight rather take a chance on catching the real criminal, even if it is a ten-to-one chance, than to go into court and have Carr kick the props out from under me."

"But why did he want you to go to court in the first place, Doug? What's the trap?"

Selby said, "Simply this. I'll bet money that if we go on trial on that Ribber case, we can't get enough evidence to get a conviction. We can't prove Ribber's guilty. Once a jury has acquitted him, he can never again be tried for that same offense. He'll come out and laugh at us and claim that our criminologist was wrong, and that his lawyer was too smart for me. He'll claim he's the guilty person, and what are we to do about it. And the answer is, we can do nothing."

"But he wouldn't do that," she said.

Selby said, "I'm not so certain. Suppose he did? It would laugh us out of office, and in view of Ribber's confession and the evidence against him, we'd then never be able to convict the guilty party, which is what Carr really wants."

"I can't conceive of a man doing anything like that," she said.

"I can," Selby told her. "That's just Carr's speed. He's one of those fast-thinking, ingenious, diabolically clever attorneys who have no conscience."

"And what are you going to do?" she asked.

"I'm going to try to upset their apple cart," Selby said. "I can't go to trial Tuesday morning with the evidence the way it now stands. I couldn't conscientiously ask any jury to convict Pete Ribber—I don't think he's guilty myself."

"But don't crooks sometime leave the gun at the scene

of the crime?" Terry asked. "Isn't that more or less unusual?"

"Sure it is," Selby said, "but they wipe the guns free of fingerprints. They wear gloves, do their killing, and nonchalantly toss the guns away. It's absolutely inconceivable to me that Pete Ribber would have placed his fingerprints on a murder weapon and dropped that weapon so near the body that the police would be certain to find it."

Rex Brandon nodded slowly. "You're right, son," he said.

Selby said, "Okay, let's go. Remember, Bob, give us five minutes and then come busting into the room."

Selby led the way into the witness room where Ribber, who had previously been summoned by the jailer, was waiting. "Hello, Ribber," Selby said.

Ribber squinted his little, glittering eyes at the trio and said, "What is this?"

"Just a visit," Selby said. "We want to talk with you."

"Well, I don't want to talk with you. I've got a lawyer to do my talking. You know where you can get him. If you want anything out of me, go ahead and call him on the phone. He'll come and do my talking for me."

"Won't you answer some routine questions?" Selby asked.

Ribber laughed. "Routine, hell! You must think I was born yesterday. What the hell do you think I got a mouthpiece for? I'm paying him to talk. Let him do the gabbing. That's what he's for."

Selby said, "He's a good lawyer too."

"You're damn right he is."

"Shrewd, cunning, resourceful."

"Say, what is this?" Ribber asked.

Selby said, "He gives me the impression of being a man who thinks his moves out a long way ahead."

"Well, what if he does?"

Selby said, "A man could be playing with him, have Carr

166

point out the next two moves, and think everything was coming fine, and then get stuck on Carr's third move."

Ribber's little, suspicious eyes moved restlessly. "If you're tryin' to say something to me," he said, "say it."

Selby said, "You're a pretty clever chap yourself."

"Oh, yeah?"

"Uh huh. That's the way you impress me."

"Just clever enough, buddy, so you can't bull me into spilling anything. Now how do you like that?"

Selby said, "Do you know whether Carr is going to represent Mrs. Artrim or not?"

"Ask him," Ribber said.

"I thought perhaps you knew. She has quite a bit of money, you know."

"So what?"

Selby said, "I heard a funny story the other day. A couple of men were talking about how it felt to be hung. They rigged a rope up from a rafter. One of the men stood on a chair. He took hold of the rope, raised himself an inch or two off the chair, and the other man took it away. Then the fellow let go the rope easy, and as soon as the rope tightened the other man slid the chair back. The first fellow described the sensations and said to his friend, 'Now you try it.' His friend put his neck in the noose, took a hold on the rope, raised himself up, and the other man moved the chair away."

"Well?" Ribber asked, interested in spite of himself.

"The other fellow just took the chair over and sat down in it," he said. "He read the morning paper, and then after a while went out. Just before he went out, he pushed the chair back so it was under the man's feet. Of course, by that time, the man didn't have any use for it. The coroner's jury called it suicide. There was nothing else they could call it."

"Well?" Ribber asked, and his voice had an odd, throaty catch.

Selby shrugged his shoulders. "That's what it was," he said. "Suicide."

Ribber raised his voice. It had a rasping quality of nervousness. "Well, cripes, why come around here telling me your bedtime stories? If you have anything to say to me, go get Carr. If you haven't anything to say, get the hell out."

Selby might not have heard him. "The moral of that story, Pete," he said, "is never put your head in a noose, for anyone."

"Nuts to you," Ribber said.

"Now in this case," Selby observed, "one of the first things which appealed to me was the fact that it was unreasonable. I said to myself, it just isn't natural for a guy like Ribber who's been in stir a couple of times to go around killing people and leaving murder guns with his fingerprints on them conveniently near the corpse. Well, I thought that over for a while, and couldn't figure why a guy would do anything like that—unless he was either protecting someone or unless it was bait for a trap.

"So then I got to thinking and said, 'Well, now, suppose Pete was either protecting someone or suppose that was bait for a trap that was being set for me. Then what?' Well, I got to thinking it over and started making investigations, Pete, and you'd be surprised at what I've found out."

"What did you find out?" Pete asked. "Oh, nuts to you, you didn't find out anything."

Selby said, "As I was remarking, Pete, you'd be surprised at what I found out, and I couldn't quite reconcile that evidence with the evidence of that gun with the fingerprints on it and the evidence that indicated your old friend Morton Taleman had been dead before that Winchester bullet was pumped into him. So then I got to thinking, and all of a sudden I thought of a lot of things. Well, Pete, I didn't intend to tell you those things. I thought I'd keep them to spring as a little surprise on you at the trial. And then this morning I stumbled onto some other evidence, and that was evidence I couldn't understand.

"I kept turning the thing over in my mind and couldn't figure it, and then all of a sudden, I remembered the story about the two friends who were going to find out what it felt like to be hung, and I started laughing. So then I said to my friend, the sheriff, 'Rex, wouldn't it be a funny thing if after Pete put his head in the noose, somebody forgot to bring the chair back for him?' Well, you know, Pete, that's the way it goes. A guy sticks his head in the noose, and has to figure his friends might get playful sometimes. Of course, as far as *I'm* concerned, I don't care, just so I get a goat. That's all I need. The taxpayers know there's been a murder. They want to see someone convicted. The man who's convicted automatically becomes the guilty guy."

Ribber said, "Say, buddy, have you gone off your trolley or . . ."

The door burst open. Bob Terry, with every evidence of excitement and breathlessness, shoved forward a wooden box he was carrying. "Here it is," he said.

Selby gave an exclamation. "You found it?"

"Yes."

"Peters bullets?"

"That's right."

Selby said, "You didn't lose any possible prints on it, did you?"

"Not a chance," Terry said. He opened the box, disclosing the manner in which the gun had been suspended by threads tied firmly to little lugs of wood which supported it.

Selby said, "That's swell. Have you tried it for latents yet, Bob?"

"Not yet. Good Lord, I broke my neck getting here!"

"Find it where I told you you would?"

"Uh huh."

Selby said, "Well, hurry up, develop those latents. Don't stand there gawking."

Apparently none of the persons in the room paid the slightest attention to Pete Ribber. They were leaning over the box, staring down at the gun with fascinated eyes, and Ribber, finding that he was not being observed, mopped a handkerchief across his forehead, slid an uneasy forefinger around the neckband of his shirt, and then leaned forward to stare as Bob Terry took some white powder and a soft camel's-hair brush from his pocket and gently dusted over the surface of the gun. As though by magic, fingerprints, a few smudged ones, then two perfect prints leapt into view.

"Those prints," Selby said breathlessly, "get them, Bob."

The deputy whipped a magnifying glass from his pocket, bent over and studied them.

Selby nodded to Rex Brandon. "Okay, Sheriff," he said. "Get the card."

Brandon stepped to the door and shouted in a loud voice to the jailer, "Get that card with Ribber's fingerprints."

Ribber recoiled as though he'd been struck. For a moment, it looked as though he wanted to bolt, then he said, "Say, what's eating you guys? My prints ain't on that gun."

The sheriff brought a card containing a set of finger-prints. Terry looked at it, compared two of the prints, and almost imperceptibly nodded his head.

Selby said crisply, "Don't say anything here, Bob. Get that gun over. Let's try the other side."

Terry untied the cords which held the gun, turned it over, and dusted powder on the other side. Once more he found smudge prints and two perfect prints. Once more he com-pared those perfect prints with the card, and once more he nodded—almost imperceptibly.

Selby shoved him sharply and said, warningly, "Watch yourself, Bob. Say nothing here."

Terry straightened, handed the card of fingerprints back

to the sheriff. He lowered the lid of the box into place, and said to Selby, "That's all of it. Where do you want this, Mr. Selby?"

Selby said, "Put it in the sheriff's safe. Photograph those fingerprints first, photograph the entire weapon, and then get Hawlins to fire a test bullet through the barrel. Tell Hawlins not to breathe a word of what he finds to anyone except the sheriff and myself. Do you understand?"

Terry nodded, picked up the box, and hurried out.

Selby took his pipe from his pocket, regarded Pete Ribber in frowning concentration as he pushed tobacco down into the bowl. "Well, Pete," he said at length, "I'm damned if I know. I don't think this is the answer any more than I thought the other was the answer, but one thing's certain. A jury will take this for an answer. . . . Well, so long, Pete."

Ribber said, "Nuts to you, wise guy."

His remark struck Selby funny. He broke into hearty laughter. "Wise guy," he said. "Wise guy."

The sheriff grinned and looked back over his shoulder at the uneasy prisoner.

Selby stood in the doorway rocking with laughter, his shaking finger pointed at Pete Ribber. "Wise guy," he said chokingly.

The door slammed, shutting off the sound of Selby's laughter.

In the witness room, Pete Ribber wiped perspiration from his forehead while Selby, in the other room, checking his well-simulated merriment, said, "All right, Rex. Now we've laid the egg and put it in the incubator, we'll sit tight for a while and see if it hatches."

"If it hatches?" the sheriff asked. "What kind of a chicken will it be?"

Selby shook his head. "I'm damned if I know, but I just have a hunch it's going to hatch."

Sylvia said, "I'm betting it hatches. Did you see his face

when you were telling that story about the friend who didn't bring the chair back?"

Selby said, "No, I was afraid he'd smell a rat if I looked at him too closely."

"He's more worried right now than he's been at any time since his arrest."

"There was nothing for him to worry about before," Selby said. "Finding that gun with his fingerprints on it was all planned in advance."

"But why, Doug?"

Selby shrugged his shoulders and said, "I think we're on the right trail, but I don't know what's at the end of it."

Brandon said, "Don't you think we'd better go back and sweat him some more after he's had a chance to think this over, Doug?"

"No," Selby said. "Leave him alone now for a while. Pretend that we have all the case we want, but keep an eye on him, Rex.

"Now then, if he telephones Carr tonight, and Carr comes rushing down to see him, we'll know that our seed didn't fall on barren ground. He'll tell Carr the story about the man who didn't put back the chair, and Carr will call him a damn fool and tell him it's part of our third degree, and reassure him."

"Well?" Brandon asked dubiously. "Then what? Wouldn't it be better to go in and strike while the iron's hot and try to make him talk?"

"He's too wise to talk," Selby said. "The only kind of a third degree which will impress him is one in which you *don't* try to make him talk. When officers actually have a good case against a man, they don't care whether he talks or not. Whenever they want him to talk, it's because they haven't got a good case and Pete Ribber knows it just as well as you do or I do."

"Well," Brandon said, "my best guess is that after Carr's talked with him, we'll never get anywhere."

"I'm not so certain," Selby said. "Carr will laugh the whole thing off and call it police third degree, but remember, Carr is clever, and after Carr's left, Ribber will have a long night to think things over. Ribber knows just how clever Carr is."

The sheriff laughed and said, "He'll think things over while he's snoring then. That chap is as accustomed to the inside of a jail as a turnkey. They say he goes to sleep and snores steadily until morning."

Selby said, "Find out what size hat he wears, Rex, and get the size of his hands. About ten o'clock tonight have one of the boys come in, rout him out of his cell, and try a hat on. It'll be a black hat with a bloodstain on it. The hat will fit. Take it away, and let Pete go back to bed. A little after midnight we'll wake him up and try an old glove on his right hand. Be certain that that glove fits. I'll wager he won't sleep after that."

"But," Brandon objected, "he won't know what that stuff is all about. Let's suppose he really *did* kill the guy. He knows how it was done and where it was done. He knows that the hat and the glove don't have anything to do with it."

"Exactly," Selby said. "He'll figure that those are bits of evidence which A. B. Carr has let fall into our hands."

Brandon's grin was more characteristic of his usual carefree demeanor than had been the case for days. "Damn it," he said, "I believe you're going to get somewhere."

Sylvia Martin was more dubious. She said, "The worst of it is, Doug, Carr will see exactly what you're trying to do, and he'll probably be shrewd enough to sense what else you're going to do and warn Ribber what to expect."

Selby's eyes indicated a flash of inspiration. He grabbed Sylvia's shoulders and hugged her. "Bully for you," he said.

"Doug, what in the world are you talking about?"

Selby said, "I'm going to tell him."

"Tell him what?"

"Just what we're intending to do."

"Doug, are you crazy?" she asked.

Brandon's voice showed admiration. "Crazy like a fox," he said.

"But I don't understand, Doug."

Selby said, "If I tell Carr what we're planning to do, Carr will naturally warn his client."

"Of course."

"And because it's the truth," Selby said, "Carr will tell Ribber exactly how he knows and exactly what I told him. In other words, he'll repeat any conversation which I have with him to Ribber."

"Well?" Sylvia asked.

Selby said, "All I have to do is to remember that with Ribber I'm dealing with a man who has given his friends so many double-crosses that he's always looking for his friends to double-cross him. If I make what I tell Carr sound sufficiently improbable so that when Carr repeats it to Ribber, Ribber will think Carr is lying—well, figure it out for yourself."

Sylvia said, "Doug, it sounds crazy, but I have an idea it may work. That isn't a third degree. That's a fourth degree."

CHAPTER XIII

Selby paced rhythmically up and down the floor of his office. Workers in the courthouse had long since departed, and the big structure was as silent as the interior of the huge vaults in which the county records were kept. On Selby's desk a large-scale road map had been spread flat under a desk light. A series of circles traced in colored ink marked distances of forty-two miles, forty-three miles, forty-four miles, and forty-five miles from Madison City.

Selby heard steps coming down the corridor, approaching his office. He listened to the sound of those steps for a moment, then hastily folded the big map and shoved it into a desk drawer. A quick knock sounded on the panels of the door. Selby crossed over and opened it.

The tall form of A. B. Carr stood on the threshold, and his face was smiling its most magnetic, friendly smile. "You're working late," he said.

Selby nodded. "Come in," he invited.

"Thanks," Carr said. "I happened to catch the janitor downstairs. He let me in the outer door—told me you were up here working."

Selby nodded.

"Hope I'm not the reason you're burning all the midnight oil," Carr said.

Selby laughed. "This is a county job. When there's work, you work hard. Then you'll have days or perhaps weeks when there's not very much to do."

Carr sat down. "What the devil were you trying to do with my client?" he asked.

"You mean Ribber?"

"Yes, of course."

Selby grinned. "Trying a third degree," he said.

"I didn't know you considered that ethical."

"I consider anything ethical," Selby said, "that will get at the truth."

"From what Ribber tells me," Carr said, "it seems you have rather a distorted idea of the truth."

"That's probably true," Selby admitted frankly. "A man trying to solve a murder mystery gets a lot of different ideas which he has to build up, consider, and discard, hoping that eventually he'll stumble on the right idea."

Carr said, "I'm not certain that I like the idea that you're playing with now."

"Indeed," Selby commented.

"Now look here, Selby. You're a nice enough chap. I don't want to get tough with you, but you went pretty far with Ribber, telling him that I was going to walk out on him and let him get hung."

Selby raised his eyes. "What gave you the impression that I told him anything like that?"

"He said you did. Of course, you told it to him in the form of a story, but the implication of that story was plain enough."

Selby said, "You must have thought the shoe was a close fit, Carr. I don't think I even mentioned your name."

"Well, you know what you had reference to."

Selby grinned and said, "I'm not certain that I do."

"What do you mean?"

In a burst of candor, Selby said, "Look here, Carr. You're representing your client. Naturally you think he isn't guilty. I'm not certain but what you're right."

Carr's eyes were veiled in caution. "So what?" he asked.

"So," Selby said, "if he isn't guilty, the question arises, who is? Now I can't conceive of a man of Ribber's intelligence killing a man and leaving the gun with his fingerprints on it at the scene of the murder."

"Neither can I," Carr said affably.

"The only other solution is that Ribber fired a shot into a dead body."

"I was hoping you'd see the logic of my contention," Carr said.

Selby nodded. "I do."

"Well," Carr asked hopefully, "are you going to dismiss the case?"

"I don't know," Selby said. "I think you're overlooking the most significant fact."

"What's that?"

"If Ribber fired a shot into a dead body, *why* did he do it? Naturally it was to protect someone. Who was that someone? Probably the murderer. Therefore, if we can find the person Ribber is protecting we can find the murderer."

"I see," Carr said noncommittally.

"Therefore," Selby said, "I thought we'd use a psychological third degree. I thought I'd let him think that the person he was protecting might not play square with him. I thought I'd let him think we'd uncovered some new clues."

Carr's eyes continued to be inscrutable. "You actually hadn't uncovered any new clues?"

Selby laughed and said, "Of course not. We figured we might be able to fool Ribber, but I didn't think we could fool you, so I'm not going to try."

"Then the gun means nothing?"

"Not a thing in the world," Selby said. "It was just a gun the sheriff picked up."

"And how about the fingerprints on it?"

"Just a grandstand," Selby said carelessly.

"Then they weren't Ribber's fingerprints?"

"Well," Selby said, and hesitated.

Carr waited for him to go on.

"Well," Selby said at length, guardedly, "Ribber didn't put the fingerprints on the gun."

Carr lit a cigar. Despite the posture of indolent ease which he tried to assume, his manner was as tense as that of a trapshooter waiting for a spinning mark to hurl out in the sky.

Selby said, "I'm not certain. I think we're going to get somewhere. I assume, Carr, that if your client is innocent, it's to your interest to convince us of that fact."

"Naturally."

"And, in the interests of your client, you should co-operate with us in finding out whom he is protecting, because in that way we'll find the real murderer."

"I see."

"Therefore," Selby told him, "if you'll co-operate a little on this, I think we can quite probably clean up the murder and dismiss the case against your client."

"What do you want me to do?" Carr asked.

Selby said, "During the night we'll probably have some other clues that we'll spring on Ribber. Now I'm acting on this theory, Carr. We don't know what happened. Ribber does. If we can start springing a bunch of clues on him that he thinks will have put us wise, and if we act on the assumption that we know all there is to know, Ribber is pretty apt to give himself away."

Carr said nothing.

"Now then," Selby said, "if you could see your client, tell him that you're satisfied that he isn't guilty, that you do think he's protecting someone, and that you think we're wise to the whole business, it may be that he'll talk."

"Why should *I* want him to talk?" Carr asked.

"Can't you see?" Selby explained patiently. "In that way, we could dismiss the case against him."

"If you think he's innocent, why don't you go ahead and dismiss the case anyway?"

"We can't because of public sentiment. Why, look here. Look at this editorial which was in tonight's *Blade*. Have you seen it?"

Carr shook his head.

Selby picked up the *Blade* which was on his desk and opened it to the editorial. "There it is," he said, "a nice piece of propaganda. The editor admits that the *Blade* has been against me politically for some time, that my record, however, in major cases has been one of consistent victories, that it is quite possible the *Blade* was mistaken, that the editor has always felt I was just unusually lucky, but that with the trial of Pete Ribber the voters in the community will have an opportunity to see how I stack up against the best legal talent. If I can get a conviction of Ribber, it will indicate that my other cases haven't been merely lucky breaks. If, on the other hand, with the iron-clad case against Ribber, with his fingerprints being found on the gun that did the shooting, Ribber is able to walk off scot-free, then it will be a pretty good indication that I haven't the maturity, the experience, or the ability which Madison County wants to see in a district attorney."

"Rather puts you on a spot," Carr said.

"It does for a fact," Selby assured him. "Now then, as I said, I can't believe Ribber would leave his fingerprints on that gun and leave the gun at the scene of the crime. I don't think that the bullet he fired into Taleman's body was the fatal bullet. Of course, this is off the record. I'm telling it to you in confidence because I want you to co-operate with me."

Carr smoked in thoughtful silence for several long seconds.

Selby said, "If you can see your way clear to intimate to Ribber that we're running down a hot trail, that we probably know a lot more about what happened than you do, that we feel he's protecting someone, and have some red-hot clues as to who that someone is, that will help. Then if you can go a step farther and point out to Ribber that this someone is probably going to double-cross him, Ribber should make a clean breast of his connection with the affair."

"You think this person he's protecting is going to double-cross him?" Carr asked.

Selby said, "I don't know, but I want to make Ribber think he is, and frankly there's no reason why that person shouldn't give Ribber the double-cross. Ribber's arrested for murder. There's some evidence against him. If this party could plant just a little more evidence that would connect Ribber with the crime, Ribber would be convicted of first degree murder and executed, and that would close the case. The real murderer would walk off, chuckling in his sleeve."

"But when that happened, Ribber would make a complete confession, wouldn't he?" Carr asked.

Selby said, "Sure he would, but who would believe him? Ribber's an ex-convict. He's a professional crook. If he didn't murder Taleman, he undoubtedly fired a slug into Taleman's dead body. It wouldn't take very much additional evidence to convict him. After he was convicted, any story that he'd tell would be considered a last-minute attempt to lie his way out of the rap. He'll have to take the stand when the case is tried in the superior court. He'll take an oath and tell a story. If he's convicted, he'll have to repudiate that story. He'll have to admit that he was committing perjury. No one's going to take the accusation of such a man very seriously."

"I see," Carr observed again.

Selby pushed back his chair. "Can I count on your cooperation?" he asked.

Carr shook hands. "I'll think it over," he said. He started walking toward the door, then, halfway across the office, paused to turn and look back at Selby, sizing him up. A frown creased his forehead, a frown which he promptly erased. "I'll see what I can do," he promised, turned, and walked through the door.

In his office, Selby sat listening to Carr's steps. Halfway down the corridor, he heard the even tempo of those steps change, heard them finally halt altogether, then after a few seconds, they were once more resumed. Selby picked up his telephone and called Sylvia Martin at the *Clarion.*

"How's it coming, Doug?" she asked when she heard his voice.

"I don't know," he said. "Carr was just in."

"What did he say?"

"He didn't say much, but he was doing a lot of thinking when he left. He's wondering if I'm as simple as I seem, or whether I'm playing a deep game, and if so just how deep the game is. I think he's worried."

"What's worrying him most, Doug?"

"Ribber," Selby said unhesitatingly. "I don't think his session with Ribber was very satisfactory."

"How long ago was he at the jail, Doug?"

Selby looked at his wrist watch and said, "It's been almost three hours."

"It took him a while to make up his mind to come and see you, didn't it, Doug?"

"He may have had something else he was doing. A deputy sheriff read the speedometer on his automobile while he was in the jail. I may get another reading after a while."

"Doug, I think you're on the right track. I think you've got him worried, and I think you've located the weak point in his armor. If Ribber thinks Carr is planning to give him a double-cross, he'll begin to crack, and if he cracks, he'll break."

"I'll keep you posted," Selby promised.

"Nice little editorial in the *Blade*, wasn't it, Doug?"

Selby grinned. "That's all in the game. Be seeing you later, Sylvia."

" 'By," she said, "and luck."

Selby hung up the telephone, once more pulled out the map and started studying it, inch by inch. An hour passed. Selby had collected a series of notes dealing with likely spots to investigate. The telephone rang. Selby heard Sheriff Brandon's voicecoming over the wire. "Doug, old son," the sheriff said, "I think you're getting somewhere, fast."

"How come?" Doug asked.

"Ribber. He's commencing to crack. Carr had a talk with him, then he came up and saw you, then he went back and talked with Ribber, then he came out, got in his car, and drove away. We took Ribber back to his cell. Ribber paced the floor for a while, then stretched out on the cot and finally got to sleep. As soon as he got to sleep, we woke him up, dragged him out into the other room, and tried the hat on him. It fit."

"Then what happened?" Selby asked, gripping the receiver tightly to his ear, his eyes glinting with interest.

"Then he started to cuss," Brandon said, "said that it was an old gag we were pulling, that it was just a bluff we were running, trying to make him talk. I laughed at him, and finally he got mad and said you had spilled the whole plan to his lawyer, and that it wasn't going to do any good to try and pull any more funny business on him because he was wise to the whole play."

"What did you do?"

Brandon chuckled. "Well," he said, in his slow drawl, "I sat down and looked at Ribber for a long time, and finally I said, 'Pete, did your lawyer tell you that?' and Ribber said, 'Yes,' and I said, 'Pete, you've had a chance to see Doug Selby. You saw him in court. You've talked with him. He's a pretty smart hombre. Now do you *really* believe that if Doug Selby were trying to pull a stunt like that just to make you talk, that he'd be a big enough damn fool to go to your attorney and tell *him* what he was doing?'"

"How did he take that?"

"Well," Brandon said, "I could see that I had him there. It was evidently a thought which had been bothering him for quite a while, and when I sprung it on him in just that tone of voice, he wilted. So I got up and shook my head sadly and called the turnkey to take him back to his cell. Just before he left, I said, 'You remember that story Selby told you about the fellow who stood on the chair and put the rope around his neck?' Well, Ribber broke away from the turnkey and started for me. He was crazy mad. He changed his mind before he'd made more than a couple of steps, but you can see he's worried sick."

Selby said, "That's fine. Let him go to sleep again, and

then try the glove on him. Did you get the speedometer reading of Carr's automobile the last time?"

"Uh huh. It was 16,302."

Selby said, "We've got Carr worried all right. He sat here in my office and looked at me, and I could see him trying to figure whether I was just dumb and inexperienced or whether I was playing a game."

"What did he finally conclude?" Brandon asked.

"I think he figured I was just young and inexperienced with a lot of goofy ideas, but I had him mumbling in his beard as he left. He walked out of the office and stopped to think things over when he was halfway down the corridor. I was a little afraid he might not tell Ribber the stuff I'd told him."

"Well, he slipped it all right," the sheriff said, "and Ribber is about half crazy. He figures he's being given the double-cross, and that Carr is in on it."

Selby said, "Keep me posted, Rex. I'm going to be here at the office for a while. There's some reading I want to do, and I'm putting in some more time studying maps."

Brandon said, "Well, go to it, Doug, but I figure a person would make only one trip to dispose of a body, and where there are more trips than that made, it may have nothing whatever to do with the case."

"I know," Selby said, "but I'm working on it just the same."

He hung up, and a moment later called Carr's residence. Mrs. Fermal answered the telephone. "This is Selby," he told her. "Isn't Carr home?"

"No, he hasn't been home tonight."

"When he comes," Selby said, "be sure to sneak out and read the speedometer on his car. Get to a telephone and give me the speedometer reading. I want it."

"All right, Mr. Selby. I'll do that for you."

Selby thanked her and returned to his study of the map.

Then he settled back in his chair and started reading the advance decisions of the supreme court in pamphlets which were put out before the cases were finally bound in official volumes. A couple of hours slipped by, and Brandon rang the telephone once more to report.

"We tried the glove on Ribber," he said, "and he's cracking some more. He even tried to argue that the glove was so small that he couldn't move his fingers."

"How did he behave?"

"He's nervous," Brandon said. "He's rattled. I told him that his case was coming up Tuesday. He said he knew it. I said, 'Carr seems to be in an awful hurry to get your case tried,' and he said, 'Of course. He knows I'll be acquitted. He wants me out of here.' "

"What did you say to that?" Selby asked.

Brandon said, "I just grinned, one of those slow, wise grins, and then after a while said, 'Maybe he wants to rush you through before you get down off that chair, Pete.' "

"Did that register?" Selby asked.

"Did it register!" Brandon said. "He blew up. He cussed and raved around a while, and finally said that no blankety blank was going to leave him standing on a chair with a rope around his neck. I thought for a minute he might talk, but I remembered what you'd told me, that I was to pretend I didn't give a hoot whether he talked or not. So I walked out and left him right in the middle of his raving."

Selby said, "Listen, Rex. He may tell the turnkey that he'll tell you something, a little later on. If he does, if he tries to make any excuse to get in touch with you, tell the turnkey that you're not interested, that you don't need to have him talk now. You've got him convicted of first degree murder, and you don't want any confessions. . . . Tell you what you do. Get something that will make him want to talk with you. Get a couple of trusties to start whispering about a plot to break jail. Ribber will figure it's a good time to get in good with you by tipping you off. He'll tell the turnkey he wants to see you personally. Have the turnkey say he'll telephone you, then you can pretend that you think it's simply that he wants to confess, and tell the turnkey you're not interested in any confession, that you've got him dead to rights now and you're not bothering about any statement he'll make."

Brandon said, "Okay, Doug. I can fix it up. I've got a couple of trusties I can depend on. I'll throw them into the adjoining cell."

"Okay," Selby said. "Keep me posted."

He hung up the telephone and had barely time to pick up his book when the phone rang, and Mrs. Fermal said cautiously, "Is this the district attorney?"

"Yes."

"I have that speedometer reading."

"What is it?"

"16,395 miles," she said.

Selby did some rapid mental arithmetic. *Carr had driven his automobile exactly ninety-five miles since leaving the county jail.*

"Listen," Selby said, "can you go out to the garage with a knife from the kitchen and scrape off the underside of the fender? See if you find any dirt mixed with oil on the underside of the fenders. If you do, call me back right away."

She said, "I may have to wait a minute or two to get a chance to get out there without his noticing."

"I'll be here," Selby said, "until you call back."

"I'll do it as soon as I can," she promised.

It was ten minutes later when Selby's phone rang again, and Mrs. Fermal, speaking in a low, cautious voice, said, "It's there."

"You mean the oiled earth?" Selby asked.

She said, "Yes. It . . ." She abruptly dropped the receiver

back into place, and as the connection went dead, Selby hastily hung up his own receiver so that the call couldn't be traced.

Selby promptly called Sheriff Brandon. "Rex," he said, "let's forget Pete Ribber for a moment. Come up to my office. I have something I want to go over with you."

Brandon promised he would be right up, and Selby called the *Clarion*, got Sylvia Martin on the line, and asked her to join the conference.

When they were grouped around Selby's desk, the district attorney took out the large-scale map and spread it before him under the desk light.

He told them the evidence he had, and then went on to explain his theory. "A person would take a body out to dispose of it once," he said. "There's an old theory that a murderer returns to the scene of his crime. That doesn't mean that a murderer would return to the place where the body was buried.

"Unless we deliberately close our eyes to the evidence in this case, we're bound to observe that somewhere within a radius of forty-five miles from Madison City there's something which is vitally connected with the crime under investigation, something which so far we've overlooked. It may be a mountain cabin. It might be something concealed in the desert, but my own idea is that it's something else.

"Most of the mountain soil in this section is of decomposed granite. The soil which is mingled with that earth is a sedementary loam mixed with bits of river gravel. Notice this circle which represents a distance of exactly forty-three miles in an air line from Madison City. That circle intersects exactly one city—El Bocano."

He paused impressively and then said, "I think we're overlooking something. I think that something is in El Bocano.

"Notice this. The automobile clubs would know of any

road repairs which were being made on any of the roads outside of the corporate limits. They wouldn't be advised of road repairs within the corporate limits of any city. The automobile clubs tell us there's no freshly oiled detour on any of the through roads within a radius of forty-five miles. Personally, I think we'll find what we want at El Bocano."

Brandon nodded and said quietly, "Okay, Doug. The county car's outside."

Sylvia Martin jumped to her feet. "Let's go," she said.

Selby folded the map, pushed it back in his desk drawer, and switched out the desk light.

CHAPTER XIV

THE COUNTY CAR ROARED INTO THE OUTSKIRTS OF EL Bocano.

"Where to, Doug?" Rex Brandon asked.

"I think we'll try the police station first," Selby said.

Brandon nodded. They swung into the main street, now virtually deserted. The last picture show was just over, and there were a few stragglers on the street. Brandon pulled into the curb and asked one of the pedestrians where he could find police headquarters, and then followed directions around the corner to an unpretentious office in the basement of the city hall.

A night sergeant on duty learned the identity of his visitors, brought out chairs, and, when they were seated, asked how he could be of service.

Selby said, "We're working on a case. The only clue we have is that apparently it centers around here, and is near a place where a roadway has been freshly oiled."

The night sergeant shook his head. "There aren't any road operations going on anywhere in the city limits," he said.

Selby fought back his disappointment. "No place near here that you know of where roads have been oiled?"

"No."

Selby thought for a moment, then, avoiding the sympathy of Sylvia Martin's eyes, pulled his pipe from his pocket, and took out his tobacco pouch.

"Wait a minute," the sergeant said. "There's a new trailer camp opened up in the river bottom. They had to oil the road into that. It's just a short stretch, probably not over a hundred feet. Would that be the place?"

Selby said, "That sounds very much like the place."

The sergeant reached for a telephone. "I'll get one of the boys to go down with you," he said.

An officer, whose name was Jenkins, entered the office in response to the sergeant's telephoned summons, and was introduced.

"How about taking these folks down to the trailer court, Bill?" the sergeant asked. "They're working on a case."

"Right now?" Jenkins asked.

"Right now," Selby said.

"Let's go," Jenkins announced.

They trooped out to the county car. Jenkins slid in beside Brandon. Selby sat in the rear seat with Sylvia Martin. Following Jenkins's directions, the sheriff ran rapidly to the outskirts of town, turned left, crossed railroad tracks, and then drove the car along a stretch of freshly oiled dirt road.

Selby, with his pipestem clamped in his teeth, smiled across at Sylvia Martin. "Looks as though we're striking pay dirt," he said.

A sign over the bank said, "Oak Grove Trailer Camp and Auto Court."

Jenkins said, "There are no lights. The manager sleeps in that first cabin. Shall we get him out?"

"We get him out," Selby said.

They stopped the car and Jenkins rang the night bell. A

sleepy voice said, "No vacancies," and Jenkins said, "This is Jenkins of Police Head . . ."

He caught himself as Selby gave him a shove. "Not so loud," Selby cautioned.

The officer said, "Get up. We want to talk with you."

"Who is it?"

"Jenkins."

"I don't know you."

"Think again," Jenkins said. "Get up. This is important." There followed the creaking of bedsprings, the sound of reluctant feet groping into slippers, and then shuffling to the door. Jenkins said in a low voice, "This is the police. I'm from headquarters. This is the sheriff and district attorney of Madison County. They want to ask you some questions."

A big-framed individual, his eyes swollen with sleep, hastily buttoned a pair of trousers over his pajamas as he saw Sylvia Martin. "All right," he said. "What do you want?"

Selby said, "You have a man staying here, probably alone. Some woman has been calling on him, from time to time, during the last week. She's thirty-two with coal-black hair, dark eyes, and good figure. She drives a thirty-nine Cadillac."

"Oh, sure," the man said. "You mean Frank Neal."

"Where is he?"

"In that trailer at the far end of the camp, the one with the awning over the door."

"How did the trailer get here?" Selby asked. "Who pulled it in?"

"Some trailer company," the man said. "It's a rent job. It's a pretty good trailer. Some of these companies that do rent business will spot a trailer for you anywhere you want."

Selby said, "I think that's our man. Suppose you come down with us and show us the place."

The proprietor said, "I'd prefer you went by yourself. I

don't want to seem to mix into this. He might think I'd been talking too much."

Jenkins said, "Never mind about that. Just take us down there."

The man consented reluctantly. "I'll have to get a flashlight."

"We have one," Brandon said, and showed him the big five-cell flashlight he was holding in his right hand.

"All right," the proprietor said.

The little group, guided by the beam of the flashlight, moved in a compact unit across the trailer court, dark except for the reddish illumination given by two lights which burned over the central building marked "Showers" and "Toilets."

"Knock on the door," Selby said as they approached the trailer.

The proprietor knocked on the door, and received no answer. He rattled the knob, and the door swung open. "That's funny," he said.

Brandon pushed him to one side, switched on the flashlight, and turned the beam on the interior of the trailer. The bed had been slept in. A man's coat and vest hung over the back of a chair. There were shoes by the side of the bed. With an exclamation Brandon jumped into the trailer and ran across to feel of the bed. "Still warm," he said.

Selby said, "He heard Jenkins say it was the police. Quick, Rex, cover the showers and toilets. Come on, Jenkins. We'll look around the back."

"There's a trail through that hedge down toward the rear over to the place where I dump the tin cans and stuff in the river bed," the proprietor said.

Brandon thrust the flashlight into Selby's hands. "You take the flashlight, Doug," he said. "I won't need it. I'll join you later, if I don't find him in the building."

Selby said, "You stay here, Sylvia, and keep an eye on things. Come on, Jenkins, let's go."

They ran down the trail, following the beam of the spotlight. Once, when it crossed a dusty patch, Selby turned the beam downward to look at the tracks. "Here we are," he said. "We're on the right trail. Someone's been running down here with slippers."

They ran on for another thirty yards and then Selby stopped abruptly and switched off the flashlight. "Listen," he said.

Ahead could be heard the sound of some object thrashing into brush. A moment later, the clatter of empty tin cans announced that the man had fallen into a pile of rubbish. Jenkins pulled back his coat and tugged out his gun. Selby gave a shrill whistle, a whistle which was answered almost immediately from behind as Rex Brandon came running up. Sylvia was just behind the sheriff.

"Showers and toilets empty," Brandon reported.

Selby swung the beam of the powerful flashlight in a half-circle, then held it steady as the pencil of bright light picked up a white blur of motion. Selby said, "Come on," and led the way across a sandy river bed.

Selby had the impression of dim motion from the darkness ahead. For a moment the flashlight wavered as he tried to center it on the figure of the man. From the darkness ahead came a stabbing spurt of flame followed almost instantly by another. Selby heard a peculiar thump on his left, sounding as though someone had dropped a custard pudding on the floor. Jenkins said, "Oh, my God!" and ran two staggering steps to pitch headlong into the sand.

He saw another flash of flame. A peculiar zinging sound was gone almost before his ears could register it. A cold whisper of air sucked past his right ear. Selby heard the deep-throated roar of Sheriff Brandon's forty-five. Deep midnight silence fell upon the river bed.

Selby switched out the flashlight, grabbed Sylvia Martin's waist. "Get down, Sylvia," he said.

She fought free.

The fingers of Sheriff Brandon's left hand slid down Selby's arm, grasped the flashlight, and wrenched it from his grasp. Selby struggled for the flashlight. Brandon shouldered him to one side. "Don't be a fool. You haven't got a gun," he said and ran out into the darkness.

Sylvia started after him.

"Sylvia, don't," Selby said. He clutched at her dress. She whirled on him like a wildcat. "Leave me alone! This is a *story!*" She wrenched free, to the sound of tearing cloth.

Selby caught a vague glimpse of Brandon's figure plunging ahead, of Sylvia Martin stumbling into a run in the ankle-deep sand. Selby lunged forward in a tackle. He missed Sylvia's waist, caught her ankle in his right hand. His left, searching blindly, clamped on her leg just above the knee. She came down hard, struggled to free herself. He held her in a hard grip.

"Doug Selby, I hate you," she cried, half sobbing.

Selby held on grimly. She kicked at him, caught him on the shoulder. He released his hold on her leg to try and catch the other ankle. She drove her foot in a vicious blow which just missed his ear.

Brandon was somewhere on ahead. Behind Selby, the city officer was groaning, an inert black blob on the white sand.

Selby wrapped both arms around Sylvia's legs. "Listen to reason, you little devil," he said.

"You let me go!"

Selby said, "I haven't time to argue with you. You stay here. It's too late to follow Rex now." He released her abruptly, ran back toward the camp ground. Sylvia struggled to her feet and plunged blindly through the darkness after Sheriff Brandon.

Selby stumbled and groped his way back toward the trail, then moved slightly to one side, crouched in the shadows, and waited.

There were no further shots from the river bed. Selby saw the beam of the flashlight stab into quick brilliance, then vanish into darkness. A moment later, ten yards farther to the right, the light again blazed into a searching beam. He heard Sylvia Martin call, "Where are you, Sheriff?" There was no answer.

Selby, panting, breathed through his mouth so that he would make less noise. He thought he heard the crunch of steps in the sand. A moment later, he was able to discern a shadowy figure moving cautiously through the darkness. He saw the form of Jenkins double up as the officer tried to get to his feet, then drop flat.

The figure was closer now. Selby crouched, tense and ready. The figure swung over to the left. Selby prepared to charge, then remained motionless as he saw that the other man was circling, looking for something. Abruptly, the man found the trail. He quickened his steps to a run. His right hand was at his side, pushed slightly to the front. The man wore dark trousers. Above them was a white shirt which harmonized with the sand of the river bed. Then as the man came closer, the shirt showed against the rim of the dark. Selby could hear his harsh, quick breathing.

Within three short steps, the other man sensed his presence, and stopped abruptly. Selby couldn't see the arm, but he knew from the set of the man's shoulder that the gun was swinging in his direction.

"Stick 'em up," Selby said, in a low tense voice, and rushed.

The sound of that grim command coming from the darkness ahead of him, made the man hesitate for just that second of indecision which enabled Selby to get momentum in his rush. Then there was a deafening roar full in his face.

Selby's mind, racing like mad, found time to wonder that
he wasn't dead even as he tackled low and hard.

The gun roared again just as Selby's impact swept the
man off his feet.

They were in the sand struggling. The man was powerful.
For a moment, Selby was on top, then his left arm was
caught in a powerful grip and forced back. He felt the weight
of the other's body. Selby's mouth opened for a quick, gasp-
ing intake of air, was forced down into the sand. The grains
gritted in his teeth, covered his tongue, choked his windpipe.

Selby twisted his arm free, squirmed to get his mouth out
of the sand. He had a glimpse of broad shoulders, of a face
blotting out the starlight, and drove his right fist upward
in a short, ten-inch blow that connected. He saw the head
snap back. Selby flung his left arm into action. Clutching
hands grabbed at that arm as he delivered a glancing blow.
The district attorney braced his right shoulder. He could
hear running steps. The beam of a flashlight illuminated
the shrubbery five yards to the left.

Selby's fist missed the chin, crashed into the man's right
eye. Selby drove his weight forward . . . was on top. . . .
His knees pinioned the other man's arms.

The light stabbed full into Selby's face, blinding his eyes.
He tried to call out, but his mouth was full of sand, and
he was choking, trying to get that sand out of his mouth.

The beam shifted, holding steady on the struggling body
beneath him. He heard Brandon's voice say, "Lie still or
I'll blow your damn brains out. . . . Here, Sylvia, take this
flashlight."

Selby's full weight was on the man's arms, but Brandon
jerked those arms out from under his knees as though the
district attorney had been but a baby. Selby heard the
businesslike click of handcuffs, and then saw the flashlight
pinwheel to the ground, and felt Sylvia's arms around his
neck. "Oh, my darling, are you hurt?"

Her face was against his. She was trying to lift him. Brandon, with a heave, jerked the big body out from under Selby.

Selby groped in his pocket for a handkerchief, wiped sand from his lips and tongue. "I figured he'd try to double back to steal our car," he croaked. "He couldn't expect to get away running. . . ."

"Where the hell's that flashlight?" Brandon muttered.

Sylvia said, "I'm sorry, Rex." She bent over, fumbled. A moment later, the flashlight stabbed full into the sullen face of a powerful man whose right eye was swelling shut.

Brandon said, "Who the devil are you?"

It was Selby who answered the questions. "Unless I'm greatly mistaken," he said, "this is James C. Artrim on whom the insurance company's paid a cool half million in life insurance."

Lights were flashing on in the trailer camp. There were confused voices. A woman was screaming. In the distance could be heard the wail of a siren.

The handcuffed man said, "All right, you son of a bitch. If you're so damn smart, figure it out for yourself. I won't talk."

Sheriff Brandon's foot, planted where it would do the most good, jarred the big frame. "Shut up, you," the sheriff said. "Ladies present." The sheriff turned the flashlight back toward the river bed. "You two stay here," he said to Sylvia Martin and the district attorney. "I'll see what I can do for Jenkins."

They heard the ground crunch under the sheriff's steps, saw the beam of the flashlight slither along the sand until it came to rest on a dark, inert bundle. Then the broad shoulders blocked out the flashlight.

The prisoner said gloatingly to Selby, "I know about you. You think you're awfully damn smart. Try and get something on me."

195

Selby slipped his arm around Sylvia Martin's waist, drew her to him, could feel the quiver of taut nerves. They heard the sheriff's steps returning, saw the red blob of light on a police car as it turned into the trailer camp. The handcuffed man said, "Go ahead. Take me back to Madison City, and see how much good it does you."

The sheriff stood beside Doug Selby looking down at the prisoner. "We don't need to take you back to Madison County," he said solemnly. "You're going to stay right here. Right in this jail. And you're going to be tried for the murder of an El Bocano policeman in an El Bocano court. If you escape the death penalty, we'll be waiting for you in Madison City. But you won't."

CHAPTER XV

Dʀɪᴠɪɴɢ ʙᴀᴄᴋ ᴛᴏ ᴍᴀᴅɪꜱᴏɴ ᴄɪᴛʏ, Sᴇʟʙʏ ᴛᴏᴏᴋ ꜱᴛᴏᴄᴋ ᴏꜰ the situation. "We can pin an insurance fraud on Mrs. Artrim and the man who posed as her father-in-law, but who was in reality her husband," he said. "That case will be tried in another county because the offense was committed there. Artrim himself will be tried in El Bocano for murder —and given the death penalty. When that happens, he may clear up the murder of Morton Taleman—and he may not. In the meantime, we have Pete Ribber in jail. We don't know his exact connection with the case. We don't know a lot of things."

Brandon said, "Somehow, Doug, I have an idea that if Artrim or Ribber or both of them ever start talking, we're going to pin a first-degree murder rap on A. B. Carr."

"Perhaps," Selby admitted. "It's going to be a job making them talk."

Sylvia Martin said, "Doug, what do you bet Carr doesn't represent Artrim on that El Bocano murder case?"

Selby said, "I think he will. I wouldn't take the other end of that bet at any odds. And he'll claim that Artrim didn't know we were officers, that he thought we were stick-up men, that we chased him out into the barranca, that he pulled his gun and started to shoot up into the air to warn us, but that at that moment he stubbed his toe, fell down, and the gun was accidentally discharged, that he had no idea the bullet had struck anyone, that he got to his feet, and shot again in the air."

Sylvia Martin said, "That's just about what he'll do, and he may be smooth enough to get someone on the jury believing it. Gosh, Doug, I'm sorry I kicked at you. But you're not the only one with a job to do. If I want to take risks I'll take them. I had to be in at the finish."

Selby said, "You'll stop a slug one of these days, and then what would I do?"

She said indignantly, "I'm as just much entitled to stop slugs as you are."

"You're a woman," Selby said.

Sylvia Martin said, "Well, well. You're finding that out, are you? I thought you always regarded me as an automatic piece of news-gathering mechanism."

Selby dropped his hand to hers. "Don't be silly," he said. "How much of what happened did you telephone in to the *Clarion?*"

"Everything," she said.

Selby frowned thoughtfully.

"There may be some of that stuff we don't want spread around. By the time . . ."

"Bunk, Doug Selby," she said. "You'll have this case cracked wide open by the time the *Clarion* is on the streets. So go ahead and get busy. If you had ten per cent of the confidence in yourself that the rest of us have in you . . ."

Selby said, "All right. All right. But it's going to mean a lot of fast work and we may strike a snag."

"If you strike a snag," she said, "you'd better plow right through it!"

"Who's first on the schedule?" Brandon asked.

"Pete Ribber," Selby said.

"Do we send out and pick up Mrs. Artrim, Doug?"

"Not yet," Selby said.

"Why?"

Selby said, "Carr will know it as soon as we do. He's a neighbor of hers, and he isn't exactly a fool." They filed into the jail. The sticky, sweet odor of jail disinfectants, the close stench of crowded sleeping human bodies assailed their nostrils, erasing the freshness of the early morning air. Selby said to the turnkey, "Get Ribber out here, and bring him fast."

Selby asked Sylvia Martin, "Can you take this down in shorthand, Sylvia?"

"If it doesn't get to going too fast," she said.

"If it goes too fast," Selby told her, "do the best you can. Don't interrupt."

They moved on into the witness room. From the interior of the jail, they could hear the sound of a key in the lock, the clang of a steel door, the voice of the turnkey, and Ribber's cursing. "What the hell is this? A game? Do you bastards think I was . . ." The voice died away into silence as there was the sound of a quick scuffle.

Brandon turned to Doug Selby and winked.

A few moments later, Pete Ribber was led in, his mouth twisted into a defiant snarl. "For Christ's sake, *you* again. I suppose you want to try on a necktie now."

Brandon snaked out a powerful arm, caught Ribber by the shirt, swung him in a half-circle, and slammed him down in a chair. "Sit down there," he said, "and don't cuss. There's a lady here."

"All right," Ribber said, "I won't cuss. I won't say a damn thing."

Selby said, "Let me handle it."

Pete said, "I suppose you've made your build-up. Now you're going to give me an opportunity to 'come clean.' Nuts to you."

Selby said, "Listen, Ribber. I'm going to give you one opportunity and only one opportunity to get out of the gas chamber. If you want to go on playing the sucker, that's all right with me. When they strap you to that chair, and you hear the hissing of the poison gas liberated by the little pellets dropping into the acid, look up at the glass windows and see the curious eyes staring in at you—when you try to keep from taking a breath as long as possible so you can prolong life for a long last few seconds—just think of me."

Ribber clamped his lips together and was silent for a long three seconds. Then he said, "Smarter punks than you have tried to scare me. They never got very far."

Selby said, "If you want to be a fall guy, it's your privilege."

"For Christ's sake, let me sleep, but don't keep busting in on me every couple of hours with some new line of crap."

Selby said, "We have the thirty-eight caliber revolver that fired the shot through Taleman's coat. The man who had it shot a cop before he surrendered. He'd been living in a trailer down at El Bocano. His name is James C. Artrim He and his wife have half a million dollars insurance at stake. He has a murder rap hanging over his head. You may be interested in knowing how we caught him."

Ribber moistened his lips, and said, "Nuts to you."

Selby said, as though he hadn't noticed the interruption, "It's exactly ninety miles from here to El Bocano and back. We noticed that the night Frank Artrim disappeared Mrs. Artrim had driven her car exactly ninety miles. We noticed that there was some oiled earth of a peculiar texture on the underside of the fenders. We combed through all the road information available and couldn't find any oiled detour within a radius of forty-five miles of Madison City. We finally picked on El Bocano. We found that the trailer camp where Artrim was holed up had a freshly oiled dirt road leading from the highway."

"What's all that to me?" Ribber asked defiantly.

"I'm coming to that," Selby said. "We've got a pretty good case against you, Ribber. It wasn't so good when it started. It's a lot better now. It's been getting better very fast. I'm not certain but what someone is planting evidence that's going to tie that murder right around your neck. However, I'm not particular. If I get a conviction, that's all the taxpayers want."

Ribber said, "I suppose you mean the hat and the glove and that stuff. Where the hell did you get that stuff anyway?"

Selby went on evenly, "When Carr came down to visit you this last time, one of the deputy sheriffs read his speedometer. When he put the car in his garage three hours later, we read his speedometer again. He'd gone just a little over ninety miles. We took scrapings from the inside of his fenders. We found the same oil composition."

"Well," Ribber asked sneeringly, "what's that to me?"

Selby said, "You figure what it is to you, Ribber. Rita Artrim and James Artrim have half a million dollars cold cash. The insurance company will sue to get it back. Right now, they have the cash. The lawyer who can beat the rap on the Taleman murder is going to get a big chunk of dough. That's the side of the bread that has the butter. There's not much of a way a lawyer can beat that rap. He's going to have a hell of a time proving Artrim innocent. Artrim's gun fired the Peters bullet into Taleman's body. Maybe there's only one way a lawyer could beat that rap. That's by having it appear that the guy who fired the Winchester bullet into

Taleman's body was the one who murdered him, and James Artrim had fired a bullet into a dead body.

"I don't suppose it's occurred to you that that little stunt that looked so slick at the time of the preliminary could be twisted so that it wouldn't look quite so slick. The Artrim side of the bread is the side that has the butter. Now I don't know Carr very well. You know him better than I do. Perhaps he's going to let some other lawyer handle Artrim's case. Perhaps he isn't going to offer to get him an acquittal by seeing that you get convicted of first degree murder. As I say, I don't know. Perhaps Carr is one of those lawyers who doesn't figure which side of the bread has the butter."

Ribber tried to keep his face expressionless and failed. His mouth corners twitched. His eyes, staring steadily at Selby, wavered.

Selby said, "When I leave here, I'm going out and arrest Mrs. Artrim. I don't suppose Carr will formally appear as her attorney. He'll keep on the record as the attorney who's defending you, but perhaps later on, if Artrim gets acquitted because you take the jolt in the death cell, Carr's bank account would show a healthy increase. I wouldn't know about those things because I'm a country lawyer, and I don't know the way these big criminal lawyers work, but I do know that after Carr saw you, he drove ninety miles and went over a road that had some oil on it."

Selby looked at his watch. "You've got three minutes," he said, "to start talking."

Gray light filtered in through the jail window, giving Ribber's face a peculiar, sickly expression. He sat silent while Selby held his watch in his hand.

The ticking of the watch grew louder as the silence became deeper.

Ribber swallowed, and the saliva seemed to rasp in his throat.

Ribber shifted his eyes as though trying to shut the others

from his mind while he thought. He still remained silent.

Selby popped his watch back into his pocket. "All right, that's that. We'll go out and get Rita Artrim." He said to the turnkey, "Take him back and lock him up. All right, Rex, let's go."

Ribber cleared his throat.

Selby paid no attention to him, but started for the door. The turnkey put a hand on Ribber's shoulder. "All right," he said, "get started."

Ribber turned his head. Sylvia Martin had gone out through the door. Brandon was following. Selby was holding the door open. None of them so much as looked back. Ribber gave a half-choked animal cry. "For Christ's sake, come back," he said. "I'll talk."

Selby turned, standing dubiously in the doorway as though half a mind to keep on going.

Ribber said, "I'll tell you the whole story. Morton Taleman and I dug up this body for Rita Artrim. It had been burned to death. Cripes, the whole deal hung fire for six months while we were trying to get a body."

Selby said, "All right, Rex. Come on back."

The three of them filed back into the room. Sylvia Martin quietly slipped a small shorthand book from her purse.

Once started talking, Ribber seemed anxious to get it all off his chest. "Well, we finally managed to get this stiff for her. That father-in-law business was part of the scheme As a matter of fact, her father-in-law had had some domestic trouble. and had taken a run-out powder. No one had seen him for years. but Rita spread the word around that her husband had heard from him, that he was coming back to live with them, and wouldn't it be nice.

"Of course. with half a million bucks in life insurance, it takes a little careful work to throw the hooks into a life insurance company, but we did it all right. In the first place, Artrim's dental work had been done by a dentist who had so many patients he couldn't remember the details. All he had was a file of card records. Well, it was a cinch. We got this stiff who had been burned to death. They can't embalm a burned body you know. Then we got a crooked dentist to make a chart of his dental work on a card we'd stolen from the other dentist's office. I'd gone in to have work done on my teeth, and it was a cinch to get the whole layout and plant the card where we wanted it.

"Right after the accident, Mrs. Artrim rushed this father-in-law of hers to a private sanitarium. She said his face was all cut up. You're damn right it was, but the cutting was done by a plastic surgeon. And he didn't have to change Artrim's map too much at that. Remember, Artrim was going to masquerade as his own father so that there'd naturally be a resemblance. All the surgeon had to do was make him look older, and make a few other changes. He was supposed to have lost his memory so the insurance company couldn't ask him any questions. Get the play?"

"But what the insurance company fell for hook, line, and sinker was that dental identification. They called on the dentist to go down and identify the corpse. The dentist took Artrim's chart from his files without having the least idea it had been planted on him. He went down and looked at the corpse, and swore to a positive identification, and just to be on the safe side the insurance company had its own dentist go down to check up. Christ, was *that* a laugh!" Ribber paused long enough to chuckle at his own smartness.

"Well," he went on, "it was a cinch after that. Of course, Mort and I started riding the gravy train from then on. They paid us five thousand bucks to put the deal across. The damn fools. They thought Mort and I were going to take five grand, and let them get away with half a million.

"Well, we started riding the gravy train like I said. We didn't want to play it too hard at first because we didn't want to bleed them white, but we made regular touches.

Well, then Mort and I had a falling out, and I got pretty drunk, and damned if I didn't stick my nose into a rap. I figured A.B.C. was the only man who could beat that rap, and I sent for him.

"Well, you know how it is with a criminal mouthpiece. The only thing that counts with him is cash, cold, hard cash. I didn't have any. I had to tell Carr that if I could get out, I could get some cash. Carr just laughed at that one. That, of course, is the line they all hand him.

"Well, cripes, what was I to do. I simply had to tell him enough to let him know that I really could raise the dough. Naturally, I talked too damn much. Everything I said was talking too much. Carr can smell a dollar as far as a turkey buzzard can smell a dead rabbit.

"Well, Carr was pretty foxy at that. He put up a bail bond, and pretended he was going to stand right back of me; but what that slick shyster was doing was figuring on railroading me to the pen on a rap I'd cooked up myself. He was just that smart. He knew damn well there was no chance of me pulling any blackmail stuff while I was in stir, and he figured he'd have most of that half million by the time I got out.

"Well, I outsmarted him. I jumped the bail and left Carr and his bail-bond stooges holding the sack. It was swell while it lasted, but it didn't last long. Mrs. Artrim settled down in Orange Heights, and you know what happened. Old A.B.C. moved right in. He pretended he was interested in astronomy. Astronomy, hell! He was planting a bunch of telescopes with cameras so he could get pictures of Artrim in his wheel chair, front views and profile views. He had cameras hooked up with those telescopes, and he had all the evidence he needed.

"Well, you know the rest. Mrs. Artrim was my meal ticket. I was broke. I had to show up to make a touch. But I was decent. I was letting her off for a thousand bucks a crack, and always figuring that I could put that dough on the ponies and make a stake of my own. But Mort wasn't like that. He was hungry. He'd gone direct to Artrim himself. Mort wanted too much. Well, you can figure what probably happened.

"I was plenty cautious, but the trouble was old A.B.C. knew that I'd be hanging around. He laid for me, and nailed me cold. Well, he had me. Because I'd jumped bond, he could pick me up and hold me, and he did, too. He made me tell him everything I knew, give him some signed affidavits, and all that stuff. He said he was going to take care of me. He said I was a damn fool, that I should have known that they wouldn't stand for a steady bleeding, that they'd take a chance on bumping me off.

"Well, it sounded reasonable all right, but after a day or two, I figured that maybe A.B.C. would bump me off, and that bothered me. So when I got the chance, I took a runout powder. I was going down to tell Mrs. Artrim to give me five grand, and I'd promise never to come near her again as long as I lived. I meant it. Things were getting too hot.

"Well, I never had the chance. She must have seen me hanging around the joint, and didn't recognize me but took me for a prowler. Anyhow, the first I knew was when I heard the grind of that cop's car coming up the grade to Orange Heights. You can tell those things as far as you can hear them. I was in a hell of a fix. I had my rod on me, and I was wanted. I'd taken a powder on A.B.C., and I'd figured he'd ease me into the pen so he could ride the gravy train instead of me.

"It was a hell of a spot. I tossed my gun into the barranca and tried to beat it, but they nailed me. At that, I was lucky. They printed me, but turned me loose the next morning because I had five hundred bucks with me—money that Carr had given me when I made the affidavit.

"But old A.B.C. wasn't asleep at the switch. When I

walked out of jail, there he was waiting in his automobile. He opened the door and said, 'Get in.' Well, I got in. I had to. Carr took me back to his house, and then read the riot act to me. He showed me that he could make a stake from the insurance company by turning in my affidavits and getting a reward. That would put Artrim and his wife in jail, and there wouldn't be no more gravy train for anyone to ride—except old A.B.C. He'd get his from the insurance company.

"Well, there I was. Carr could kill the goose that was laying my golden eggs and put me into stir on the one hand; or, on the other hand, if I wanted to play along with him, he could milk Artrim white and give me a little dough on the side. The thing that bothered both of us was Mort. I knew he'd be hanging around sooner or later—and, sure enough, he popped up, and he sure as hell got what was coming to him.

"I heard the shot that night, and I knew what it was just as well as though I'd been standing there looking on."

"Who did it?" Selby asked.

Ribber shrugged his shoulders and said, "Carr probably, but it may have been Artrim. Pay your money and take your choice. I don't know."

"Then what?" Selby asked.

"Then Carr told me he'd decided it wasn't safe for me to stay there any more. He said he'd heard a shot, and he was afraid something might have happened. He said for me to get out."

"So what did you do?"

"Like a sucker," Ribber said, "I went out and put in an hour looking for my gun. It wasn't there. Of course it wasn't. I'd told Carr all about tossing it away, and asked him to get it for me. He told me I'd better forget it, that I shouldn't be packing a rod. Well, you know what Carr did. He slipped out and got that rod of mine. He had gloves on so that he wouldn't leave any prints. He fired another bullet into Mort's body, then he dropped my gun with my fingerprints still on it, went back into the house, and probably had a damn good breakfast. You get the point. He figured he'd pinned it on my neck.

"Well, he had, all right. As soon as I read in the papers about my gun being found there, I went to Carr for a show-down. He promised me ten grand if I'd stand the rap. He guaranteed to beat it, and then after I'd been acquitted so I couldn't be tried again, I was to sign a confession that I'd done it. That would put everyone else in the clear."

"Did he tell you he'd killed the man?" Selby asked.

"Don't be funny," Ribber said. "Old A.B.C. never tells anyone anything."

Selby glanced thoughtfully at Brandon.

Ribber went on, "I stood it all right until you got to show-ing me about how Carr could jerk the chair out from under me, and leave me with my neck in a noose—a noose that I'd tied myself. That bothered me. Then when you let me know that he was playing ball with Artrim, that was too much."

"And you don't know definitely who killed Morton Tale-man?"

"So help me, Mr. Selby, I don't."

Selby said to Sylvia Martin, "Have you got that all down, Sylvia?"

She nodded.

"Want to write it up?"

"For you or the paper?" she asked.

"For the paper," Selby said.

"It can wait for about an hour," she told him. We'll get out an extra. If we wait an hour, will we have more to put in it?"

Selby said, "I think so," and then to Ribber, "All right, Ribber. I want you to go over to that desk. The jailer will give you a pen, ink, and paper. I want you to write down in your own language exactly what you've told us."

Ribber said, "Okay. Now listen, I'm tying the can on A.B.C. I don't want him for my mouthpiece. He's too smart, and he'll get himself in the clear by putting me behind the eight ball. Can you keep him away from me?"

"He isn't your lawyer any more?" Brandon asked.

"No."

"And you tell me that you don't want to see him?"

"That's right."

Brandon grinned. "There's only one way A. B. Carr can get to see you," he said.

"What's that?" Ribber inquired.

"That," Brandon said, "is when he goes into the tank as a prisoner."

Ribber said, "And I don't want to see him even then."

The jailer brought writing materials. Ribber sat down at the desk, dipped the pen in the ink, and said to Selby, "Where do you want me to begin?"

Selby said, "At the beginning."

"When I first met Artrim?"

"Yes, all about the insurance fraud, and what happened after that. Write the whole story."

Ribber said, "Okay. You want everything, is that it?"

"Everything," Selby said. He nodded to the others, and they quietly withdrew into the outer room.

Brandon grinned and said, "Well, it looks as though we give A. B. Carr a jolt he'll remember for a long time."

Selby shook his head.

Sylvia's eyes widened. "Why not, Doug?"

Selby said, "In the first place, I don't think he's guilty of anything that we can pin on him. He probably intended to do some fancy blackmailing, but the thing got away from him."

"You don't think he killed Taleman?"

Selby shook his head. "Artrim did that," he said.

"But how could he? Wasn't he in bed when the police came?"

Selby said, "Artrim killed Taleman, down in that liquor closet. Carr could never have got Taleman into that room. Artrim could have done it by arranging a secret rendezvous. Once having killed Taleman, Artrim tried to escape detection by fooling the police, first as to where the murder was committed, second as to the time at which the murder was committed."

"And you want to go see Mrs. Artrim now, Doug?" Sheriff Brandon asked.

Selby nodded. "Let's go," he said.

The freshness of morning sunlight was gilding the higher points of land, but long, purple shadows were cast over the lowlands. As the county car climbed up to Orange Heights, Selby could look down over the long sweep of well-kept orange groves, out across the long valley to the purple mountains rising against the clear blue black of a calm Southern California sky.

Sheriff Brandon said, "I'd rather take a beating than do this to Rita."

Selby nodded wordless assent.

"I keep thinking of her folks," Brandon said.

Selby said, "That's what comes of being an instrument of the law, Rex. We have to function impersonally and uniformly. After all, she went into this with her eyes open."

The county car drew up in front of the Artrim residence. Sheriff Brandon seemed willing to hold back and let Selby take the lead in walking up the cement steps and in pushing the doorbell.

After a while, Selby said, "She's probably been tipped off."

"Don't you think she might be asleep?" Sylvia Martin asked.

"Not after the way we've been ringing that doorbell," Selby said.

"What do we do?" Brandon asked. "Send out a general alarm for a pickup?"

"It's the only thing for us to do, Rex," Selby said. "Of course, she may have gone to El Bocano."

They walked down off the porch and around to the side of the house. Selby tried the garage door. It was unlocked. He swung it back, and pointed to the car which was standing in the garage. The men exchanged glances. Wordlessly, Selby crossed the garage and tried the door which led into the house. It, too, was unlocked. The three of them crossed the kitchen, the serving pantry, and dining room. They found Rita Artrim in the living room.

She looked tranquil and calm in death as though she had at the last found surcease from the powerful emotions, the conflicting interests which had ruled her life.

A portable typewriter was on a table. A chair had been drawn up to the typewriter. A signed sheet of stationery lay beside it. Selby picked it up and read it aloud.

I have gambled and lost. Mr. Carr has just given me the news. He is on his way to El Bocano to represent James. He says that if I sit tight, I can, as he expresses it, "beat the rap."

I don't want to beat the rap.

I guess I've been traveling the wrong side of the street. I got so tired of a country town, I thought I'd be willing to do anything to get away. I married Jim. It was fun for a while. I liked the idea of gambling for big stakes. Every day was twenty-four hours of exciting thrills. Then I burnt out. Things couldn't excite me any more. Jim hit a run of hard luck. He got the idea of beating the insurance company. He said we'd have to lay low for two years, then we'd have a real stake.

It was gambling with the penitentiary, but we were both gamblers. We realized the risk and took the chance. That part of it was all right. Then the thing happened that we hadn't figured on. People started blackmailing us. It kept getting worse and worse. There was no let-up to it. I wanted to run away, but Jim said it wouldn't do any good. They'd find us no matter where we went.

We'd made easy money, but we couldn't keep it. We were being bled white. Our nerves got raw. Once when I made some crack at Jim, he lost his head, went crazy, and tried to choke me. I carried black and blue marks on my throat for a week. The situation was simply impossible. Jim said he was going to fix it up. I swear before God that I didn't know what he meant to do. I thought he'd decided to take a chance on running away. He had me plant a trailer at El Bocano, and we drugged the nurse, and I drove Jim down, then called the police and claimed he'd been kidnaped.

Afterwards I found out what Jim had really done. He'd killed Taleman, taken off all of his clothes, and all of Taleman's clothes, carried the body over to the barranca, and planted it. Then he kept prowling around the house naked until he heard me telephone for the cops. He ran over to the other side of the barranca, using a little trail he'd worked out, and marked with bits of white paper so he could follow it in the dark. When the officers drove up, he fired a shot, then ran back across the barranca, slipped in through the bedroom window and started pounding on the floor for the nurse.

About daylight he heard another shot from the same place. He got up and went to the window, but could see no one. And then Carr moved in on him. Carr wanted big blackmail. The others had wanted a little money from time to time. Carr wanted half of it, all at once. The other men had been blackmailing for an insurance fraud. Carr was blackmailing for murder.

It was an awful mess. Carr offered to have Ribber tried for the murder, acquitted, and then get a confession out of Ribber and get Ribber out of the country.

Jim had concealed Taleman's clothes under an old suit in the back of his clothes closet, intending to cut them up and burn them a few pieces at a time, and then that dumb nurse, when I told her to give the gray suit he'd been wearing to the cleaners, got the wrong suit. Jim supposed, of course, the authorities had been able to trace the clothes and were waiting to clamp down on him when they got more evidence. Selby has had us guessing until we don't know where we stand, and has had Carr half crazy.

I'm writing this because I'm hoping that my mother can understand. Father never will. I inherited my disregard of conventions from Mother. She was strong enough to overcome her own impulses. Sometimes I think she's been sorry that she did. Anyway, I couldn't follow the middle of the road. I had to start cutting corners—and this is where it's led me. I've had the poison for months. It's supposed to be swift and painless. I'm taking it now. Good-by, Mother.

Selby lowered the confession to the table. "That," he said, "winds it up."

Sylvia Martin looked at the still figure on the couch and blinked back tears. She said, "Doug, I'm an awful b-b-bawl baby for a newspaper w-w-woman. But how I can go to town on that story."

Selby walked across the room, picked up the telephone, and called the coroner's office.

A. B. Carr sat across the desk from Doug Selby. "Of course, Selby," he said, "the woman was hysterical. I'm trying to believe that she was sincere in writing that confession, that it was the product of a disordered mind, and not an attempt to absolve herself of responsibility. What really happened is this: She killed him. Her husband tried to dispose of the body so that the police would be fooled. I suppose she left this confession to try and protect her parents. In any event, it isn't evidence. It isn't a dying declaration which you can introduce. But it does make it damned embarrassing for me. People here will think I really am crooked.

"That was damn clever of you, finding Artrim by reading speedometers and drawing circles on a map. I, of course, had no intimation myself that he was the husband who was supposed to have been killed. I accepted him in good faith as the father-in-law."

"You're going to represent him in that murder case?" Selby asked.

"Homicide," A.B.C. corrected quickly. "Not murder. Homicide. Justifiable homicide. The man was pursued across the river bed by persons who had routed him out of his trailer in the dead of night. He thought you were blackmailers, and he shot only to defend himself. But at that, Selby, I'm damned glad the case isn't going to be tried in your county."

Selby opened a drawer in his desk. He took out a map of the city and a small pair of compasses.

Carr watched him with alert, inscrutable eyes.

Selby laid the map on the desk. "Carr," he said, "I've drawn one circle in this case. It was a big circle. Now, I'm going to draw a small circle." He indicated a point on the map with the needle-sharp point of the compass. "Know what that is?" he asked.

Carr looked and said, "Why, yes. That's about the place where I have bought my house."

Selby narrowed the compass so that it would draw a circle a scant half inch in diameter. Slowly, deliberately, he drew the circle around that point on the map. "Carr," he said, that's your limit. You stay inside that circle. I haven't anything now that I can take up before a grand jury. You were blackmailing Artrim, but you patched up a deal with him by which he would deny his wife's confession and you'd represent him on that murder case. Now that she's dead, the two of you have decided to throw all the blame on her. That isn't going to set well in this county. It doesn't set well with me. As it happens, I'm not called on to do anything about it. The insurance fraud occurred in another county. Artrim is held for murder at El Bocano. If you get him acquitted, or beat a death sentence, I'm going to try him for murder in this county. And when I try him here, I'm going to convict him. You mark my words, Carr. Artrim is going to the death cell in San Quentin, either from El Bocano or from Madison City."

Carr said, "I can't guarantee results. All I've agreed to do is to defend him."

"I know," Selby said, "and you're going down to El Bocano and try some of the tactics you've used in the big cities. They aren't going to go across in El Bocano. There's a lot you have to learn about country justice. People in the country don't appreciate the slick ingenuity of pettifogging criminal lawyers."

Carr showed no flicker of expression on his face, but he swallowed—hard. Abruptly he said, in a strained voice, "All right, Selby. You're the district attorney here. I want those newspaper articles written by that Sylvia Martin stopped. They're doing me a lot of harm, and they're going to keep me from getting any place in that trial in El Bocano. It's a criminal defamation of character. I'm calling on you as district attorney to protect me."

Selby extended his forefinger to the small circle he had drawn on the map of Madison City. "Carr," he said, "you get back in that circle and stay in it. Don't stick your nose outside of it. Sylvia Martin is going to continue to write those articles. If you think they're libelous, go ahead and sue for libel, and see what a jury in Madison City has to say about it."

"You're not going to stop her?" Carr asked.

Selby shook his head. "You're clever, Carr," he said. "You're cunning, and you're ingenious. Your mind has a daring twist to it. But that stuff doesn't go across in Madison City. This is an agricultural, rural community. We're probably country hicks, but we've learned to value sincerity a lot more than ingenuity."

Carr pushed back his chair. "All right, Selby," he said.

"If you want to make an enemy of me, go ahead. You were lucky on this case. One of these days you won't be so lucky. When that time comes, you may find A. B. Carr on the other side of the case from you."

Selby smiled, a hard, mirthless smile. "Carr," he said slowly and impressively, "when Sylvia Martin gets done with that series of articles, you couldn't get a juror in Madison County to even listen to your eloquence, let alone be swayed by it. There, Carr, is your circle, right there on the map. Stay within it, and you won't be molested. Start moving around outside of it, and you'll wish you hadn't."

Carr turned without a word, walked to the door, and opened it. On the threshold, he turned, bowed, and smiled sardonically. "I should have expected that," he said. "You could make a killing at criminal law in the city, but you're damn fool enough to go on working for a bunch of hicks, at the salary the taxpayers can afford to pay. I should have known you wouldn't listen to reason. But, in case it's any comfort to you, you're the toughest—oh, hell! Good morning."

Amorette Standish heard the door close. She opened the door from the outer office and said, "Sylvia Martin's here. I didn't want to announce her while Mr. Carr was here. I was afraid there might be—well, trouble."

"Send her in," Selby said.

Sylvia Martin came hurrying into the office. "Doug," she said, "do me a favor. I have another article here I want to run. Carr has warned the editor that what we're doing is criminal libel. The editor's getting cold feet. Would you . . ."

Selby took the typewritten copy from her hand. Without reading it, he scrawled across the top of it, "Okay for publication," and signed his name.

"But, Doug, you haven't read it."

"I don't need to read it," Selby said. He indicated the map of Madison City with the little circle drawn on the

Orange Heights subdivision. "From now on," he said, "A. B. Carr is going to stay within the circle so far as his professional activities are concerned."

Sylvia Martin looked at him for a moment with starry eyes, then she said, "Doug, look at me. No, a little more this way. Raise your chin. Tilt your head a little bit."

Selby frowned. "What's that matter? he asked.

"Hold still," she said. "Don't move."

"What . . ."

Her laugh rang out clear as a bell. "I'm going to kiss you, you big oaf."

>>> If you've enjoyed this book and would like to discover more great vintage crime and thriller titles, as well as the most exciting crime and thriller authors writing today, visit: >>>

The Murder Room
Where Criminal Minds Meet

themurderroom.com

9 781471 909368